"MADELINE BAKER IS SYNONYMOUS WITH TENDER WESTERN ROMANCES."
—*Romantic Times*

PRAISE FOR HER NOVELS . . .

Under Apache Skies

"[An] exciting western romance."
>—*Midwest Book Review*

Lakota Love Song

"Poignant. . . . Lovers of Indian stories should not miss this one."
>—*Affaire de Coeur*

"Warm romance . . . as only Madeline Baker could so vividly describe. . . . Charming."
>—*Midwest Book Review*

"A touching story, full of emotion. . . . Ms. Baker's books are always a pleasure to read. It is known that each story will be unique—a masterpiece—and *Lakota Love Song* does not disappoint."—The Best Reviews

"All the intriguing detail of Native American life we've come to expect from this talented author, as well as characters who are likable. . . . A captivating love story about people who come from very different worlds but find a way to blend their lives and their hearts. . . . Fans of Native American romances will find *Lakota Love Song* a pleasurable reading experience."
>—Romance Reviews Today

continued . . .

Wolf Shadow

"Will delight her legions of readers. . . . Baker's depiction of Native Americans is respectful, and her Old West setting rings true." —*Booklist*

"Award-winning Madeline Baker provides her readers with an exciting and insightful tale. The lead protagonists are a charming pair . . . a warm Indian romance."
—*Midwest Book Review*

Apache Flame

"Delightful. . . . A first-class historical romance."
—BookBrowser

"Baker is justly renowned for her portrayals of American Indians." —*Publishers Weekly*

"Ms. Baker has written another captivating and emotional romance that captures the true magic of love and the Old West." —*Romantic Times*

Hawk's Woman

"Powerful. Tender. Poignant. *Hawk's Woman* is a beautiful love story full of warmth, compassion, and innocent sensuality. Another Baker triumph!"
—*Romantic Times*

"Ms. Baker is wonderful!" —*Bell, Book & Candle*

Other Books by Madeline Baker

Under Apache Skies
Wolf Shadow
Lakota Love Song
Apache Flame
Hawk's Woman

DAKOTA DREAMS

Madeline Baker

A SIGNET ECLIPSE BOOK

SIGNET ECLIPSE
Published by New American Library, a division of
Penguin Group (USA) Inc., 375 Hudson Street,
New York, New York 10014, USA
Penguin Group (Canada), 90 Eglinton Avenue East, Suite 700, Toronto,
Ontario M4P 2Y3, Canada (a division of Pearson Penguin Canada Inc.)
Penguin Books Ltd., 80 Strand, London WC2R 0RL, England
Penguin Ireland, 25 St. Stephen's Green, Dublin 2,
Ireland (a division of Penguin Books Ltd.)
Penguin Group (Australia), 250 Camberwell Road, Camberwell, Victoria 3124,
Australia (a division of Pearson Australia Group Pty. Ltd.)
Penguin Books India Pvt. Ltd., 11 Community Centre, Panchsheel Park,
New Delhi - 110 017, India
Penguin Group (NZ), cnr Airborne and Rosedale Roads, Albany,
Auckland 1310, New Zealand (a division of Pearson New Zealand Ltd.)
Penguin Books (South Africa) (Pty.) Ltd., 24 Sturdee Avenue,
Rosebank, Johannesburg 2196, South Africa

Penguin Books Ltd., Registered Offices:
80 Strand, London WC2R 0RL, England

First published by Signet Eclipse, an imprint of New American Library,
a division of Penguin Group (USA) Inc.

First Printing, January 2006
10 9 8 7 6 5 4 3 2 1

For
Kathleen Graves
Shirley Brashear
and
Linda Farris

Thank you for your love and your friendship
And for making me feel at home
In your midst.

Chapter 1

Yuma Prison
Arizona Territory

Nathan Chasing Elk stared out the window, his hands fisted around the bars as he watched the setting sun slip behind the distant mountains in a blaze of bright crimson.

One more day gone.

Moving away from the window, he paced the confines of his cell. Three long strides took him from one end to the other. There was nothing to impede his progress save the wooden beds that were stacked three high on the long sides of the cell. He glanced at one of the narrow cots with its bug-infested straw tick. Given a choice, he would have preferred sleeping outside on the ground; it would have been cleaner, he mused, and far more comfortable.

He paced for hours, restless as an animal in a cage, but it did nothing to cool either his rage or his frustration. Or calm the fear that threatened to engulf him. The fear that, in the end, he would stop fighting and they would win.

Sweat dripped from his brow, ran down his back. The summers in Yuma were like hell, with temperatures soaring above a hundred degrees.

How long until he lost the will to keep fighting, the will to live, and simply gave up?

He stared at the walls that surrounded him on three sides. They were made of granite he had helped quarry with his own two hands. The granite had been plastered over and whitewashed. The doors were made of strap iron. Four years, six months and thirteen days since they had arrested him, four years of it spent in this hellhole. How much longer could he survive being locked in a cage, a cage that he had been forced to help build?

He swore under his breath. He thought it ironic that a number of the men who now inhabited the prison had helped to build it. The prison, situated on a bluff above the Colorado River, was located in what was surely the hottest, most isolated stretch of ground in the territory. The nearest town was Phoenix, which was more than a hundred and fifty miles away. Prisoners from all over the country had been sent to the hellhole in the four years since the place had been built. There were even a few women confined behind its walls. One had been convicted of killing her brother, another of attempted robbery.

He stared out the barred door of his cell. Across the way, another prisoner stared back at him. Chasing Elk's hands tightened around the bars. Did he wear the same disconsolate expression? Were his own eyes as sunken and devoid of hope?

Despair settled on his shoulders at the thought of never seeing his home or his daughter again. He knew that other prisoners had obtained pardons and been released early. So far, he'd had no such luck. But then, he'd been convicted of a far more serious crime than robbery or theft.

Escape. The word whispered through his mind, as fervent as the prayer of a dying man. Escape. It was his one hope. His only hope.

His hands tightened around the bars until his knuckles were white. There might come a time when he could no longer withstand the cold walls, the wormy food, the beatings, when thoughts of suicide would tempt him to put an end to his misery.

But it would not be today.

Chapter 2

Chasing Elk walked the perimeter of the prison yard. A ball and chain, punishment for trying to escape the week before, hampered his steps. How he hated dragging that damn thing around! The rattling of the chain was a constant irritation. He hated the sound, hated the feel of the cold iron cuff scraping against the skin of his ankle.

Other prisoners moved around the yard, their feet shuffling, while guards kept watch from the observation towers located at each corner of the enclosure.

Chasing Elk looked up at the vast blue vault of the sky, his gaze lifting past the walls of his prison as he followed the graceful flight of an eagle as it dipped and soared high overhead. Would he ever know that kind of freedom again? Or would he die here, lost and forgotten, far from the Black Hills, where he had been born? He had hoped to take his daughter there one day so she could meet her grandparents and learn the ways of the People. It didn't look like that would ever happen now.

Lost in despair, he didn't see the guard approaching from his left until it was too late.

The guard known as Fat Tom yelped as hot coffee spilled out of his cup and splashed down the front of him. "Why the devil don't you watch where you're going, you dirty half-breed?" he bellowed.

Knowing anything he said would be the wrong thing, Chasing Elk clenched his hands at his sides and kept his mouth shut. The punishment for touching a guard, by accident or design, was a week in the dark cell, which was just what its name implied—a narrow cell completely devoid of light, where recalcitrant prisoners were chained to the floor. But Fat Tom had his own method of punishment.

There was no need for words. The guard jerked his head toward the dead tree at the far end of the yard, the tree that he used as a whipping post. Whipping the inmates was against prison policy, but who was going to complain? Fat Tom's cronies wouldn't rat on him, and the prisoners certainly weren't going to say anything. Squealing on a guard would only bring a worse punishment, or death.

There was a sudden hush from the other prisoners as Chasing Elk walked toward the dead tree, his stomach churning with dread. Two of the other guards fell in step beside Fat Tom.

When Chasing Elk reached the tree, he removed his shirt and tossed it aside.

"You know the drill," Fat Tom said. "Hug the tree."

Chasing Elk spread his arms. The other two guards stepped forward, grinning expectantly as they tied Chasing Elk's hands together. One of them tossed the whip to Fat Tom, who was well named. He was near as wide as he was tall. There were squint lines around his deep-set brown eyes. His bulbous nose had been broken at least twice and looked it.

Chasing Elk sucked in a deep breath. He knew the feel of that whip, had endured the kiss of that long black lash countless times before.

The other two guards made small talk, laughing now and then, while Fat Tom cracked the whip a few times to get the feel of it.

Chasing Elk waited in terrible anticipation. He didn't know which was worse, being tied and helpless, waiting for the first breath-stealing stroke of the lash, or the humiliation of being whipped by a white man.

He broke out in a cold sweat as Fat Tom cracked the whip again. There was a sudden, ominous silence from the other two guards. Chasing Elk's whole body went rigid. And then the whip whistled through the air again, striking his flesh, wrapping around him like a tongue of fire. The first stroke was always the worst. And always something of a surprise, because the pain was inevitably worse than he remembered.

It was pain beyond description.

"Two."

As the whip bit deep into his flesh, Chasing Elk heard one of the guards grunt softly. Blood splattered through the air, dotting the earth at his feet like drops of red rain.

"Three."

His fingernails dug into the bark, finding and deepening the furrows his nails had left before.

"Four."

His knuckles went white.

"Five."

His back was on fire.

"Six."

Blood dripped down his back, a river of heat threading through the cold sweat that covered every inch of his flesh.

"Seven."

He pressed his cheek to the cool bark, his legs shaking, his whole body quivering from the pain and the effort to keep from crying out.

"Eight."

"He never makes a sound," one of the guards complained. "Come on, Tom, really lay it on him."

Chasing Elk closed his eyes, his jaw tightly clenched. His back was a solid sheet of flame. Blood ran freely down his back, seeped inside his trousers to run down his legs. He bit down on the inside of his cheek to keep from crying out as Fat Tom put all the strength at his command behind the next stoke of the lash. The whip whistled through the air, landing with a sickening wet smack against torn flesh.

"Nine."

Chasing Elk swallowed the groan that rose in his throat. *One more*, he thought. *Just one more.*

"Ten."

Chasing Elk sagged against his bonds, his forehead resting against the tree trunk. One of the guards stepped forward to cut him loose. It took all the willpower Chasing Elk possessed to remain upright. He couldn't give in now, couldn't let them know how badly he was hurting, how much he wanted to curl up on the ground and give voice to the pain. The blood of chiefs ran through his veins. He would not let the *wasichu* win, would not give them the satisfaction of knowing how close he was to breaking.

Pushing away from the tree, he squared his shoulders and made his way to his cell, the insufferable ball dragging behind him, the chain rattling like mocking laughter with every step. Inside, he lowered himself onto his cot. Knowing the worst was not yet over, he closed his eyes and waited.

A few minutes later, one of the old cons came in with a length of cloth and a bucket of salt water.

Chasing Elk buried his face in the mattress, smothering the groan he couldn't suppress as Pappy dipped the rag in the salt water and began washing the blood from his back.

"Try to relax," the old man said gruffly.

Chasing Elk grunted.

"Ya got to be more careful," Pappy admonished as he gently wiped the blood from Chasing Elk's back. " 'Specially around Fat Tom. You know he's got it in for ya."

"I know." Chasing Elk hissed the words between clenched teeth.

"I'll sneak ya in some dinner later," Pappy said.

Chasing Elk nodded, his body rigid as Pappy laid a damp cloth over his back, then covered him with a threadbare blanket.

Taking up the bucket and rag, Pappy shuffled out of the cell.

"Someday." Chasing Elk ground the word through clenched teeth. Someday Jim Buckner would pay for every hour, for every degrading, agonizing minute he had spent in this godforsaken place!

But it would not be today.

He spent the rest of the afternoon lying face down on his cot, trying to pretend that his back belonged

to someone else. Closing his eyes, he imagined he was
lying on his back, floating in a pool of cold water. The
Black Hills rose in the distance. Tall trees and the scent
of pine rose all around him. He could hear the chatter
of squirrels, the cheerful song of a bird. His favorite
paint horse grazed on a patch of greening grass. . . .

He muttered an oath, shuddered convulsively as a
fresh wave of pain speared through his back. Never
again, he vowed. Never again would he submit to
being bound to a tree and whipped like a cur dog.

In spite of the whipping and the fact that his back
was still almost raw, he was back at work two days
later, making little rocks out of big ones. It was te-
dious, backbreaking work, work that required little
concentration, leaving him way too much time to think
about things best forgotten. Like the last time he had
seen his daughter, more than four and a half years
ago. Pain twisted through his gut. She would be eight
years old next week. Another birthday missed, he
thought bitterly. Had she forgotten him? Jaw
clenched, he swung the sledgehammer again and
again. Each blow sent pain lancing through his lacer-
ated flesh. Blood oozed down his back as the day
wore on.

His whole body tensed as Fat Tom strolled up. Fat
Tom hated all the cons, but he took special delight in
tormenting those prisoners whose skin wasn't lily-
white. He especially hated Indians, Mexicans, and
half-breeds.

Chasing Elk stared at the bucket in the guard's
hand, grimaced with the knowledge of what was
coming.

"Looks like you're bleeding," Fat Tom observed

with a malicious grin. "This'll help." And so saying, he doused Chasing Elk's back with the contents of the bucket.

A low groan erupted from Chasing Elk's throat as the cold salt water sprayed over his bare back. He lifted the sledgehammer in his hands. One swing, he thought. One swing would wipe that smirk from the bastard's face.

Fat Tom drew his Colt. "Try it."

Slowly, Chasing Elk lowered his arm. The sledgehammer hit the ground with a muffled thud.

"Want a shot at me?" Fat Tom asked.

"Damn right."

Fat Tom glanced around the yard. "Meet me behind the shed in five minutes."

"Right."

"Afraid?"

Chasing Elk glanced at one of the other guards standing nearby. "I can't just walk away."

"I'll fix it," Fat Tom said with a shrug.

"What happens if I win?" He had to ask, though he knew there wasn't a chance in hell of that happening, especially now, when his back was still practically raw. But then, he might never get another chance to take a swing at Fat Tom. "You gonna lock me in solitary, or beat the shit out of me again?"

"You ain't gonna win. Five minutes," Fat Tom said, and walked away.

Chasing Elk stared after him. He flexed his hands and arms. Did he dare? How could he not? It was an opportunity that might never come his way again.

With a casual glance around, he headed toward the shed.

Fat Tom was waiting for him. The first thing Chasing Elk noticed was that the guard wasn't wearing his gun.

Fat Tom made a "come here" gesture with his hand.

"How about removing my chain?" Chasing Elk asked.

Fat Tom shook his head.

"Kind of gives you an unfair advantage, doesn't it?"

Fat Tom's eyes narrowed; then, muttering an oath, he pulled a ring of keys from his back pocket and tossed them to Chasing Elk.

Chasing Elk quickly unlocked the iron cuff around his ankle and tossed the ball and chain aside, along with the keys.

He was turning to face Fat Tom when the guard plowed into him. Driven off-balance, Chasing Elk fell backward. He landed hard on his back, muttered an oath as dirt and rocks were ground into his already battered flesh.

Four and a half years of rage welled up inside him. Four and a half years of scummy water and wormy meat. Four and a half years of being whipped, of being caged, of being treated as if he was less than human.

A low growl rose in his throat. Gathering all his anger, all his suppressed pain and fury, he threw the guard off and scrambled to his feet. Fat Tom was still trying to rise when Chasing Elk slammed a hard right into his face. Fat Tom reeled backward from the force of the blow, and Chasing Elk drove his fist into the guard's face again and again. Blood spurted from the guard's nose and mouth.

With a roar, Fat Tom lumbered to his feet. He shook his head to clear it, grunted as Chasing Elk struck him again and yet again. Fat Tom staggered backward. His foot caught in the chain Chasing Elk had tossed aside and he fell heavily, striking his head against a corner of the shed. He started to rise, then fell back and lay still.

Breathing hard, his knuckles bruised, his back bleeding, Chasing Elk stared down at the guard. One minute passed. Two. And still Fat Tom didn't move.

Damn. There would be hell to pay if the bastard was dead.

Grabbing the shackles and Fat Tom's keys, Chasing Elk made his way around the barn and back to his place on the work detail. No one remarked on his absence.

"Wagon coming in!"

Chasing Elk's head jerked up as the gates to the prison swung open to admit the monthly supply wagon, giving him a view of the desert beyond. Freedom. It was only a few yards away.

Save for one, all the guards watching the prisoners started toward the supply wagon, eager to receive their mail and hear the latest news from town.

Chasing Elk glanced at the sentries posted at the four guard towers. All attention was on the wagon that was now parked in front of the Mess Hall.

His gaze moved to the gates, still open, and then to the lone horse tethered near the stable. One of the prisoners had just finished saddling the stud. It was a beautiful horse, a long-legged black that belonged to the captain of the guards. The captain took the stud out for a run once a week.

Chasing Elk looked over at the guard who had stayed behind with the prisoners. The man's attention was on the men gathered near the wagon, obviously trying to overhear what the driver was saying. Something about a bank robbery in town. Moving as inconspicuously as possible, Chasing Elk walked toward the horse.

The prisoner who had saddled the horse blinked in surprise as Chasing Elk picked up the stud's reins. "What the hell do you think you're doing?"

"Getting the hell out of here." Holding the reins in one hand and grasping the horn with the other, Chasing Elk put his mouth next to the horse's ear and let out a bloodcurdling war cry.

Startled, the horse spun on its hocks and lined out in a dead run. Swinging into the saddle, Chasing Elk jerked on the reins, turning the horse toward the gates that two of the guards were closing.

Leaning low over the horse's withers, Chasing Elk drummed his heels against the horse's flanks.

He heard the guards hollering as he thundered through the narrow opening, the sharp report of a rifle. A sudden stinging in his upper thigh told him he had been hit at least once.

And then, miraculously, he was through the gates and racing across the desert.

Chasing Elk took a deep breath, his first breath of freedom in over four and a half years. It was sweet indeed.

Glancing over his shoulder, Chasing Elk thought his bid for freedom might be over before it began. Strung out behind him were a half-dozen armed and mounted men, all firing in his direction. He had no weapon and little hope of outrunning them. Desperate to escape, he offered a fervent prayer to *Wakan Tanka*. It had been years since his vision quest, but he had nowhere else to turn.

"*Wakan Tanka*, hear me! My enemies pursue me like foxes after a hare. I have nowhere to hide, nowhere else to turn. Oh, Great Mystery, have mercy on me. Let the four winds blow my enemies away. Let Mother Earth hide me from their sight lest I perish!"

Bullets whined past his ear, sounding like angry hornets. Chasing Elk bent lower over the stud's neck. He would escape or he would die, but he would not go back to prison.

Heart pounding, his thigh oozing blood from where he had been shot, he rode determinedly onward. If they caught him, they would have to kill him.

Gray clouds swirled overhead, blocking out the sun, stealing the warmth from the day. A blast of cold wind stung his face, sending dust devils and tumbleweeds spinning across the desert. Thunder rumbled overhead.

Chasing Elk looked over his shoulder again, startled to see that a wall of dust now stood between him and his pursuers.

Hope, that feeling he thought had been forever extinguished, rose within him. With a heartfelt prayer of thanks to the Great Spirit, he raced across the desert. Behind him there was a crash of thunder followed by a sudden downpour. Rain, he thought with a grin. It would wash away his tracks.

A short time later, he reached the river, a river that was already rising. He urged his horse into the water, and it struck out swimming strongly. Lightning flashed overhead, and Chasing Elk urged the horse toward the far shore. After scrambling up the bank, the horse shook itself.

Chasing Elk patted the horse's neck while he considered which way to go. There was little to see but sand and sage in either direction, save for the mountains in the distance. Tall craggy mountains that called to something primal deep within him even as they reminded him of the home he had not seen in more than ten years.

Kicking the horse into a gallop, Chasing Elk headed toward the high country. The rain, welcomed as an answer to his desperate plea only moments ago, now became another discomfort. Raindrops pelted his bare back and shoulders, and he hunched forward, shivering uncontrollably as a cold wind blew across the desert.

Even though he was certain he had lost his pursuers, he kept the horse at a gallop for several miles. He was grateful once again for the rain that would have washed out his tracks. No doubt his pursuers had turned back: Only the most foolhardy would endeavor to cross the river in such a downpour.

Now that the first rush of adrenaline had passed, he grew increasingly aware of the pain in his thigh. It burned as if all the fires of hell were lit within it. Chin resting on his chest, it was all he could do to stay upright in the saddle as the weary horse plodded on.

He lost track of time. He dozed and woke and dozed again. He shivered with chills, burned with fever, and only the thought of seeing his daughter again kept him going, but even that hope couldn't keep the pain and the thirst at bay. After a day and a night in the saddle, without seeing any sign of life in the barren desert, he was ready to admit defeat.

It was time to give up, he thought bleakly, time to surrender to the hunger and the pain and the hopelessness that had been his constant companion for the last four and a half years. Death whispered to him, beckoning him with the promise that the next world was better than this one.

It was then, when despair sat on his shoulder like a carrion crow, that he saw smoke rising from the chimney of a farm house in the distance.

Chapter 3

Catharine Lyons stood on the front porch, her heart pounding with fear and trepidation as two dozen Indians rode up to the front of the house. She clutched her shawl closer to ward off the chill evening wind. Dark clouds hung low in the sky, promising more rain before the day was through. A shiver ran down her spine, whether from the cold or the approach of the Indians she couldn't say. She told herself there was nothing to fear. It wasn't the first time Marteen and his Apache warriors had come here. They often stopped to water their horses in the stream that ran behind the house. Sometimes they ran off a couple of head of cattle. A few weeks ago, they had taken her horse, thereby depriving her of her only means of leaving the ranch once and for all, as she had been planning to do.

She crossed her arms over her breasts as Marteen broke away from the others and rode toward her. He was a fearsome-looking warrior, with piercing black eyes and a sharp slash of a nose. A long scar ran from his left shoulder to his waist. He wanted her to be his woman. He stopped at the ranch whenever he was in the area, sometimes with a handful of warriors, sometimes with dozens. He always brought her gifts: a beaded necklace, a pair of moccasins, furs.

She had told him, as best she could, that she couldn't be his woman because she already had a man. Of course, it was a lie. Her younger brother, Mark, had been the only man in her life since her father died two years ago, and she hadn't seen Mark since he had gone into the Crossing for supplies a little over a month ago. Mark hated life on the ranch: the solitude, the never-ending work, the cattle. She shook her head ruefully. You really couldn't call the ranch a ranch. People with ranches ran hundreds of head of cattle. They had hired help and actually turned a profit. She and Mark had less than a hundred head of cattle left, and only the two of them to look after the small herd.

She glanced at the Indians surrounding her. Had they killed Mark, or had her brother simply gone back East, as he had so often threatened to do?

Marteen dismounted in a single lithe movement. Reaching into a rawhide pouch at his side, he withdrew a pair of jeweled combs and placed them in her hands.

Catharine stared at the combs, a shudder of horror sliding down her spine. She wanted to ask him where he had gotten the combs, but she was afraid of what the answer might be. The Apache didn't make jeweled combs, leading her to believe that he must have taken them from the body of a woman he had killed.

He was looking at her expectantly.

She forced a smile as she nodded her thanks.

"Be winter soon," he said. "If your man does not return by then, I will take you to my wickiup."

She shook her head vigorously. "No."

He nodded once, curtly, his dark eyes burning into hers. "Yes. You are strong woman. You will give me many sons."

Grabbing a handful of his horse's mane, he swung onto the animal's bare back and rode away.

Catharine stared after him. Maybe she was wrong to refuse him. At least he wanted her. At twenty-three, she was well on her way to being an old maid.

Good Lord, what was she thinking! The man was a savage. With a shake of her head, she went into the house. She placed the combs on the kitchen table, knowing she would never wear them. Perhaps she could sell them at the Crossing. Heaven knew she could use the money.

Well, there was no help for it. She had to leave here as soon as possible. Tonight she would gather her few precious belongings and what little cash money she had, and tomorrow morning, she would make the long walk to Finley's Crossing, some twelve miles away. The Crossing didn't qualify as a town; it was just a wide spot in the road on the way to Tucson, a place where a body could order goods from back East through a mail-order catalog. You could order almost anything through the catalog. Old Angus Macintosh had ordered a bride! Finley also carried a supply of canned goods, yardage, and a few farming supplies.

All the neighboring farmers and ranchers frequented Finley's Crossing. Once a month, most of the people roundabout went to the Crossing to barter goods or just to visit. It was a lonely life, living in the West, where your nearest neighbor might be ten or twenty miles away. It wasn't like the East, where there were neighbors on every side, where a town meant churches and schools and dress shops and restaurants.

Finley had expanded the trading post in the last year due to the fact that stagecoaches had begun using his place as a layover. He had built a small, three-room hotel and, much to the disapproval of the farmers' wives, added a saloon. Some of the men opined that if Finley kept expanding, the day would come when Finley's Crossing would be more than just a wide spot in the road; why, it might even become a real town. Catharine hoped to be gone long before that happened! She'd had enough of life in the West. It was time to go back East where she belonged.

She glanced around the parlor. Was she doing the right thing? Should she try and sell the ranch? How could she just walk away and leave Mama's pianoforte and all of Papa's books? What if Mark came home after she left? And yet, what other choice did she have? She couldn't stay here, not now. She had no defense against Marteen. She would leave a note for Mark, telling him that she was going back to Boston.

It might take a couple of days for her to make the trek to the Crossing on foot. The roads would be treacherous after the rains. There were other dangers, as well: She could get lost, be attacked by wild animals, or run into another band of Indians. She shuddered at the mere idea of being taken captive. She had heard stories of what happened to white women captured by the Apaches, although she doubted that being taken as Marteen's wife would be much better.

Well, there was no help for it. Come morning, she would shoulder her belongings and head for the Crossing. She should have done so long ago. Even with Mark's help, they had barely eked a living out of the cattle and their meager garden. Now that Mark was gone, the place was quickly going to seed. She couldn't keep the place up by herself; she had been a fool to try.

Catharine took one last look at the house, then turned away. She had left a note for Mark, telling him that she intended to go back East as soon as she could get enough money together. Lifting the poke that held all her worldly goods to her shoulder, she started walking. She was surprised by the sharp sting of tears behind her eyes. She hadn't expected to feel anything at leaving the place behind; she had never been happy there. It had never really been home, and yet she had lived there for almost five years. She had cooked and cleaned, stood on the porch to watch the sunset, all the while letting herself hope that things would get better, but they never did. She felt guilty leaving the two milk cows behind, but they could look after themselves, same as the cattle and the chickens and the barn cats.

She blew out a sigh as she trudged across the wet, muddy ground. It had been her father's idea to move west. He had bought the homestead sight unseen, convinced that it was everything the former owner had claimed it was, when it was just the opposite. Both Catharine and her mother had been against moving west. Neither had wanted to leave their church or their friends or their comfortable home in Boston. Mark had been excited at the thought of trekking westward, but then Mark had always been a dreamer, not a doer.

Nothing had turned out the way her father or Mark had planned. Her mother had died in childbirth the year after they arrived. And the baby died with her. After that, her father, who had always been strong, gradually lost interest in the ranch and everything else. He had turned to alcohol for solace and passed away six months later. It was after their father's death that Mark discovered just how much work ranching really was. She hadn't expected him to stay on after their father passed away. Nor had she expected him to leave her behind when he finally decided he'd had enough.

She plodded onward, wondering what she would do when she reached the Crossing. She had very little money. Perhaps she could go to work for Mr. Finley until she had earned enough money to buy either a horse or a ticket on the stage to Tucson. Tucson was a good-sized town. She could certainly find work there, perhaps at the mercantile or one of the restaurants. She didn't know how long it would take to earn enough for a ticket to Boston, but she was willing to do whatever she had to. Of course, there was always a chance that no one would hire her, but it was a chance she was willing to take. She had no choice. Anything was better than staying at the ranch, waiting for Marteen to make her his squaw.

She had been walking for perhaps forty minutes when she saw the horse, a beautiful black horse. It stood with its head hanging, the reins trailing on the ground.

A horse! It was like an answer to a prayer. She

could ride to Tucson and when she got there, she could sell the horse, perhaps for enough money to buy a ticket east.

Murmuring softly, she walked toward the animal, careful not to make any sudden moves that might spook it and cause it to run off.

The horse lifted its head, its foxlike ears twitching, nostrils flaring as she drew closer.

"There now, that's a good boy." She held out her hand, palm up. "Easy now, I'm not going to hurt you."

She was reaching for the reins when the horse snorted and darted to one side. It was then that she saw the man. Clad in nothing but a ragged pair of prison-issue trousers and a pair of heavy brogans, he was lying facedown on the wet grass. Long black hair fell across his shoulders and hid half of his face. Her stomach churned when she saw the fresh cuts and welts that crisscrossed his back. His skin, where it wasn't torn, swollen, or bruised, was a smooth reddish-brown.

She stared at him in horror. He was an escaped prisoner. Even worse, he was an Indian.

Moving cautiously around him, she reached for the horse's reins again, and again the contrary animal backed away from her. She was about to try one more time when, with a low groan, the man rolled over, and she found herself staring down into a pair of pain-glazed smoke-gray eyes.

He stared at her for stretched seconds, unmoving, unblinking.

He was broad through the shoulders. His arms were long and well-muscled. In spite of that, he was so thin she could almost count his ribs. There was a dark stain on his trousers that looked suspiciously like dried blood.

Moving ever so slowly, he pulled himself into a sitting position.

Catharine took a wary step backward. Even though he was obviously in pain and looked weak and feverish, she didn't trust him.

"You . . . got any . . . water?" The words were low and raspy, as though they had been torn from his throat.

She hesitated a moment, then reluctantly pulled a canteen from inside her poke. She really couldn't spare the water, but she couldn't bring herself to refuse. She passed it to him, staying as far away from him as possible as she did so.

He took a few sips of water. "Don't worry, lady. . . . You've got . . . nothing . . . to fear from me." He took another drink. "Couldn't catch you . . . even if . . . I was . . . of a mind to."

She was not reassured. Even sick and feverish, he looked dangerous, like a wild animal that had been wounded and cornered.

He took another, longer drink, wiped his mouth with the back of his hand, then handed her the canteen. "Obliged." He glanced at the pack she had dropped on the ground. "You going somewhere?"

"I don't see as how that's any of your business."

"Reckon it's not." Looking past her, he muttered an oath.

Catharine was about to ask him what was wrong when she heard the sound of hoofbeats. Turning, she felt a chill run down her spine when she saw Marteen and some of his warriors riding toward her.

In moments, the Indians had surrounded her and the stranger.

Dismounting, Marteen swaggered toward the wounded man. Reversing the lance in his hand, he jabbed the wooden end against the stranger's thigh.

The stranger gasped and fell back, all the color draining from his face. A fresh flood of crimson spread over his pant leg.

"No!" Catharine screamed the word as Marteen drew his knife.

Marteen paused in midstrike. "You know this man? He means something to you?"

Catharine glanced at the stranger. Though he was only inches from death, she detected no fear in his eyes, no sign of the pain she knew he must be feeling, save for the fine white lines etched around his mouth.

"Yes, I know him," she replied, her voice trembling. "He's my husband."

Marteen kicked the stranger in the side. "Is this true?"

"You doubting . . . the lady's words?" the stranger replied through clenched teeth.

Marteen regarded him for several taut moments, then turned his attention to Catharine once again. "What is your man doing out here?"

"He was on his way home." To her surprise, the lie rolled easily off her tongue. "He was attacked in town because . . . because he's part Indian, and they hate him for that. I was on my into town to look for him when I found him out here."

The Apache's deep-set black eyes bored into her.

Catharine held his gaze, her mouth dry, her palms damp. Did he believe her? If he didn't, would he kill the two of them on the spot? Would he spare her if she told him the truth? She glanced at the stranger again, wondering why she was risking her life for a man she didn't know.

Marteen grunted, then motioned two of his warriors to come forward. None too gently, they lifted the stranger onto the back of his horse. Marteen picked up her poke and hooked it over the saddle horn.

"Here," he said, offering her the reins of his mount.

Head high, she took the reins and swung onto the horse's back. She would not thank him for the horse: It was the chestnut mare he had stolen from her weeks ago.

"Go home now," Marteen said. He glanced at the stranger, who was slumped forward in the saddle, one hand pressed hard against his bloody thigh. "I will come in a few days to see if your man still lives. If he does not . . ."

There was no need for him to finish the sentence. If the stranger died, she would become Marteen's woman.

Chapter 4

The stranger was nearly unconscious by the time Catharine got him to the farm. Dismounting, she carried her belongings into the parlor, then returned to the stranger's side, wondering how she was going to get him off his horse and into bed.

"Mister?" When he didn't answer, she reached up and shook his arm. "Mister, can you hear me?"

Slowly he lifted his head and opened his eyes. He blinked at her several times, his gaze unfocused.

"If I help you, can you get off your horse?"

"What?" he asked groggily. "Oh, sure." He lifted his right leg over the black's withers and sort of slid out of the saddle to the ground.

Catharine put her arm around him to steady him, and he sagged against her. She staggered under his weight. He might be thin and undernourished, but he still outweighed her by a good thirty or forty pounds. His skin beneath her hand was far too warm.

Moving closer to him, she propped her shoulder under his arm, praying for the strength to get him inside before he collapsed. Step by slow step, she guided him into the house and down the narrow hall toward Mark's bedroom. Crossing the threshold, she gave the stranger a little push, and he fell face down on the mattress.

Catharine grimaced, thinking that she would never get all the blood and dirt out of the patchwork quilt that covered the bed. She felt a moment's regret. Her mother had made that quilt. It was one of the few things they had brought with them from the East.

Catharine stood there a moment, wondering what to do next. One thing was certain. No matter who this man was, she couldn't let him die. Right now, he was the only thing standing between her and life as an Apache squaw.

Leaving the room, she went into the kitchen. Removing her cloak, she tossed it over a chair and then rolled up her sleeves. Moving quickly, she filled a pan with water and put it on the stove to heat. She found a bar of hard yellow soap, a clean cloth to wash his wounds, another length of cloth to use for bandages. In the cupboard, she found half a bottle of whiskey that Mark had left behind. Ladies did not drink spirits, but today she was not a lady. Opening the bottle, she splashed some in a glass and took a swallow. It burned all the way down. How did men abide the taste?

When the water was warm, she poured it into a bowl. Placing it on a tray with the other items, she took a deep breath, then made her way back to the stranger's side.

He lay as he had fallen. She stared at the half-healed cuts and welts on his back and shoulders, a shiver of revulsion running through her as she tried to imagine what it must have been like to have been so brutally whipped. And not just once, judging by the spiderweb of old scars that crisscrossed his back, but many times.

After placing the tray on the table beside the bed, she dipped a cloth in the bowl. She washed away the dirt and blood as carefully as possible. He winced at her touch, and she winced with him.

It took all the strength she possessed to roll him over. His face and chest were dotted with perspiration. Thick black bristles shadowed his jaw. Blood, old and new, stained his pant leg from thigh to knee. She could see the ugly wound through a jagged rip in the coarse material of his trousers. She only hoped the bullet was not lodged in his flesh.

Uttering a quiet prayer, she pulled off his heavy work shoes and then unfastened his trousers. She eased them down past his hips and, as gently as she could, over his injured thigh. He wore nothing beneath his trousers.

He was not the first naked man she had seen: Once, when she was thirteen and Mark was twelve, she had inadvertently walked in on him when he was undressing. To this day, she didn't know who had been more embarrassed. They had laughed about it later. But this man was a stranger, and much older than Mark had been. Feeling a flush rise in her cheeks, she quickly covered his loins with a corner of the quilt. Then, closing her mind to everything else, she set about washing away the sweat and dirt from his face, chest, and belly, and the blood from his thigh. So much blood.

The wound that slashed across his thigh was long

and deep, though thankfully not deep enough that it would require stitching. She was relieved to see that the bullet had only grazed him.

He groaned softly as she thoroughly washed the wound with strong yellow soap, but he didn't regain consciousness. When she finished, she wrapped his thigh in several layers of cloth, and then washed his neck and his arms. While drying him off, she wondered how long he had been in prison and when he'd last had a bath. And a shave.

Easing the soiled quilt out from under him, she covered him with a blanket, then stood staring down at him. He had long black hair and dusky skin, a wide, generous mouth, a strong jaw, a fine blade of a nose, well-defined cheekbones. If he hadn't been so gaunt, his face lined with pain, he might even be handsome. She shook her head, annoyed with the turn of her thoughts. What was she thinking? The man was an outlaw. He might be a murderer for all she knew, and she had him tucked all safe and sound in her brother's bed as if he was an invited guest!

Tapping her foot, she considered her options. She couldn't throw him out, nor could she let him die. But she certainly wasn't going to give him an opportunity to steal the few belongings she possessed or murder her while she slept.

Leaving the house, she led the horses toward the barn. She was glad to see that the milk cows she had turned loose the night before hadn't wandered away. They grazed contentedly on a patch of grass a short distance from the house.

Inside the barn, Catharine put the horses in adjoining stalls. After removing their saddles and bridles, she tossed both animals some hay and filled the water barrels. When that was done, she cut two lengths of rope from the coil in the corner and tucked them into her skirt pocket.

She was about to leave the barn when one of the cows ambled in, mooing softly.

"Need to be milked, do you, girl?" Catharine murmured. The cow followed her docilely into a stall, stood with her tail swishing from side to side while Catharine found a stool and a bucket and proceeded to milk her. The second cow came in just as she finished milking the first.

After putting the milk in the springhouse, Catharine went into Mark's bedroom and tied the stranger's hands to the bedposts and then, feeling a good deal safer, she took the quilt outside. She filled her washtub with cold water and dumped the quilt inside, hoping a good soaking would get rid of the bloodstains. Next, she went into the kitchen to make a pot of chicken broth. She checked the dough she had left rising on the window sill, glad now that she hadn't thrown it out. She kneaded it a few times, dropped it into a pan, and put it in the oven.

Sitting down at the table, she rested her head on her folded arms. It had been a long day.

Chasing Elk woke to the smell of baking bread. With a low groan, he tried to sit up, only to discover that his arms were drawn behind his head and his hands were tied to the bedposts.

Where the hell was he?

Muttering an oath, he glanced around. The room wasn't much bigger than his cell at the prison. The walls were painted a dull green. Gingham curtains hung on the single window, and a picture of a sailing ship hung on the wall. There was a rag rug on the floor and a white china dry sink sat on the cherrywood dresser across from the bed.

Where the hell was he?

He tugged on the ropes that bound his hands, cursing as the movement sent shards of pain skittering down his back and through his thigh. Damn. He hurt all over.

He took a deep breath, and his nostrils filled with the faint scent of lavender. He frowned as the memory of a woman rose in his mind, a woman who had smelled of lavender.

It came back to him in a rush: his escape from Yuma, the rainstorm that had come like the answer to a prayer. The Indian. The woman . . .

As though summoned by his thoughts, the door opened and she entered the room.

She stood in the doorway, a bowl in one hand, her expression uncertain. She wore a white apron over a simple brown dress. Her hair, unbound, fell to her waist in rippling waves of auburn silk. He hadn't noticed how pretty she was before, but that wasn't surprising considering the condition he'd been in when he had first set eyes on her. But pretty she was, with her smooth clear skin, sky-blue eyes, and a mouth made for kissing. He knew her hands were warm and gentle; he remembered the touch of them on his skin.

The same hands that had tied his to the bedposts.

She regarded him warily. "How are you feeling?"

"Like a hog trussed up for butchering."

Her gaze darted to his bound hands, but she made

no apology. "I brought you some broth. I thought you might be hungry."

"You gonna feed me?"

"Yes." With her free hand, she pulled a chair over to the bed.

"I can feed myself."

"I'm sure you can, but I'm not untying you."

"Why the hell not?"

"Because I don't know who you are. Because I don't trust you. Because you're an escaped convict."

"If I'm such a desperate character, why'd you tell that Apache I was your husband?"

"That's none of your business."

"I think it is."

"I don't care what you think. Do you want to eat or not?"

He wanted to tell her to go to hell, but he was hungry and it had been far too long since he'd had a home-cooked meal. Swallowing his pride, he lifted his head and opened his mouth.

She propped a pillow behind his head, then sat down beside him. Her hand trembled a little as she fed him, making him wonder if he was in danger of being drowned in broth.

She was a good cook, and when he finished the first bowl, she brought him a second one.

It was humiliating, being hand-fed as if he were an infant, having her wipe his mouth for him. Yet he couldn't blame her for being cautious. Everything she had said was true. She didn't know him, and he was an escaped convict.

"Just how long do you intend to keep me tied up?"

"I . . . I don't know." Catharine stared at him. What

had she been thinking when she told Marteen this stranger was her husband? She couldn't keep him tied up in her brother's bed forever. Sooner or later she would have to let him go. And when she did, what then? There was an air of danger about him. For all she knew, he could be a murderer, or worse.

He was watching her, a hint of amusement in his dark eyes. She had the feeling that he knew exactly what she was thinking.

Picking up the bowl, she started toward the door.

"Hey, lady?"

Pausing, she glanced over her shoulder. "Yes?"

"You got a bedpan?"

Catharine pulled her nightgown over her head, then went into the kitchen to brew a pot of tea. The last two days had been the most unsettling of her life. Whether cooking or cleaning or looking after the livestock, she had been acutely aware of the stranger in Mark's bedroom. Though she would have avoided him completely if she could, that hadn't been possible.

Now, sitting at the kitchen table, sipping a cup of tea, she asked herself again what she was going to do about him. If only he were a gentleman instead of a rogue! If only he weren't so handsome. Yes, handsome, though she was loathe to admit it. Even his coarse beard didn't detract from his bold good looks. Amazing what a couple of days of rest and some hot food had done for Nathan Chasing Elk. That was his name. It was the only thing she knew about him, for he was decidedly closemouthed about his past and the reason he had been imprisoned, which led her to believe that he was hiding something so horrible he was afraid to tell her what it was. Either that, or he was simply too ashamed to talk about it.

She was going to have to release him soon. It wasn't healthy for a body to stay abed so long. But would it be healthy for her if he were free? Perhaps she could ask for his word that he wouldn't hurt her, but even if he swore an oath on the Bible, what good was the word of a convict? No doubt he would say anything, promise anything, to obtain his freedom.

She had thought of untying him while he slept, taking the horses, and riding to the Crossing. And she would have done so if it weren't for the Apaches. Each time she stepped out of the house, whether to gather vegetables for dinner or to feed the stock, she had seen one of Marteen's warriors in the distance, watching her. It was obvious that Marteen wanted her to know that his men were there, for the Apache were masters at hiding from their enemies when they chose to do so. With nothing more than a handful of dirt and a few branches, they could become virtually invisible.

With a sigh, she rose and carried her cup to the dry sink. It was time to look in on her unwelcome guest one last time before going to bed.

Chasing Elk stared at the ceiling, wondering how much longer the woman intended to keep him tied up. He was damned sick and tired of lying there. He tugged on the ropes that bound his wrists. The binding on his left hand didn't seem quite as tight as it had been. He was about to give it a good tug when the door opened and the woman stepped into the room.

He glared at her.

She glared back. "I'm going to bed, Mr. Elk. Do you need anything before I go?"

"My freedom."

"Good night."

"Dammit!"

"Don't curse at me, you brigand!"

"Then turn me loose!"

She didn't bother to reply. Head high, she turned on her heel and swept out of the room, slamming the door behind her.

Muttering an oath, Chasing Elk jerked against the ropes that bound him.

And smiled as his left hand slid free.

Chapter 5

Easing into a sitting position, Chasing Elk untied his right hand. He rubbed his wrists a moment, feeling a wave of dizziness when he swung his legs over the side of the bed. He waited for it to pass, then stood, holding the bedpost for support. The wound in his thigh started throbbing when he put his weight on it. He stayed where he was, braced against the bedpost. His back ached, his leg ached, but by damn, he was standing on his own two feet again.

He glanced at his trousers, draped over the back of the chair. It appeared the woman had washed them. Grimacing at the thought of wearing anything that reminded him of Yuma, he moved to the armoire and opened the doors in hopes of finding something else to wear. He stared at the shirts and trousers hanging inside. Reaching for a pair of whipcord britches, he pulled them on, wondering whom they belonged to. Husband? Brother? Father? Not that it mattered, he thought wryly; they were his now. The trousers were a little too snug around the middle, a little too short in length, but better by far than the prison-issue britches he had worn for the last four and a half years.

Padding barefooted across the floor, he opened the door and stepped out into the hallway. The house was dark and quiet.

Ignoring the ache in his thigh, he moved silently through the house toward the front door. Lifting the latch, he stepped out onto the porch and drew in a deep breath.

He was free. It was a heady feeling. Free to come and go as he pleased, free to see his daughter. Leah. What could he say to her? How could he make her understand what had happened? What would he do if she refused to listen to what he had to say? What if she refused to believe him, or worse, refused to forgive him?

A movement to his left drew Chasing Elk's attention. Peering into the darkness, he froze when he saw two dark shapes ghosting through the shadows of the night. Apaches, he thought. The warriors were making no effort to conceal their presence. Chasing Elk frowned. Were they there to keep an eye on the woman, or on him?

Well, it didn't matter. What mattered was that he was free. He would rest here for another two or three days and then be on his way.

He leaned one shoulder against the porch upright and drew in a deep breath. No more whippings. No more chains. No more gray walls and iron bars. Nothing to keep him from going after Leah.

Suddenly feeling fatigued, he went back inside and stretched out on the bed.

Free. It was his last thought before he drifted off to sleep.

*   *   *

He woke to the scent of bacon frying. The aroma tickled his nostrils, drawing him out of bed and into the kitchen. He paused in the doorway.

The woman stood at the stove with her back toward him. Her hair fell down her back in a riot of waves. He was sorely tempted to reach out and run his fingers through the thick strands. It had been years since he had been close to a woman. And this one was all woman. His gaze moved over her slim shoulders to her narrow waist.

Just then, she turned away from the stove to reach for something on the counter. She gasped, one hand flying to her throat, when she saw him standing in the doorway.

"You!" she exclaimed, her eyes widening. "What are you . . . how did you . . . ?"

"I got tired of being tied up," he said curtly.

"But . . ." She took a step backward, her gaze darting around the room like a rabbit seeking a hidey-hole.

"Relax," he said quietly. "I'm not going to hurt you."

It was obvious from her expression that she didn't believe him.

"Think you could fix me some breakfast?" Moving slowly so as not to alarm her, he pulled a chair out from the table and sat down.

She stared at him uncertainly.

"I hope you don't mind my borrowing a pair of your husband's trousers."

"They're my brother's."

He grunted softly. "Where is he?"

"He went into town. He'll be home soon."

"Uh-huh. You got a name?"

She hesitated a moment.

Chasing Elk waited patiently. There were those who believed that knowing another's name gave you power over them. He wondered if she was one of them.

"Catharine," she said. "Catharine Lyons."

He glanced past her. "The bacon's burning, Miss Lyons."

"Oh!" Whirling around, she snatched the pan from the fire, and yelped as the handle burned her palm. She jerked her hand away, and the pan hit the floor with a crash, sending strips of bacon and hot grease flying through the air.

Rising, Chasing Elk caught her by the forearm. "Come sit down and let me look at it."

"I'm fine."

He pulled her over to a chair and sat her down in it. Moving to the counter, he found a pot of lard. He scooped out a little, then smeared it ever so gently over the palm of her hand. His touch sent a little thrill of pleasure skittering down her spine.

"I need to clean up the mess," she murmured, not meeting his eyes.

"Just sit tight," he said. "I'll take care of it."

Still stunned by the fact that he had somehow managed to free himself and that she was now at his mercy, Catharine watched as Chasing Elk quickly cleaned up the mess on the floor. He cut a dozen fresh slices of bacon, and put the pan on the stove. He pulled another skillet from the rack, cracked a dozen eggs, scrambled them in the pan, and put it on the fire.

As though feeling her scrutiny, he turned to look at her. "How's your hand?"

She shrugged. It still hurt a little, but she saw no need to tell him that. As casually as she could, she glanced around the room, looking for something she could use as a weapon. There was nothing close at hand.

Her gaze moved over him, drawn to the patchwork of silvery scars, many of which were only half healed, across his back and shoulders. She watched his muscles ripple as he turned the bacon and eggs, then poured himself a cup of coffee.

Looking over his shoulder, he held up the coffeepot. "You want a cup?"

She did, but not from him. She shook her head.

With a shrug, he turned back to the stove.

A short time later, he filled two plates with bacon and eggs and set them on the table, along with a couple of forks. Sitting in the chair across from hers, he gestured at her plate. "Eat."

She glared at him.

With a shake of his head, he picked up his fork and began to eat.

Catharine picked at her food, her appetite ruined by his nearness and the fact that he was free to come and go as he pleased. And therein was her dilemma. She wanted him gone, but she needed him to stay.

Feeling his gaze, she looked up. "What are you going to do?" she asked.

He lifted one brow. "About what?"

"About me."

He frowned at her. "What do you mean? What do you think I'm gonna do?"

"I don't know!"

"Listen, lady, you've got nothing to worry about

from me. I reckon you saved my life. I'm obliged to you for that."

"Are you planning to leave soon?"

"Anxious to be rid of me, are you?"

"Yes, but . . ."

He lifted one brow. "But?"

"I need you to stay."

"Is that right?"

She nodded.

"You want to tell me why?"

"Marteen thinks you're my husband."

Chasing Elk nodded. "Go on."

"He . . . that is . . . he wants me to be his squaw."

His gaze moved over her, lingering on the thick fall of her hair that begged his touch, her mouth, her breasts, her tiny waist. "Can't say as I blame him."

She flushed under his appreciative gaze.

He grunted softly. "So, that's why you told him I was your husband."

"Yes."

"I'll be happy to pretend to be your husband, Miss Lyons," he replied with a wicked grin.

She stared at him blankly for a moment; then, as his meaning sank in, she sprang to her feet. "I think you had better go. Now."

"Calm down, darlin'," he said mildly. "I was just joshing with ya."

"You are a lowdown, despicable . . ."

He held up his hand. "I know what I am." He gulped down the last forkful of scrambled egg, pushed away from the table, and stood facing her. "Like I said, you've got nothing to fear from me."

She nodded curtly. The burn on her palm stung a

little as she gathered the dishes from the table then moved past him toward the dry sink. She was keenly aware of him standing behind her as she filled a pot with water and put it on the stove to heat. His presence made her small kitchen feel even smaller, until it seemed as if the walls were closing in on her. She stared at the water in the pot, willing it to boil, ever conscious of his gaze on her back. Her skin prickled under his regard.

She knew the very moment that he left the room. Feeling weak with relief, she sagged against the counter. She had a sudden horrible feeling that she would be safer in Marteen's lodge than she was here, in her own house, as long as Nathan Chasing Elk was living under the roof.

All that day she was plagued with a restless yearning that she didn't understand, whether she was dusting the furniture, which was a never-ending task out here in the West, or kneading dough for biscuits. Time and again she found herself thinking about Chasing Elk, wondering what he was doing, thinking, feeling; wondering why she cared, and why she couldn't put him out of her thoughts.

Finally, unable to resist her curiosity a moment longer, she took off her apron and went outside. Standing on the front porch, she glanced around the yard. He was nowhere to be seen.

Frowning, she walked down to the barn and peered inside. She was about to leave when she heard his voice.

"Easy now, mama," he crooned softly, "everything's gonna be all right."

Walking on tiptoe, Catharine followed the sound of his voice to the back of the barn, and there, in one of the stalls, she saw Chasing Elk. He was hunkered down beside a pile of straw, talking to one of the cats while he endeavored to rub some life into a tiny gray kitten.

Catharine felt an odd shiver run down her spine as she watched his big hand move lightly over the kitten's body. It reminded her of the gentle way he had rubbed lard into her hand earlier in the day. Thinking of it now made her palm tingle.

"Come on, cat," he muttered. "Take a breath." He massaged the kitten's chest one more time, and a shudder ran through the furry little body.

Catharine felt the sting of tears in her eyes when the kitten took a shallow breath.

He rubbed the tiny kitten for another minute or so and then placed it in the straw with the others. The mama cat licked the kitten, then looked up at Chasing Elk and meowed, almost like she knew what he had done and was saying thank you.

Catharine was about to tiptoe away when Chasing Elk glanced over his shoulder. When he looked up, their gazes met and something warm and exciting and totally unexpected passed between them. Feeling suddenly flushed and flustered, Catharine turned and hurried out of the barn.

Chasing Elk sat on the top step of the front porch, basking in the warmth of the sun and in the knowledge that he could sit there for as long as he damn well pleased.

He leaned back on his elbows, wincing as the movement sent a sharp twinge of pain lancing through him. In spite of the constant aches in his back and his thigh, he felt better than he had in years. There were no guards to order him about, no gray walls to block his view of the distant mountains.

He could hear the woman, Catharine, moving around inside the house. Pretty name, he thought with a smile. A pretty name for a pretty woman. A woman who looked at him as if he were some sort of wild animal who was going to take a bite out of her first chance he got. He laughed softly. He wouldn't mind taking a nibble here and there.

He closed his eyes, utterly relaxed for the first time since he'd been arrested just over four and a half years ago. That was a day he wasn't likely to forget, he thought bleakly.

It had been a cool day in late spring. He had left to go hunting early that morning. He had mounted his horse, then paused to look back. Ellenora had been standing in the doorway, holding Leah in her arms. Nora had looked so pretty standing there in her long white cotton nightgown, her hair falling in wild disarray over her shoulders, that he had been tempted to stay home. He frowned. Had he known, even then, that he would never see Nora alive again?

It had been just before dusk when he returned home. The house had been dark. No smoke rose from the chimney. A shiver of unease had trickled down his spine as he stepped from the saddle and drew his Colt.

A sound from behind the house caught his attention. Moving cautiously, he rounded a corner in time to see a man run out of the barn, swing onto the back of a horse, and ride away.

"Buckner!" Lifting his weapon, Chasing Elk fired at the fleeing man, cursing when he missed.

He'd heard his daughter sobbing then. Hurrying into the house, he went to her bedroom. The door had been locked from the outside.

"Ellenora? Ellenora, where the hell are you?"

There was no answer.

Frowning, Chasing Elk unlocked and opened the door.

Leah looked up from where she sat huddled on her bed, her eyes wide with fright as he entered the room.

"It's all right, honey," he said, holstering his gun. "Where's Mama?"

Fresh tears cascaded down his daughter's cheeks.

"It's all right," he said again. "We'll find her."

Lifting his daughter into his arms, he had carried her into the living room. "Nora?"

He had checked the kitchen and their bedroom, but Ellenora was nowhere to be found.

Suddenly feeling sick to his stomach, he had gone out to the barn. He paused at the door, then put Leah down. "Wait out here for me, sweetheart," he said. "I'll be right back."

She looked up at him, mute, her eyes still damp with tears.

Taking a deep breath, Chasing Elk had stepped into the barn's dusky interior. His nostrils filled with the scents of hay and manure. And the coppery scent of blood.

"Nora?"

He found her sprawled on her back in a pile of straw, her skirts hiked up to her waist, her eyes wide and staring. Blood oozed from the knife wound in her chest.

He stared at her in horror; then, mindful of his daughter, he closed Ellenora's eyes and pulled her skirt down over her legs. Taking a deep breath, he withdrew the knife from her breast.

He had stared at the bloody blade and then lifted his shirt. "I will avenge you," he vowed, and then he had dragged the bloody blade across his chest.

And that was how his daughter and his neighbor had found him.

He'd had nightmares for months after that. Vivid dreams where he saw Nora's death over and over again, but it had been his hand plunging the knife into her breast while Leah stood nearby, screaming . . .

"Mr. Elk?"

He looked up to find Catharine staring down at him.

"Something wrong?" he asked.

"I'm going into the Crossing for supplies."

He sat up. "I'll go with you."

"Do you think that's wise?"

"Probably not."

"Then why don't you stay here?"

"And have you go running to the sheriff? I don't think so."

"There is no sheriff at the Crossing. Anyway, I wouldn't do that. I need you here."

"Darlin', if you make it into town, I doubt you'll be coming back here."

"Why do you say that?"

He lifted one brow. "You were running away from this place when you found me, remember?"

Crossing her arms over her breasts, she glared at him.

"I'll go hitch the horses to the wagon."

With a little "humph" of exasperation, she turned on her heel and went back into the house.

Smiling with amusement, Chasing Elk stared after her, admiring the sway of her hips. Still smiling, he stood and headed for the barn.

Chasing Elk took one look at Finley's Crossing and knew he had nothing to fear. Catharine had spoken the truth. There was no law here. Save for a couple of ramshackle buildings and a few scraggly-maned horses in a peeled-pole corral, there was nothing here. He glanced at the buildings. Signs proclaimed that the larger of the two buildings was Finley's Trading Post, the smaller one was Finley's Hotel and Saloon.

Chasing Elk shifted on the hard wooden seat, uncomfortable in his borrowed clothes. The brown twill trousers were too short, the scuffed black boots too big, the brown plaid shirt tight through the shoulders. He grinned wryly. At least they weren't prison-issue and crawling with vermin.

He reined the team to a halt in front of the trading post, set the brake, and wrapped the reins around the handle. Vaulting to the ground, he reached up to help Catharine down. Lips pursed, she ignored his hand and climbed down on her own.

With a shrug, Chasing Elk followed her into the store, then trailed along behind her while she shopped. She bought sacks of sugar, flour, and coffee; a can of baking powder; a round of cheese; a side of bacon. He didn't know what shopkeepers were charging in

Tucson or Tombstone these days, but Finley's prices seemed like highway robbery.

Catharine paused in front of a rack of ready-made clothing, her fingers caressing a dress of pink-flowered muslin; then, with a sigh, she moved on.

"Afternoon, Miss Lyons," the proprietor said when she reached the counter. "Did you find everything you were looking for today?"

"Yes, thank you, Mr. Finley."

Walter Finley was tall and lanky, with a shock of wheat-colored hair and muttonchops. His eyes were blue behind a pair of round spectacles.

He added up her purchases, then wrapped them in brown paper and string and packed them in a couple of boxes. "Junior, come carry these things out for Miss Lyons."

"Yessir!" A boy of perhaps thirteen emerged from a back room. He was tall and thin, with curly brown hair. Picking up one of the boxes, he carried it outside. He returned for the second one a couple of minutes later.

Finley added her current bill to his book, wrote a figure down on a piece of paper, and handed it to her with a smile.

"I trust our usual agreement is still acceptable?" Catharine asked, returning his smile.

"Yes, indeed, Miss Lyons."

"Very well. Good day to you, Mr. Finley."

"Good day, Miss Lyons."

She smiled and nodded at the boy who had loaded the wagon, then left the building.

Curious about her "usual agreement," Chasing Elk followed her outside. She again refused his offer of assistance, preferring to climb onto the wagon seat on her own.

Chasing Elk shook his head at her stubbornness. Climbing up beside her, he unwrapped the reins from around the brake. Clucking to the horses, he pulled away from the trading post.

The ride home was as long and quiet as the ride to the Crossing had been. Chasing Elk glanced Catharine's way from time to time, noting the stiff set to her shoulders, the stubborn jut of her chin, the way the sunlight danced in the burnished wealth of her hair. He noted the sweet curve of her breast, the warmth of it when the wagon hit a rut in the road and her body brushed against his shoulder. There was something about her, he thought, something that reminded him of Ellenora, though he couldn't say what. Perhaps it was the way she moved, sort of graceful and elegant. Perhaps it was the slight lilt in her voice, or the way she sometimes looked at him, her eyes filled with warmth and understanding.

"So," he said after awhile, "what's your usual agreement with Finley?"

"I don't have much cash, so he takes part of his payment in trade." She blushed when he lifted one brow. "Not that kind of trade. He comes out to the house with his son once a month. I make them dinner and send them off with a pie to take home and another pie to sell at the store."

He grunted softly. "You lived out here long?"

"Almost five years."

Her answer was curt, but at least she was talking to him again.

"You don't seem to like it much," he remarked.

"No."

"So, why did you come here?"

"My father decided we should move West after he lost his job. My mother died in childbirth a year later. My father drank himself to death."

"Where's your brother?" he asked, thinking that she'd had more than her share of heartaches and troubles.

"I don't know."

Chasing Elk shifted on the hard seat, wondering if she had forgotten that she had told him her brother would be coming home soon, or if she had decided against lying to him a second time.

"How long has he been gone?"

"Just over a month." She looked at him anxiously. "He was going to Finley's Crossing to pick up supplies, but he never came back. Mr. Finley said he bought a few things . . . I haven't seen him since. You don't think that he's . . . that Marteen . . . ?"

That was exactly what Chasing Elk thought, but he didn't tell her that. Why destroy her hopes?

"Why were you in prison?"

A muscle worked in his jaw. His hands tightened on the reins. "They said I killed my wife."

She looked at him, her eyes wide. "Did you?"

"No."

"Why do they think you did?"

"They found me kneeling beside her, holding the knife that killed her."

"Oh." That one softly spoken word clearly revealed her horror at what he had told her. "How long were you in prison?"

"Four years, six months, and thirteen days, not

counting the three weeks I spent in jail while they waited for the judge to arrive and try my case."

"Was it awful?"

He stared at her. "Awful? Honey, it was a hell of a lot worse than awful."

"You have a lot of scars."

"Yeah." Some that showed, he thought bitterly, and some that didn't.

They were approaching the farm when three Apache warriors rose up out of nowhere. They didn't say anything, just stood there watching as he turned the horses onto the road that led to the house.

"Do you think they followed us to the Crossing?" Catharine asked, her voice hushed.

"I know they did." He had spotted them from time to time but had seen no reason to worry her.

"Why didn't you tell me?"

"Figured it would have upset you," he said with a shrug. "Nothing you could have done about it anyway."

He pulled up in front of the house a few minutes later. This time, he didn't offer to help her down. Instead, he went around to the back of the wagon, lowered the tailgate, and picked up one of the boxes.

He followed her to the door, waited while she unlocked it, then followed her into the kitchen. He put the box on the table and went back out for the other one.

There was no sign of the Apaches.

He carried the second box into the house and dropped it beside the first one. Catharine was standing in front of the pantry, putting the canned goods on the shelf. Unable to resist, he walked up behind her, close enough that the hem of her dress brushed the toes of his boots.

"I'll go out and put the horses away."

She shivered as his breath stirred a few strands of hair along her nape.

He took a deep breath, his nostrils filling with the scent of lavender and woman. Desire rose up within him, hot and quick.

He didn't move, didn't speak, yet he knew she was aware of the sudden tension between them. She went very still. He noticed her knuckles were white around the can she held midway between the box and the shelf.

He took the tin from her hand and placed it on the shelf, and then, taking hold of her shoulders, he turned her around to face him. She stared up at him, her eyes wide and wary, like a doe about to be set upon by wolves. A wordless sound that might have been a protest escaped her lips.

"I haven't been this close to a woman who smelled as clean as you do in a long time," he said, his voice little more than a rough whisper. "A very long time."

And then he lowered his head and kissed her.

Startled, Catherine didn't move, only stood there, her eyes open, while his mouth moved over hers. His lips were warm and firm, evoking feelings she had never experienced in places she had not known existed. His beard was softer than it looked. Liquid heat flowed through her. And then, to her horror, she closed her eyes and kissed him back.

His arm snaked around her waist, drawing her body fully against his. It was only when his tongue slid across her lower lip that sanity returned.

With a cry, she twisted out of his embrace, drew back her arm, and slapped him.

The sound of her slap seemed to hang in the air, and even as she watched, the print of her hand bloomed on his cheek.

"You could have just said no," he remarked.

And then, flashing a wry grin, he left the house.

Chapter 6

Catharine stared after Chasing Elk, her mind in turmoil. Her first kiss. She wasn't sure if she was more shocked by the hot, sweet intimacy of his mouth on hers or her unexpected reaction to it. She had kissed him back, kissed him with a passion she hadn't known she possessed. And then she had slapped him, something propriety demanded she should have done far sooner than she had.

What was she going to do? She couldn't stay here with him, not after the way she had behaved. She had to get away from him, the sooner the better.

Tomorrow morning, she would go into the Crossing and beg, borrow, or steal a ticket on the first stage heading east.

Going to the front window, she gazed into the distance. She didn't see any Apaches, but she knew they were out there. Would they let her leave the farm alone? Would she be foolish to try?

Blowing out a sigh of exasperation, she went back into the kitchen and put away the rest of the supplies. When that was done, she hiked up her skirts and scrubbed the kitchen floor, hoping it would keep her from thinking of him. It didn't, of course.

Why had he kissed her?

Worse, why had she kissed him back?

Just the memory of his kiss caused a flurry of excitement in the pit of her stomach. She had waited a lifetime to be kissed, had imagined it a thousand times. But the reality was nothing like her dreams. She smiled faintly. She had imagined being kissed on a moonlit balcony, or swept off her feet by a man in uniform, or wooed with soft words and poetry. She had never envisioned being kissed in her kitchen by an escaped convict! Why did *he* have to be the one to give her her first kiss? And what was wrong with her, that the kiss of a total stranger could make her yearn for so much more?

With a rueful shake of her head, she went into the living room and began to dust the furniture. Doing housework had always been her answer to whatever was troubling her, whether it was a problem that needed to be solved, anger at her brother for some slight, real or imagined, or just sheer frustration at being stuck on a farm in the middle of nowhere.

She paused at one of the windows, her gaze captured by the sight of Chasing Elk currying his horse. He had removed his shirt, allowing the sunlight to caress his broad back. Muscles rippled under his skin as he drew the brush over the stallion's back in long, even strokes. Setting the brush aside, he checked the horse's feet, giving Catharine an unobstructed view of his backside. She felt a rush of heat flood her cheeks as she realized just what she was staring at. What was wrong with her? She had seen men before. The Crossing was full of them. Tall, short, young, old, smart and not so smart. She had never given any of them a second look. Again she asked herself, *why him*?

Just then, he glanced over his shoulder toward the very window where she was standing. She jumped backward, knocking a vase from a table.

Mortified, she stood with her back pressed against the wall, broken pieces of crockery scattered at her feet. Oh, Lord, had he seen her ogling him? How could she explain . . . ? How could she sit across from him at dinner and make small talk? Maybe she could insist he eat in his room. Or plead that she had a headache, or just lock herself in her room and never come out again!

Easing away from the wall, she went into the kitchen for the broom and the dust pan and quickly cleaned up the broken vase. When that was done, she returned to her housecleaning with a vengeance.

She was in the midst of changing the sheets on Chasing Elk's bed when she heard the front door open.

Stars above, he was here! She froze, her heart pounding like a blacksmith's hammer, when she heard his footsteps coming down the hall.

Chasing Elk stopped abruptly when he reached his room and found Catharine standing by the bed where she had obviously been changing the sheets. When she saw him standing in the doorway, her face went white, then red.

He lifted one brow in wry amusement. He had seen her at the window earlier, watching him. She might be embarrassed to admit it, but there was no denying it. She was as attracted to him as he was to her. The question now was, what were they going to do about it?

He glanced at the half-made bed. He knew what he wanted to do, but he doubted she was the kind of woman to succumb to a quick tumble between the sheets.

"I . . ." She cleared her throat. "Is there something you wanted?"

He glanced at the bed again. Oh, yeah, there was something he wanted, all right.

Catharine followed his glance, then looked up at him, wide-eyed, her cheeks flushed. With a wordless cry, she tossed the sheet she was holding in his face and ran out of the room.

His laughter followed her down the hallway to her own room. Even after she slammed the door, she could hear his laughter echoing in her mind. Oh! The man was despicable! But then, what could she expect from a convict? He had to leave here now, and she would tell him so tonight, at dinner. Marteen or no Marteen, she refused to have Chasing Elk under her roof for one more night.

She stayed in her room the rest of the day. She changed the sheets on her bed. She rearranged the furniture. She caught up on her mending, which had been woefully neglected since Mark left. She read from the Bible. She sorted through her dress patterns, and all the while she told herself that she wasn't hiding from that despicable man; she was merely catching up on a number of chores that she had been putting off for far too long.

With a shake of her head, she dumped the patterns

back in the box. Rising from the edge of the bed, she lifted her chin and squared her shoulders. What was she doing? This was her house, after all. She wouldn't let that man make a prisoner of her in her own home! It wasn't against the law to look out the window, and it wasn't her fault that he had been in her line of sight when she did!

Opening the door, she marched into the kitchen, put on a clean apron, and began peeling potatoes for dinner.

He entered the kitchen a few minutes later, his footsteps ringing in her ears like thunder.

"Dinner won't be ready for at least an hour," she said, not turning around. "I'll call you when it is."

Though she had clearly dismissed him, he didn't take the hint. She could feel his presence in the room, feel him watching her like a cat at a mouse hole.

Glancing over her shoulder, she saw him straddling a chair, his arms folded across the back.

"What do you want?" she asked curtly.

He shrugged. "A little company? A kind word? A smile?"

"I'm busy." She tossed a peeled potato into the pot of water on the old wood-burning stove. Placing the knife carefully on the table, she turned to face him, her hands fisted on her hips. "But as long as you're here, we need to talk. I want you to leave. Now. Tonight."

He raised one brow in a gesture that was becoming all too familiar. "Is that so?"

"Yes."

"What about the Apache?"

"That's none of your concern. I was wrong to get you involved. I want you to go, the sooner, the better."

He grunted softly. "I see."

"Do you?"

"More than you think. You're afraid of me."

She lifted her chin defiantly. "Don't be ridiculous."

He rose very slowly and walked toward her. He was a big man, tall and broad-shouldered, with big, capable-looking hands. Hands that could easily break her in two. He had been convicted of killing his wife. Of course, he had claimed he was innocent, but was there ever a guilty man who didn't?

Overcome by a sudden rush of panic, Catharine picked up the knife she had been using to peel the potatoes and thrust it out in front of her. "Stay away from me!"

He stopped where he was, a look of amusement on his face as he gestured at the knife in her hand. "Not afraid, huh?"

"N-no." Her voice was trembling; so was the hand holding the knife.

Taking half a step forward, he plucked the knife from her hand and dropped it in the sink. "Shall I tell you what you're afraid of?"

She shook her head. She knew what she was afraid of but she didn't want to hear him put it into words, didn't want to have to deny it.

"Catharine." His voice was soft, seductive, reminding her of the kiss they had shared and her ardent response to it.

"Go away!"

"Is that what you really want?"

Of course it was, she thought, so why did the words stick in her throat? Would it be so bad to let him kiss her again? But what if he refused to stop after one kiss? Even worse, what if she didn't want him to stop? She was starting to care for him and she didn't want to. He was only passing through. If she let him get too close, it was going to hurt when he left.

Torn with indecision, she stared at him, not knowing what to do or what to say.

He solved the problem for her by simply taking her in his arms and kissing her.

It was exactly the solution she had hoped for. Since she hadn't initiated it, she couldn't be held accountable.

Her arms remained at her sides, though her eyelids fluttered down. His lips moved over hers softly at first, then grew more and more ardent. His tongue slid over her lower lip, teasing, tempting, until her curiosity overcame her hesitance and she opened for him.

Heat shot through her from head to heel. With a gasp, she leaned into him, her body yearning for something unknown and out of reach. She had no knowledge of men, little understanding of what went on between a man and a woman. She had seen the cattle breed out on the range, but that hadn't given her much enlightenment.

She had asked Mark, but he had been horrified by her questions and almost as embarrassed as she had been to ask them. It had never occurred to her to ask her mother, and certainly not her father!

Muttering an oath, Chasing Elk drew back. "Damn, woman."

She stared up at him, her legs suddenly unsteady,

her senses reeling. She felt hot and tingly all over, as if she had a fever. "Did I do something wrong?"

Chasing Elk shook his head to clear it. "No, darlin', you did everything just right."

She swayed toward him, her lips parted, her eyes cloudy with passion. He would have bet his right arm that she was a maiden untouched, but she sure didn't kiss like one. He was debating whether to hightail it out to the safety of the barn or sweep her off her feet and into bed when someone knocked at the door.

Instantly alert, Chasing Elk moved toward the kitchen doorway. Peering around the jamb, he saw a man standing on the front porch.

Catharine smoothed a hand over her hair; then, with a quick glance at Chasing Elk, she went to answer the door.

"Evening, Miss Lyons. I'm Sheriff Hogan from Tucson."

She stared at the badge on his shirt front. How did he know who she was? Could he tell, just by looking at her, what she had been doing in the kitchen?

"Good evening." She cleared her throat. "Is something wrong?"

"Yes, ma'am. We received word from the Yuma pen that one of their convicts escaped. He's a half-breed, just over six feet tall, black hair, gray eyes, wearing a pair of prison-issue trousers. Have you seen him?"

Her mind in turmoil, Catharine's hand curled around the edge of the door. She could practically feel Chasing Elk's gaze burning into her back. What should she do? What should she say?

"Are you all right, Miss?"

"What? Oh, yes. Yes, of course. It's just frightening, you know, to think of such a man on the loose." She smiled up at the sheriff. "Me being alone way out here and all."

The sheriff nodded. "Perhaps you should go stay at the Crossing until he's caught."

"Perhaps I will," she said, though she had no intention of doing any such thing. "Is there anything else?"

"Do you mind if I have a look around outside?"

"No, of course not."

The lawman touched the brim of his hat with his forefinger. "Sorry to have bothered you. I'll let you know if I find anything."

"Thank you. Good night."

Biting down on her lower lip, she closed the door, wondering what on earth had possessed her to lie to the sheriff. She was breaking the law by keeping a known criminal in her house. It was on the tip of her tongue to call the sheriff back, but then she remembered the horrible scars on Chasing Elk's back and shoulders. She couldn't abide the thought of his being imprisoned again, being subjected to that kind of punishment.

"Is he gone?"

At the sound of Chasing Elk's voice so close behind her, she practically jumped out of her skin. "Yes."

"What's he doing?"

Moving to the window beside the door, she watched the sheriff's progress as he went into the barn, only to emerge a short time later leading the black horse.

Catharine heard Chasing Elk mutter a vile oath. When she turned to look at him, he was gone.

Moments later, the sheriff was knocking at the door again.

Taking a deep breath, she opened the door.

"Where did you get that there horse?" He gestured at the stallion he had tied to the hitching post.

"I . . . that is, it just wandered into the yard one day. I didn't know where it came from, so . . ." She lifted one shoulder and let it fall.

"It was stolen in the escape."

"Oh, dear."

"You didn't see the man riding it?"

"No."

"Uh huh. Mind if I look around inside?"

Catharine stared at him, her heart pounding with trepidation. She didn't want to let him in, but how could she refuse? To do so would make him think she had something to hide.

Well, it was out of her hands now.

She stepped away from the door, then trailed after the lawman as he went from room to room, checking under the beds, in the armoire, in the pantry. Going out the back door, he looked in the springhouse and the outhouse.

Catharine's heart was beating double time when they returned to the front of the house. Where was he?

"I'll be going now," the sheriff said. He took up the reins of the stolen horse, then mounted his own bay. "Keep your doors locked good and tight."

"Yes, I will."

"I'll be out to check on you again in a week or so."

With a nod, she watched him ride out of the yard leading the stolen horse.

Catharine watched the sheriff until he was out of sight, then went into the house. Where was Chasing Elk?

She let out a startled cry when she entered the kitchen and saw him sitting at the table.

Chapter 7

Chasing Elk regarded her curiously. "Why didn't you turn me in?"

"I don't know," she said with a shrug. It was a lie, of course. She hadn't turned him in because she just didn't believe he was capable of cold-blooded murder. She dropped into the chair across from him. "Where did you go?"

He shrugged. "Just decided to make myself scarce for awhile."

"But there's nowhere to hide out there, at least not near the house."

"Sure there is," he said with a grin.

She recalled then that he was part Indian. No doubt he had the ability to make himself invisible, just like Marteen and his warriors.

She was suddenly very curious about Chasing Elk's heritage. Though she had lived in this part of the country for almost five years, she knew little about the Indians and their lifestyle save what she read in the weekly paper. If everything she had read was to be believed, Indians were godless savages who spent all their time raiding and stealing and killing innocent women and children. It was said that the Apache could hide themselves so well that unwary travelers never saw them until it was too late. She thought that part must be true, since the Army couldn't seem to find them. The Indians could run farther than a horse and exist on whatever food and water they could find. Some said they would ride a horse into the ground, and then eat the carcass. It was also said that they considered everyone who was not Apache to be the enemy. While she couldn't say for sure if all that was true, she couldn't say it wasn't true, either.

Chasing Elk lifted one brow. "What?"

"Excuse me?"

"Why are you lookin' at me like that?"

"Like what?"

"Like I'm about to take your scalp."

How had he known what she was thinking? "I don't know what you're talking about. Anyway, I have to finish fixing dinner."

Rising, she went back to the dry sink and picked up a potato.

"Something's bothering you," he said. "So, what is it? The sheriff's visit? The fact that the horse is gone? Or the fact that I'm still here?"

He was far too perceptive!

"You can ask me anything," he said, leaning back in his chair, his arms crossed over his chest, his legs stretched out in front of him. "Of course, I don't promise to answer."

"Well, if you must know, I was just curious about, well, about the Indian part of you."

"Not interested in the rest of me, huh?"

She heard the barely suppressed laughter in his

voice and knew he was teasing her. It was a new experience, being teased by a man who wasn't her brother
or her father.

"Sorry," he said. "What do you want to know?"

"Are you Apache, like Marteen?" She finished
peeling one potato and started on another.

"No. I'm Lakota."

"Oh." She glanced at him over her shoulder. "Like
Crazy Horse."

Chasing Elk grunted softly. Everyone knew about
Crazy Horse. Back in '76, when Chasing Elk had been
breaking his back putting the finishing touches on his
cell in the hellhole that was Yuma Prison, Crazy Horse
and his people had been at war with the Seventh Cavalry. In June of that year, the Lakota, the Cheyenne,
and the Arapaho had wiped out General George
Armstrong Custer and more than two hundred of his
men at the Little Big Horn. Following the battle, the
tribes had scattered. Sitting Bull had taken his people
and gone north to Canada, but Crazy Horse had continued to fight.

"Yeah," he said with a sigh. "Like Crazy Horse."
Only Crazy Horse was dead. He had been killed at
Fort Robinson, Nebraska, in 1877, bayoneted by a sol-
dier while he was trying to escape captivity.

"Were you there when Custer was killed?" she
asked, the potato in her hand forgotten.

"No."

"You sound sorry."

"Believe me, I'd rather have been fighting at the
Greasy Grass than locked up in Yuma."

She supposed she could understand that. Even

fighting would be better than being locked up. "Were you living with the Indians when they arrested you?"

"No."

"Have you ever lived with them?"

"I spent the first nine years of my life with the Lakota."

"And after that?"

"When I turned nine, my old man decided I should move into town with him. He ran a freight line. My mother didn't want me to go, and I didn't want to leave her, but my father insisted. He sent me to school in town. I hated it there, and they hated me. It seemed that practically everyone in the town had lost a loved one in a battle or a massacre, and there I was, the only Indian in town. I was the butt of every joke and every dirty trick you can imagine."

"Didn't the teacher . . . ?"

Chasing Elk snorted derisively. "He was as bad as everyone else. He didn't want me there any more than I wanted to be there." He shook his head. "I must have got beat up after school by the older boys in class at least once a week. When I told my old man what was going on, he told me to stop whining, that it would make me stronger. He was right about that, too. When I got a little older, I beat the sh— I got even with all of them, one at a time."

He shook his head. "The teacher had looked the other way when I was on the losing end, but when I got big enough to fight back, he suddenly decided fighting was wrong.

"Later, I was grateful to my old man for making sure I learned how to read and write and speak his language fluently. But I hated him for it at the time, and I resented the fact that the only time I was allowed to see my mother was during the summer."

She looked thoughtful for a moment before asking, "If your father was white and your mother was Lakota, how did they meet?"

"My old man was hauling freight across the plains when his wagon broke down. A hunting party found him and took him back to their camp."

Catharine dropped the potato and the knife in the sink, wiped her hands on a towel, and then sat down at the table, more interested in hearing about Chasing Elk's past than in fixing dinner. "Why didn't the Indians kill him?"

"Because it was a hunting party, not a war party."

"Go on."

"Well, they took him home and fed him, and sometime during the course of the evening, he met my mother and . . . Anyway, he went back to their camp every chance he got that summer. He married her that winter. Of course, it wasn't recognized by the whites."

"I guess she couldn't live in town with him."

"Not hardly."

"Why didn't he stay with her?"

"He was a man of vision, my old man. He knew that the Indian way of life wouldn't last forever, and he wanted me to be as comfortable in the white world as I was in my mother's. Then, too, he had a pretty good business, one that he hoped I'd take over when I got older."

"Did you?"

"No. I never forgave him for taking me away from my mother's people."

"Why didn't you go live with the Lakota when you were older?"

It was a question he had often asked himself. When he turned sixteen, he'd had every intention of going to live with his mother's people summer and winter. But somewhere along the way, he had gotten sidetracked, once by the lure of gold, another time by a pretty woman. When he turned nineteen, he found himself in Tucson dealing cards for a gambling house. He had been thinking about quitting his job and going home to see his mother that summer, only that was the year he had met Ellenora. He had bumped into her one afternoon when he was coming out of the general store. One look at her and he knew he wouldn't be leaving Tucson anytime soon. He had insisted on walking her home, and when he left her at her front door, he had an invitation to dinner for the following night. After that, any thoughts he'd had of going back to the Dakotas were forgotten.

He ran his hand through his hair. How differently his life would have been if he had gone to live with the Lakota the way he had planned. He would never have met Ellenora. She wouldn't have given him a daughter. He wouldn't have gone to prison. He wouldn't have lost touch with his mother. What with one thing and another and the time he'd spent in prison, he figured it had been close to thirteen years since he had seen her—something he intended to rectify as soon as he got his daughter back.

He shook his head. "I had my reasons."

She couldn't help feeling a little bit resentful that he didn't want to share his reasons with her. "Are your parents still alive?"

"My father was killed in a freight accident the year after I was sent to Yuma."

"What about your mother?"

"I don't know." He dragged the back of his hand over his jaw. "Most of the Lakota have been forced onto the reservation. If she's still alive, that's probably where she's living—if you can call that living."

"What do you mean?"

"Living on a reservation is like living in prison."

"Why is that?"

"My people have lost their freedom. Back in 1868, the government agreed that the Paha Sapa, the Black Hills, would belong to the Lakota people forever. They also agreed to keep white settlers out of the area. As written, the only way the treaty could be reversed was if three fourths of the warriors signed away the land, something my people would never do. As usual, the treaty wasn't worth the paper it was written on. Within four years, miners were roaming the area. Then Custer discovered gold in the Hills, and thousands of miners swarmed into the area like flies on a carcass. My people fought to keep their land.

"The year after Custer was killed, Congress passed the Black Hills Act, which not only took the Black Hills away from the Indians but millions of acres of their hunting grounds as well. White hunters have killed off most of the buffalo. Now my people are wards of the government, dependent on the white man for food and clothing that never comes. My people are starving while dishonest Indian agents are getting rich by selling wagonloads of food and supplies meant for the reservation."

"That's terrible."

He nodded, his anger rising as he thought of his mother living in poverty, forced to rely on charity from the enemy. The warriors could no longer hunt what few buffalo the whites hadn't killed. Deprived of hunting and warfare, the men looked for solace in the white man's whiskey. The women scavenged for food and firewood. The old people turned their faces toward death.

Muttering an oath, he pushed away from the table and left the house. He had failed both the women in his life. God willing, he would be able to make it up to them before it was too late. Thoughts of his daughter filled his mind.

He paced back and forth in front of the porch until his anger cooled. One thing at a time, he thought, rubbing his aching thigh. Sitting down, he stared into the gathering darkness. It was a long walk to town.

A movement in the distance caught his eye. Turning his head, he saw two mounted warriors in the distance.

Chasing Elk smiled inwardly. Maybe he wouldn't have to walk, he mused. The Apaches had horses. Among the Lakota, stealing horses from the enemy was considered a great coup. And he had been one of the best horse thieves in the tribe.

It was almost eight o'clock that night when Catharine went looking for Chasing Elk. She found him outside, sitting on the top rail of the corral.

"Dinner's ready if you're hungry," she said, coming up behind him.

He glanced over his shoulder. "I'm always hungry these days."

"I guess the food wasn't very good," she remarked. "In prison, I mean."

"Honey, nothing was good in prison," he said, his voice bitter.

Moving carefully, he climbed down off the fence.

Wordlessly, they made their way back to the house. Walking beside him, Catharine was aware of how tall he was. All her senses came alive at his nearness. When his arm brushed against hers, it sent little shivers of excitement running through her.

He held the door open for her, then followed her into the house and the kitchen. She gestured for him to sit down while she dished up two plates of fried chicken, mashed potatoes, corn on the cob, and freshly baked biscuits.

He really was hungry, she thought. He ate so quickly, she wondered if he tasted any of it. Had they starved him in prison, she wondered as she filled his plate again, or was his enormous appetite merely a sign that his wounds were healing?

He looked up at her as she refilled his plate a third time. "Why do I get the feeling that I'm eating tomorrow night's dinner, too?"

"Maybe because you are."

He smiled at her. "It's your own fault, you know, for being such a good cook."

She smiled back at him, and something hot and vibrant passed between them, something that suddenly made it hard for Catharine to draw a breath.

She was about to go back to her own seat when his fingers curled around her hand. Slowly, he drew her down onto his lap. His arm slid around her waist.

"What are you doing?" she asked, startled.

He shook his head. "Nothing."

The look in his eyes made her heart skip a beat.

"Nothing?" Her voice was little more than a squeak.

His hand slid up and down her spine, making slow, lazy circles. "Nothing that you don't want me to do."

She stared into his eyes. What *did* she want him to do?

He didn't wait for an answer. Cupping the back of her head in his hand, he kissed her, a long, deep kiss that made her toes curl inside her shoes. She gasped as his tongue slid across her lower lip. It was a good thing she was sitting down, she thought, dazed, because it felt like her blood was on fire and her bones were melting from the heat. A soft moan filled her ears. To her astonishment, she realized it had come from her own throat.

"Does that give you any ideas?" he asked, his voice gruff.

She blinked at him. "What?" Ideas? How could she think of anything at a time like this? She pressed a hand to her cheek. Her skin felt like it was burning, and she felt hot and achy in the strangest places.

"You all right?" he asked.

She shook her head. "I don't think so."

He looked at her oddly for a moment, and then he grinned. "Haven't you ever been kissed before?"

"Of course I have!" She slid off his lap and smoothed a wrinkle from her apron, suddenly embarrassed by the truth. She was twenty-three years old and until he came into her life, she had never been kissed. Not that it was any of his business!

"Have you got a beau I don't know about?" he asked.

She lifted her chin defiantly. "Maybe I have."

"Uh-huh."

She glared at him. "You don't believe me?"

"I would never call a lady a liar."

She fisted her hands on her hips. "But you don't believe me?"

Slowly, he shook his head.

"Oh! It's because I don't kiss very well, isn't it?"

Rising, he drew her into his arms. "Honey," he drawled, "believe me, there's nothing wrong with the way you kiss."

"Really?"

"Really."

She smiled, feeling terribly pleased by his praise, and then she frowned. "I guess you've kissed a lot of women."

"A few," he admitted with a wry grin.

"Oh."

"Jealous?"

"Of course not! Why would I be jealous? I hardly know you."

He laughed softly. The sound was full and rich, and it made her insides turn to mush.

"Seems to me we're getting acquainted right quick," he remarked, a wicked gleam in his eyes.

At a loss for words, Catharine pushed him away, embarrassed and confused by his teasing words and by her shameless response to his touch, his kisses. She had been raised better than that! Head high, she swept past him. Only her pride kept her from running down the hall to her room.

Once inside her bedroom, she closed and locked the door, then sank down on the foot of the bed, her fingertips pressed to her lips. She could still feel his kisses. She should get up, she thought, find a washcloth and scrub his taste away. That's what she should do.

But she didn't. Instead, she fell back on the mattress, smiling a foolish little smile. Three kisses in one day, and each one better than the last!

Chapter 8

Chasing Elk stood in the middle of the kitchen, wondering what the hell had just happened. Not to Catharine. He was pretty sure he knew what had happened to her. Unless he missed his guess, she was still a virgin, one who had never been kissed until he came along, and it had shaken her right down to her toes.

What he didn't know was what had happened to him. He wasn't a virgin, and it wasn't his first kiss, but damned if he didn't feel shaken right down to his toes as well. He shook his head. Maybe it wasn't such a surprise. He hadn't had a woman in over four years. He was surprised he even remembered how to kiss. He did remember a few other things though, things he'd like to do with Catharine. . . .

Dragging a hand over his beard-roughened jaw, he jerked his thoughts from that path. She had saved his life, and he wasn't going to take advantage of her. Besides, she was a maiden, untouched, and though he hadn't lived with the Lakota in years, the lessons he had learned as a young warrior were still strong within him. A warrior protected and provided for the women of his lodge. He didn't defile them. And while this wasn't his lodge, and she wasn't his woman, he couldn't disregard what he had been taught.

Sometimes it wasn't easy being a warrior.

Needing some fresh air, he stepped out onto the front porch. He stood there a moment. Then, having nothing better to do, he walked down to the barn to check on her horse, only to discover that Catharine's horse was gone. Save for one of the cows, who mooed softly, the barn was empty.

The next few days passed peacefully enough. Thanks to Catharine's good cooking, Chasing Elk quickly regained his strength, and when boredom set in, he began doing chores around the farm. He repaired the gate on the corral and fixed the broken hinge on the barn door. He patched a hole in the roof, weeded her garden and repaired some tack for the horse he intended to steal back. Catharine had burst into tears the night he told her that the Indians had stolen her horse. Again. Sobbing, she had fallen into his arms. Holding her, comforting her, he could almost be grateful to the thieving Apaches. Almost, but not quite.

The tension between himself and Catharine grew stronger with each passing day. He had caught her watching him on more than one occasion. She always blushed. He found it most becoming. Of course, he spent a fair amount of time watching her, too, imagining what it would be like to take her to bed and make love to her all night long.

She was watching him now. He could feel her gaze on his bare back as he sawed a fallen branch into two-

foot lengths for firewood. He knew she was attracted
to him and didn't want to be. She was ripe, he thought,
like an apple ready for picking. He also knew she
liked his kisses and that she was curious about where
those kisses might lead. And he was eager to be her
guide, to show her just how good loving could be between a man and a woman.

If only she had been a widow woman instead of a
maiden, someone who knew what went on behind
closed doors and might be willing to ease a lonely
man's need for a woman's touch.

Damn! With each passing day, he found more to
love about her. Her smile, her laugh, her very innocence drew him. He wanted to take her in his arms
and teach her how good it could be between the two
of them. He wanted to watch her eyes glow with passion, hear her cry his name as he aroused her, feel the
warmth of her skin against his own.

Muttering an oath, he tossed the saw aside, picked
up the ax, and turned his attention to a seasoned log.
Swinging the ax made his back hurt like the very dick-
ens, but it took his mind off the woman.

Catharine stood at the window, watching Chasing
Elk as he chopped firewood. He had found Mark's
razor and shaving mug and shaved off his beard. She
had thought him handsome before but he was beyond
handsome now. His jaw was firm and square, his lower
lip full and enticing. She didn't know what there was
about watching him work that drew her gaze again
and again, but there it was. Maybe it was because he
moved so beautifully, almost like a dancer. Maybe it
was the way the sun seemed to caress his sweat-

sheened flesh and cast blue highlights in his long black hair. Maybe it was his easy strength that fascinated her.

Maybe it was simply that he was the first man she had ever met who excited her. She dreamed of him at night, thought of him every waking moment of the day. Maybe she could have ignored both him and her feelings if he wasn't so outrageously handsome, or if his smile wasn't so devastating, or if his voice didn't remind her of warm, sweet molasses.

She moved away from the window before he caught her staring at him again. No matter how it embarrassed her to be caught, she couldn't seem to stop watching him.

Going into the kitchen, she checked on dinner. She was making chicken and dumplings again because he had remarked that he liked it the last time she had served it to him.

She paced the kitchen floor a moment. It was time to go out and milk the cows and feed the chickens. She would have to pass by Chasing Elk to get to the barn. She chewed on a fingernail a moment, willing herself to be calm. She put on her apron, then grabbed the milking pails and went outside.

Chasing Elk looked up when he heard the back door slam. Straightening, he rolled his shoulders, wincing as he did so. Though he felt a lot better, his back was still sore. He watched the woman walk toward the barn. Catharine. She got prettier every time he saw her.

She stopped in front of him, the buckets in her hands swinging back and forth. "Dinner will be ready soon."

"What are we having?"

"Chicken and dumplings."

"My favorite."

A familiar blush pinked her cheeks. "I guess I'd best go milk the cows."

"I'll see you up at the house as soon as I finish here and get washed up."

They shared a smile, then she continued on toward the barn.

Chasing Elk stared after her, admiring the sway of her hips, the fall of her hair down her back.

Blowing out a sigh of exasperation, he swung the ax again.

A short time later, he washed up in the tub beside the back door before putting on his shirt and going into the kitchen. She was standing at the stove, stirring something with a big wooden spoon. He stood there a moment, thinking how quickly he had grown accustomed to her presence, to living in her house. He might have considered asking her if he could stay on if he hadn't been an escaped convict, with a daughter he hadn't seen in more than four years.

She smiled at him over her shoulder. "Sit down. Dinner's ready."

With a nod, he took his place at the table. It was covered with a checked cloth. There was a jar of wildflowers in the center of the table.

Catharine served him and then sat down across from him.

He had to get out of here, he thought, before leaving her became impossible. He didn't want to leave her behind, not with Marteen waiting to pounce on her first chance he got. But he supposed that decision was up to her.

"How soon can you be ready to leave here?"

"Leave?" She looked at him across the table. "How can we leave?"

"You let me worry about that. How much time do you need? A day? Two?"

"But . . . what about Marteen? He won't just let us go."

"Like I said, you let me worry about that. I'm leaving here as soon as I can get a horse. You can come with me or not, it's up to you."

"I'm ready now."

He grinned at her. "Good."

Catharine wandered through the house later that evening, wondering where Chasing Elk had gone. He had left right after dinner. She assumed he had gone to find some horses, though she had no idea where he planned to find them. The only horses around here belonged to the Apaches. . . .

She stopped in midstride. He wouldn't! He couldn't! She pressed a hand to her chest. Surely he didn't mean to try and steal horses from the Indians! If he was killed . . . Oh, Lord, if he was killed, she would be at Marteen's mercy. Even worse, she would never see Chasing Elk again.

Sitting down on the sofa, she tried to relax, but to no avail. The slightest sound sent her to the front window in hopes that Chasing Elk had returned, but it was either the whistling of the wind, the creak of the eaves, or the leaves rustling on the tree outside the window.

An hour passed. Two. Where was he? She imagined that he had been caught by the Apaches, that even now they were torturing him, skinning him alive, using him for target practice, or doing any one of the hundred other atrocities she had heard about. If anything happened to him . . . She tried to imagine what it would be like to be Marteen's captive. But he didn't want a captive; he wanted something much worse. He wanted a wife. And sons. She shuddered at the thought of sharing Marteen's bed, bearing his children in some hide lodge with no doctor to help her, or worse, out in the open, like some wild animal.

She curled up on the sofa. She would kill herself before she became Marteen's woman. She was almost asleep when a hand covered her mouth, stifling the cry that rose in her throat.

"Shh," Chasing Elk whispered. "It's me."

Relief washed over her, leaving her feeling momentarily light-headed.

"Are you ready?" he asked. "We need to go, and we need to go now."

"Go?" She stared at him blankly, and then she bounded to her feet. "You got a horse?"

"Two of them.

"But how . . . ?"

"Not now, darlin'." He lifted the rifle from the rack over the mantel, checked to make sure it was loaded. "You got any other weapons?"

"There's a pistol under my pillow."

"Get it and whatever else you want to take along, and let's get the hell out of here."

With a nod, she ran into her room. She pulled the Colt that had belonged to her father out from under her pillow and placed it into her poke, along with all the clothing she could stuff inside. She grabbed the photograph of her parents that had been taken on their wedding day, her mother's cameo locket, and her father's pocket watch and added them to the contents of her bag. She pulled the blankets off her bed and carried them and her poke into the parlor and dropped them by the door. Going into the kitchen, she found an old feed sack and filled it with as much food as it would hold, then added a frying pan, the coffeepot, a box of matches, and a couple of knives and forks. She wondered briefly what the Tucson sheriff would think when he came to check on her again. No doubt he would assume that she had gone to Finley's Crossing. She wondered what he would do if he checked and discovered she hadn't gone there. Would he search for her? Well, no matter. She couldn't worry about that now.

Hefting the heavy sack, she returned to the parlor. Chasing Elk was waiting for her by the front door, the rifle in his hand. For the first time, she noticed the knife on his belt. It was tucked into a beaded sheath, similar to the ones she had seen used by the Apaches.

When she started to put out the lamp, he shook his head.

She nodded. No doubt he hoped leaving the light on would make the Indians think they were home. She noticed he had left the lamp lit in Mark's bedroom as well.

"You ready?" he asked.

"I guess so." Taking her coat from the coat rack, she put it on and then picked up her poke.

Taking her by the hand, he hurried her out the back

door to where two horses waited for them. Then he lifted Catharine onto the back of a long-legged bay. "Can you ride bareback?"

"A little late to be asking," she retorted, "but yes, I can."

"Good." He tied the ends of her poke and the burlap bag together and draped them over her mount's withers, and then he swung up onto the back of the second horse. "Stay close behind me," he said. "And no matter what happens, keep riding north toward the Crossing."

Clucking to his mount, he struck out for the deer path that ran along the stream behind the house.

Catharine urged her horse after his, her heart pounding like thunder in her ears. She had never ridden in the dark before, and she decided almost immediately that she didn't like it. She knew how well the Apaches could blend into their surroundings. Marteen's warriors could be hiding behind every tree, every bush, waiting to strike them down, and they would never know it until it was too late. The sound of her horse's hoofbeats sounded very loud in the stillness of the night. She flinched when a jack rabbit bounded across her path, nearly jumped out of her skin when an owl swooped down out of a nearby tree.

She fixed her gaze on Chasing Elk's back, her hands tightly around the reins. He was strong. He was part Indian. He would keep her safe. She repeated the words in her mind over and over again, trusting that he knew where he was going, that he wouldn't be trekking through the darkness in the middle of the night if he thought they were in any danger.

After an hour or so, he turned his horse away from the stream and away from what little cover the trees had provided.

Feeling like a sitting duck, Catharine glanced over her shoulder time and again, reassuring herself that there was no one there.

She wondered where they were going. Chasing Elk had told her that if anything happened, she was to ride for the Crossing, but surely that couldn't be their destination. There was nothing there. Did he intend to go to Tucson? It was over two hundred miles away, but it was the nearest town of any size, and she decided that must be where he was headed. She had gone there once with her father to buy supplies. It was a small town, the buildings made of adobe, most with flat roofs. The ceilings were made from saguaro ribs, with large wooden beams spaced twenty-four inches apart for support. Her father had told her that the beams were so valuable that they sometimes appeared as bequests in people's wills. Catharine had never been sure if her father had been joking with her about that or not.

She reined her horse to a halt as Chasing Elk came to an abrupt stop in front of her.

Gesturing for her to be quiet, he slipped off the back of his horse and disappeared into the night.

The darkness closed in on her, thick and quiet and filled with menace. She shivered as a wolf howled in the distance.

Fear fluttered like butterflies in her stomach as a dark shape rose up from the ground and moved toward her. She leaned forward, peering into the darkness. Was it Chasing Elk? She was about to whisper his name when she saw the flash of a knife in the moonlight.

She was going to die. It was her first thought as the warrior ran toward her.

She opened her mouth to scream, but no sound emerged.

And then a second figure rose up from the ground behind the first. Even in the dim light cast by the moon, she knew it was Chasing Elk.

Shaking off her fright, she dug the pistol from inside her poke, aimed it at the first figure, and drew back the hammer. She was about to pull the trigger when Chasing Elk hurled himself at the Apache. The two of them went down in a tangle of arms and legs. They rolled away from her, making it impossible for Catharine to determine who was winning the fight. The sound of steel against steel rang out as the blades flashed in the moonlight. She heard a grunt laced with pain. The smell of blood drifted on the wind. She stared at the two men, one hand pressed to her heart.

The fight ended as quickly as it had begun.

One of the figures rose up from the ground and walked toward her.

"Dammit, woman, I thought I told you to keep riding, no matter what."

Relief rushed out of Catharine in an audible gasp. Dropping her pistol back in her poke, she dismounted and ran toward him. "Are you all right?" Her gaze moved over him. There were shiny wet spots on his shirt.

Lifting her skirt, she tore a ruffle from her petticoat and ripped it in half. "Take off your shirt."

"We don't have time for that now."

"You're bleeding."

Knowing it would be quicker to do as she asked than to spend time arguing with her, Chasing Elk removed his shirt.

Using the torn ruffle, she bandaged a shallow gash across his chest with one half and a cut in his left forearm with the other.

"I'm always patching you up," she muttered as she tied off the ends on the second bandage.

"Why didn't you keep riding?"

"I . . . I forgot."

"You forgot? Dammit, what if I'd lost?"

She stared at him, and then shrugged. "But you didn't."

With a shake of his head, he shrugged into his shirt. "Come on," he said gruffly, "let's get the hell out of here."

She didn't argue. She pulled herself onto the back of her horse, waited while Chasing Elk swung onto the back of his.

Once again, she followed him through the darkness, her gaze darting nervously from side to side. Were there more Apaches lurking out there in the darkness? Chasing Elk couldn't possibly fight them all and win, not now, when he'd been wounded. More scars, she thought sadly, when he already had so many.

They rode for what seemed like hours. She was afraid she was going to fall asleep in the saddle when Chasing Elk reined his horse to a halt just after dawn. Catharine looked around. They were in a sandy wash, out of sight of anyone who might be passing by.

She dismounted, then watched as Chasing Elk eased

off his horse's back. He looked bone-weary, reminding her that he wasn't fully recovered from his other wounds yet. His face set in grim lines, he hobbled the horses. Now, in the gray light of early morning, she saw that there was dried blood in several places on his back. There was little point in trying to bandage those wounds now, she thought. The bleeding had already stopped.

Rummaging through her poke, she handed him a slice of bread and a piece of cheese, then spread a blanket on the sand while he ate. She offered him a drink from one of the canteens, then urged him to lie down and get some sleep. He didn't argue. Moments later, he was snoring softly.

Catharine regarded him for several minutes, noting the dark shadows under his eyes, the fine lines of pain etched around his mouth. His wounds, both old and new, needed tending, but that would have to wait.

Smothering a yawn, she stretched out on the blanket beside him, careful not to touch him. Certain she would never be able to sleep out in the open when there might be Indians or wild animals creeping up on them or lurking behind every bush, she closed her eyes. . . .

She woke to the warmth of the sun on her face and a hard male body pressed against her back. One of Chasing Elk's arms was beneath her head, the other lay heavy on her waist. His breath feathered against her cheek, warm and soft.

Her first instinct was to push him away but that would wake him, and the last thing she wanted was to have him wake up and find them lying so close together. She frowned. After all he had been through, he needed his rest. On the other hand, they really needed to be on their way before the Apache he had killed the night before was missed and his friends came looking for revenge.

Catharine was about to wake Chasing Elk when she realized it wouldn't be necessary. She wasn't sure how she knew he was awake—a subtle change in his breathing, a shift of the weight of his arm—but she knew.

Her breath caught in her throat, all her senses suddenly alert and waiting. . . .

The arm that had been resting on her waist slowly wrapped around her, holding her in place.

"You smell good," he whispered.

Somehow she doubted that, but it pleased her that he thought so. "We . . . we should be . . . shouldn't we be going?"

He blew out a heavy sigh. "Yeah." But he didn't release his hold on her.

When she tried to wriggle out of his grasp, he muttered, "Dammit, stop that."

"Am I hurting you?" she asked, her brow furrowing with concern.

With a low groan, he let her go. "You have no idea."

Sitting up, she looked over at him. "I think you need a doctor."

"Believe me, honey, a doctor couldn't help."

She frowned at him. "I don't understand."

"I know. Let's keep it that way. We'll leave as soon as you're ready."

Grimacing with pain, Chasing Elk eased himself into a sitting position and reached for the canteen, but a

drink of cold water didn't help. He could still feel
Catharine's fanny pressed intimately against his groin.
He'd thought he might explode when she'd wriggled
against him. What he needed was a dip in the river,
though he wasn't sure even that could put out the fire
she had stirred within him.

Muttering an oath, he gained his feet and went to
remove the hobbles from the horses. No matter what
he felt for Catharine, physically or otherwise, the last
thing he needed in his life was another woman to
worry about.

They neared the outskirts of Finley's Crossing just
before noon. It was a long trip to Tucson, and while
Chasing Elk didn't mind roughing it himself, he had
Catharine's needs and comfort to think about now.
They could stock up on foodstuffs and whatever else
Catharine thought she might need and then strike out
for Tucson. Once there, he would get her settled and
she would be on her own. No doubt she would light
out for Boston the first chance she got.

A few wisps of gray-black smoke rising in the air
were the first indication that something was wrong.

Chasing Elk reined his horse to a halt, and Catharine pulled up beside him.

"What's wrong?" she asked, shading her eyes with
one hand.

"Stay here."

"Why?"

"Just do as I say." He paused, considering the risk
of leaving her there alone against the risk of taking
her with him and perhaps running into any Indians

who might be lingering at the site of the carnage. His decision made, he said, "If I'm not back in half an hour, get the hell out of here. And keep your pistol handy."

Clucking to his horse, he rode on, his rifle at the ready.

The smell of smoke grew stronger and more acrid as he drew nearer the Crossing. He knew what had happened even before he saw the burned-out buildings and the bodies.

Smoke hung heavy in the air. He found Finley's body lying outside the trading post, a dozen arrows protruding from his back. A second body, badly burned, was sprawled across the threshold of the saloon. He glimpsed two more bodies inside. There was no sign of Finley's son, and Chasing Elk figured the Apaches had taken the boy to raise as one of their own. The Apaches, like all Indians, had strong feelings for children.

Dismounting, Chasing Elk poked around the trading post, looking for anything he might salvage, and came away with a number of canned goods that he dumped into a burlap bag. He also found a sheepskin jacket that had miraculously escaped the flames.

He wasn't surprised to find that the saloon had been looted of its stock. No doubt the Apaches would be as drunk as lords on the white man's firewater by nightfall.

The corral out back was empty, but he found two saddles draped over the top rail. He threw one over the back of his horse and cinched it up, then tied the burlap bag around the horn. Balancing the other saddle on his uninjured thigh, he rode back to where he had left Catharine. She was still there, the pistol clasped in one hand.

"What is it?" she asked. "What's happened? Is Mr. Finley all right?"

"The Apaches burned him out. He's dead."

The blood drained from her face. "Dead?"

"Yeah." He dropped the saddle to the ground, then dismounted and lifted Catharine from the back of her horse.

She stretched the kinks out of her back and shoulders while he saddled her horse. "Did you . . . did you bury him?"

Chasing Elk shook his head. "Even if I'd wanted to, the ground's too hard, and I've got nothing to dig with. Mount up."

She did so, and he adjusted the stirrups, then looked up at her. "How's that?"

"Fine. But it's our Christian duty to bury Mr. Finley. We can't just leave him laying there in the dirt. . . ."

"Honey, I'm not up to digging a grave with my bare hands." Chasing Elk stepped into the saddle and clucked to his mount, and the horse moved out at a walk. "Besides," he said over his shoulder, "I don't think it's wise for us to be hanging around here."

Catharine urged her horse after his. "What about Mr. Finley's son?"

"I didn't see any sign of the boy. I think the Apaches took him."

Her eyes widened. "What will they do to him?"

"They won't hurt him. Apaches set a store by young 'uns. They'll raise him as one of their own."

"Was it Marteen?"

"Most likely."

Chasing Elk urged his horse into a lope, eager to put the Crossing behind them.

He kept up a fast, steady pace for close to an hour. When he slowed, Catharine rode up beside him. "How long will it take us to get to Tucson?"

"Eight or nine days. Once you're settled in, I'll be going on to Tombstone."

"Tombstone? Whatever for?"

"I've got business there."

She looked at him askance, but he didn't seem inclined to elaborate. Lost in thought, she fell back a little. Poor Mr. Finley was dead. His son had been abducted. And Chasing Elk was going to drop her off in Tucson like a sack of dirty laundry and then travel on to Tombstone for reasons he didn't see fit to share with her.

Hours passed. Sweat trickled down her neck and back and pooled between her breasts. They stopped only once to rest and water the horses, and then they were riding again. The desert stretched out before them, seemingly endless. Heat shimmered in the distance. A lizard sunned itself on a rock, its beady eyes unblinking as she rode past. Now and then a jackrabbit bolted from cover.

Catharine took a drink from her canteen. Her back and shoulders ached; her backside felt numb. Were they ever going to stop?

Just when she thought he intended to ride all night long, Chasing Elk drew rein near a shallow water hole.

Catharine climbed wearily out of the saddle, then made a grab for her horse's mane as her legs threatened to give way beneath her. Any more days like this, she thought glumly, and she wouldn't be able to walk!

She glanced over at Chasing Elk. Though he was in much worse shape than she was, the long ride didn't seem to have affected his ability to stand up. He unsaddled the horses and hobbled them, and then removed their bridles so they could graze on the sparse vegetation.

After a moment, she spread one of the blankets on the ground, then rummaged around in the burlap bag, pulling out the frying pan, matches, and coffeepot.

He shook his head when he saw the matches. "No fire. The smoke can be seen for miles."

They made do with biscuits and cold beans for dinner, and washed it down with water from one of the canteens.

"You'd best turn in," Chasing Elk said. "I want to get an early start in the morning."

She didn't argue. Wrapping herself in one of the blankets, she stared up at the sky, certain that she would never be able to get to sleep out there in the open, not with the memory of Mr. Finley's death fresh in her mind, not when Marteen and his warriors might still be lurking nearby, ready to attack them while they slept.

Chasing Elk sat cross-legged on the ground, a blanket wrapped around his shoulders, his rifle close at hand. Time and again his gaze was drawn toward Catharine, to the rise and fall of her breasts beneath the covers, to the curve of her cheek, the tantalizing fullness of her lower lip.

Ah, Catharine. What was he going to do about her? He didn't need another female to look after. Once he located Leah and his mother, he would surely have his hands full. Still, he didn't like the thought of leaving Catharine in Tucson to fend for herself.

He shook his head. It really wasn't up to him to decide what she did or where she went. Once he got her safely to town, she could make up her own mind about what she wanted to do. If she didn't want to stay in Tucson, he'd find a way to get enough money to put her on a stage and send her wherever she wanted to go.

But first he had to get her out of the Apaches' reach.

Chapter 9

After three days on the trail, Catharine was beginning to wish she had stayed home and taken her chances in fending off Marteen. She was heartily tired of sand and cactus, tired of riding for hours on end. She had forgotten to bring her bonnet, and her face and neck were sunburned.

Chasing Elk woke her at dawn each morning, and after a hurried breakfast, they were riding again. Once, when she complained about being tired, Chasing Elk told her that it was over two hundred miles to Tucson and that, because of their meager supplies and the threat of Indian attack, they didn't have time to dawdle. Mention of Indian attack reminded her that there were other bands in the area besides Marteen's, and she stopped complaining. The thought of being taken as Marteen's wife was bad enough; the thought of being captured and tortured or killed was far worse.

She grew increasingly grateful for Chasing Elk's knowledge about living off the land as the days went by. He managed to find game—rabbits, birds, and the like—to add to their rations, and he knew how to find water where it seemed there was none.

Now, riding across the desert, she wondered what awaited her when they arrived in Tucson. She had no money, and when Chasing Elk left for Tombstone, she wouldn't know a soul in town. She wondered again what business he had there. She had heard stories of the town, of gunfights in the saloons and in the streets, of con men and gamblers and women of easy virtue. Tucson wasn't much better. What would she do there on her own? She didn't intend to stay one minute longer than she had to, but the question remained, what was she going to do until she managed to earn enough money to pay for a ticket back East?

An even bigger question was what she was going to do when she got to Boston. She was certain that Mrs. Montgomery would put her up for a few days, perhaps a few weeks, but she couldn't impose on the woman's kindness indefinitely.

Catharine shifted in the saddle. She had no experience, no skills to speak of. Perhaps she could get a job waiting tables in a restaurant or working as a chambermaid in one of the hotels. She clung to the slim hope that she might find Mark there.

Catharine shook her dreary thoughts aside. Plenty of time to worry about Tucson and Boston when the time came.

She glanced over at Chasing Elk, admiring the set of his shoulders, his strong profile, the way he rode in the saddle, relaxed and easy, as if he were a part of the horse. Just looking at him filled her with a strange excitement. She knew so little about him, only that he was part Indian and that he had been accused of killing his wife. She was certain now that he could never have done such a terrible thing, though why she felt that way she couldn't say. True, he was tall and dark and dangerous-looking; but he had treated her with kindness and respect. He knew how to take care of himself, and her, and for that she was grateful. She knew without doubt that no matter what happened, he would protect her with his life. And she knew just as surely that he would never harm a woman.

When he looked her way, warmth spread through her. And suddenly she wasn't so anxious to leave Arizona and go back to Boston, even if Mark was there, because it meant she would never see Chasing Elk again.

That night they camped in the shelter of a rocky overhang. Dinner was roast rabbit and the last of the biscuits, washed down with a shared cup of coffee. It was the first night since they had left Finley's Crossing that Chasing Elk considered it safe enough to keep the small fire going after she had cooked the rabbit.

It was, Catharine thought, rather pleasant sitting there in the moonlight. The night was warm, the sky clear. Millions of stars twinkled overhead, sparkling like the finest diamonds in the night sky. Chasing Elk sat across from her, his expression impassive. She wondered what he was thinking about, what he thought about her.

"There's a little coffee left," she said. "Do you want it?"

"Yeah, thanks."

She refilled the cup and handed it to him. His fingers brushed hers, sending a little thrill of excitement racing through her. Did he feel it, too, that rush of heat each time they touched?

His gaze met hers. Awareness sparked between them.

Catharine's heart seemed to skip a beat, then pounded like thunder in her ears as he put the cup aside and reached for her.

She went into his arms willingly, eager for his kiss.

She wasn't disappointed. Murmuring her name, he settled her on his lap and lowered his head.

She closed her eyes with a sigh, surrendering to the pleasure of his mouth on hers, the stroke of his tongue across her lower lip, the feel of his arms tight around her. There were no words to describe the wonder of it, the way her whole body came alive at his touch, making her yearn for more than kisses. She was a woman untouched, a maiden with a maiden's burgeoning curiosity. Right and wrong no longer seemed important when his hands were moving over her, each caress stoking her desire. His touch felt so right, so wonderful—how could it possibly be a sin?

Drawing her closer, he deepened the kiss, his tongue tangling with hers in a sensual duel that enflamed her still more.

Somehow, she found herself lying on the ground, his body covering hers, his breath warm upon her skin as he whispered her name, telling her that she was beautiful, desirable.

She gasped, startled when his hand slipped under her skirt, his strong hand moving over her ankle, sliding up her calf.

She broke the kiss, her eyes going wide when his fingers curled around her thigh.

"Change your mind, darlin'?" he drawled.

"No. Yes. I mean . . . I . . ." She stared up at him, her body feeling hot and cold and shivery at the same time.

"You've never done this before, have you?" he asked drily.

She shook her head, ever aware of the heat of his hand on her thigh.

Chasing Elk grunted softly. He had suspected as much, had known he should have backed off long before things went this far, but she was so tempting, so incredibly sweet.

Muttering an oath, he gained his feet. "I'm going to check on the horses," he said, and strode into the darkness.

Catharine stared after him. She felt both relief and disappointment that he had walked away, leaving her body aching and her virtue intact.

Catharine avoided Chasing Elk as best she could during the next few days. It wasn't easy, of course, since they were always together. When riding, she stayed a few yards behind him. At night, she went to bed right after dinner. She didn't go to sleep, of course. Instead, she lay wrapped in her blanket, watching him. He stayed up late each night, the rifle close at hand. She wondered what he thought about while he sat there staring out into the darkness.

Late one night she found the courage to ask him.

"I thought you were asleep," he replied.

She shook her head. "No. So, what do you think about?"

"Lots of things. Like whether they're still looking

for me, and where that bastard who killed my wife is hiding out."

"Do you know who did it?"

"Oh, yeah."

"He was an acquaintance of yours?"

"He was in love with my wife."

Catharine sat up. "He was?"

"Yeah. I knew he came around from time to time when I wasn't home. He was always trying to convince Nora to run off with him. He was just a kid, eighteen, nineteen." He shrugged. "I wanted to confront him, tell him to leave Nora alone, but she said it was just an innocent infatuation and that no harm would come from it." He shook his head. "I never should have listened to her."

"But if he loved her, why did he kill her?"

"I don't know. Maybe they had a fight. Maybe it was an accident. Maybe . . ." He lifted one shoulder and let it fall. "Who the hell knows?"

"I'm so sorry. It must have been horrible for you, finding her like that."

He nodded. "It was worse for Leah."

"Who's Leah?"

"My daughter."

Catharine stared at him. His daughter! "You . . . you've never mentioned her before."

"She was only four when it happened."

"How awful!"

"Yeah. I guess I should have gone after Buckner when I saw him riding away, but at the time I didn't know what he'd done. I thought he was just afraid of being caught at the house again. I heard Leah crying and I went inside. I found Leah locked in her room. I picked her up and went looking for Nora. She wasn't in the house. When I got to the barn, I left Leah outside. Nora was dead when I found her.

"As it happened, our neighbor, Deirdre Watkins, stopped by to visit Nora shortly after I went into the barn. She found Leah standing outside where I'd left her. Leah was crying. I guess she told Mrs. Watkins I was inside, because the two of them came in together." He paused, seeing it unfold all over again in his mind. "Like I said, Mrs. Watkins came in with Leah, and they saw me holding the knife. I didn't think anything of it at the time. I hadn't done anything wrong. I wanted to go after Buckner right then, but I couldn't leave my daughter."

He took a deep breath. "When I went to Leah, she wouldn't come near me. She wouldn't speak to me. When I was arrested, Mrs. Watkins testified that she'd seen me in the barn holding the knife. After the trial, she came to the jail and offered to look after Leah.

"Three years ago, I got a letter from the Watkins woman saying she and her husband were moving to Tombstone to open a bakery and they were taking Leah with them, if it was all right with me." He snorted softly. "Like I had any choice in the matter. She said she would write to me when they got settled, but I haven't heard a word from her since. I don't know if they made it or not."

Catharine blinked back her tears. It was the saddest story she had ever heard. Even worse, his daughter had spent the last four and a half years thinking her father had killed her mother.

She looked at Chasing Elk. He was staring into the distance again, his face set in hard lines.

She was sorry now that she had wanted to know what thoughts kept him awake. She hadn't known the answer would revive unhappy memories for him.

Drawing the blanket around her, she stretched out on the ground and closed her eyes.

Later, she woke to the sound of a tortured cry. Sitting up, she glanced over at Chasing Elk. He was thrashing around in his blankets, his face twisted in pain, every muscle in his body taut.

"No!" The word was torn from his throat. "Leah . . ."

Reaching over, Catharine shook his shoulder lightly. When he didn't wake, she shook it again, harder.

He bolted upright, his eyes wild in the moonlight. For a moment, he stared at her as if he didn't know who she was.

"It's me, Catharine," she said. "Are you all right?"

"Catharine." The tension seeped out of him, and he scrubbed his hands over his face.

"You were having a nightmare," she said.

"Yeah."

"Do you want to talk about it?"

He looked at her, his face drawn and haggard. "It's the same nightmare I had every night for weeks right after Nora died," he said. "I see her struggling, fighting for her life, and then I see the knife . . . and the blood, it's everywhere." He took a deep breath, one hand tightly clenched. "But it isn't Buckner holding the knife. It's me, and I'm stabbing her over and over again and Leah's there, watching . . ."

Catharine laid her hand on his arm. "It's only a dream."

"Yeah."

Moving closer, she wrapped her arms around him. He rested his head on her shoulder, and she stroked his back, wishing she could say something to ease his pain.

Chasing Elk closed his eyes. He hadn't had the nightmare in the last year or so, but talking about Nora's death had stirred up all the old memories and revived his guilt. He should have been there. Nora had asked him to spend the day at home, but he had been determined to go hunting. He'd wanted some time away from town, wanted to enjoy the thrill of the hunt, to pretend, for a little while, that he was still Chasing Elk the warrior.

A sob tore at his throat. If he had stayed home that day, she would still be alive.

Tucson was just as Chasing Elk remembered it: hot and dry, with narrow dusty streets lined by adobe houses, saloons, and churches topped with wooden crosses.

Chasing Elk stopped in front of a weathered hotel. Dismounting, he turned and lifted Catharine from the back of her horse. He lifted her poke and the burlap bag from the saddle horn and thrust them into her hands, then grabbed his rifle and went into the hotel.

Catharine followed him inside, waiting quietly while he spoke to the desk clerk, who, after looking them over, asked Chasing Elk to sign the register.

"Rooms five and six, Mr. Rossiter," the clerk said. He handed Chasing Elk two keys, then gestured to his right. "Just down the hall."

"We'd like some hot water right away," Chasing Elk said, hefting his rifle.

The desk clerk nodded. "Yessir."

"Rossiter?" Catharine queried softly as she followed Chasing Elk across the lobby.

"I'm a wanted man, remember?"

"Oh. I didn't think of that."

Rooms five and six were located across from each other. Chasing Elk handed Catharine one of the keys. "Keep your door locked."

She nodded.

"Why don't you wash up and get some rest before dinner?"

"All right." She opened the door and stepped inside, then glanced over her shoulder. "You won't leave town without telling me, will you?"

"No."

She smiled faintly.

"See you in a couple of hours," he said.

With a nod, she closed the door. She stood there a moment, glancing around the room. It was small and reasonably clean. Limp lace curtains hung at the single window. There was a fine layer of dust on the sill. A colorful rag rug covered the floor beside the bed. A plain white pitcher and bowl sat atop a scarred three-drawer mahogany dresser. There were a couple of clothes hooks on the wall next to the bed.

With a sigh, she put her poke and the burlap bag on the floor, then sat down on the edge of the bed and burst into tears.

Chasing Elk glanced around the room. It was nothing much. Four walls, a double bed, a four-drawer

dresser, a worn rag rug on the floor. Compared to his
cell at Yuma, it looked like a palace. He wondered
idly how long it would be before he stopped compar-
ing everything to Yuma.

He propped the rifle in a corner, then sat down on
the bed and pulled off his boots. A boy brought him
a bucket of hot water a short time later. After filling
the bowl on the dresser, Chasing Elk washed
quickly, dried his face, hands and arms, then took
up the rifle and left the room. He needed money
and a change of clothes. With that in mind, he led
the horses down the busy street to the Double T
Stable and Corral.

After twenty minutes of haggling with the owner
over the price of the horses and the saddles, Chasing
Elk left the stable with four hundred and fifty-five
dollars in his pocket.

Stopping at the general store, he purchased a new
shirt, a pair of whipcord britches, a pair of long-
handles, socks, a new pair of boots, and a hat. He put
on the boots and the hat, paid the clerk, then tucked
the package holding the rest of his purchases under
his arm and left the store.

Walking back to the hotel, he paused to glance at
the bulletin board outside the sheriff's office. He was
relieved to see that his name wasn't on any of the
wanted posters. But that didn't mean they weren't
looking for him.

He slowed as he neared a saloon. It had been years
since he'd had a drink of good whiskey or relaxed
over a game of poker. He hesitated a moment, then
pushed his way through the swinging doors and made

his way to the bar. He dropped his package on the bar, set the rifle beside him within easy reach.

The saloon was crowded. Men stood at the bar or sat hunched over tables. Chasing Elk closed his eyes for a moment and drank it all in, the tinny discordant notes of an off-key piano, the acrid scent of cigarette smoke and stale perfume and perspiration.

A heavy-set bartender wearing a pair of pinstripe trousers, a white shirt, and sporting a pair of pearl-handled Colt revolvers stopped in front of Chasing Elk. "What's your pleasure?"

"A whiskey and a beer."

"Coming up."

"Don't think I've ever seen a bar dog packing iron," Chasing Elk remarked.

The bartender filled a shot glass and slid it across the bar. "Helps to keep out the riffraff," he said with a grin.

Chasing Elk picked up the shot glass. He regarded the contents for a moment, then downed the liquor in a single swallow. The whiskey slid down his throat, warm and smooth.

The bartender grinned as he set a tall glass of beer on the bar. "That's prime whiskey, wouldn't you say?"

"Best I've had in years."

"They don't serve whiskey like that in the pen, that's for sure."

Chasing Elk looked at the bartender sharply.

"I recognize that look in your eye," the bartender said. "I'd say you're on the run. If I'm wrong, the whiskey's on the house."

Chasing Elk dropped a silver dollar on the bar, then reached for the beer. "You the law, too?"

The bartender laughed. "Only in here." He glanced at the clock on the wall. "Sheriff comes by twice a day. He won't be making his nightly rounds for a couple of hours yet."

Chasing Elk nodded, wondering if he dared trust the barkeep.

"I've got nothing to gain by turning you in," the bartender said. "Just keep your eyes open. The sheriff ain't too bright, but he's not a fool."

Chasing Elk drained the glass and put it on the bar. "Obliged."

"If you're a gambling man, you might come back around ten. Always a good game going on about then."

With a nod, Chasing Elk picked up his new duds and his rifle and left the saloon. He paused outside the swinging doors, glancing right and left before he crossed the street toward the hotel. The sooner he got out of town, the better.

Catharine stood at the window, gazing out into the street. She had taken a sponge bath, washed her hair, and put on clean clothes for the first time in days. She wondered what time it was and when Chasing Elk would come for her, and how long it would be before he bid her good-bye and walked out of her life for good. Fresh tears stung her eyes at the mere thought. Though she had known Chasing Elk only a short time, she was very much afraid that she was falling in love with him and that his leaving would break her heart.

She was about to turn away from the window when she saw him striding toward the hotel. He was wearing a new hat. She wondered what he had in the package under his arm.

She went to the door, expecting him to knock any moment, frowned when several minutes passed. Had he forgotten they were going out to dinner?

She was about to go across the hall when she heard a knock at the door. Stomach fluttering with excitement, she opened it.

"Ready?"

She nodded, her gaze moving over him. He wore a pair of black whipcord trousers, a dark green shirt, and a pair of new boots. And he looked more handsome than ever.

"Let's go," he said, and offered her his arm. "There's a little Mexican café down the street. I thought we'd eat there, if that's all right with you."

"Fine with me."

The café was small and dimly lit. Eight tables spread with bright red cloths filled the room, most of them unoccupied. Candles flickered in wrought-iron wall sconces. A man sat on a stool in one corner, idly strumming a guitar.

A Mexican woman wearing a white blouse and a long red skirt emerged from the kitchen to take their order. Catharine had never eaten Mexican food before, so she let Chasing Elk order for her as well.

"Have you eaten here before?" she asked.

"Once or twice."

"How soon are you leaving?" She hadn't meant to ask, but the words popped out of her mouth, seemingly of their own volition.

"As soon as I know you've got a ticket to wherever you want to go—unless you're planing to stay here."

"I'm not going anywhere. I don't have enough money for a fare."

"You do now. I sold the horses and tack."

"You did?"

"Yeah." He reached into his pocket and pulled out a handful of greenbacks. He counted out two hundred and thirty dollars and handed it to her.

Catharine stared at the money lying in the palm of her hand. It was more than she had ever seen at one time, certainly more than she had ever had. "I . . . thank you."

He gestured at the greenbacks. "So, now that you've got the wherewithal to buy a ticket, where do you want to go from here?"

"With you."

"What?"

"I want to go with you. To Tombstone."

Chasing Elk stared at her, wondering if he'd heard right. She wanted to go with him? To Tombstone?

He shook his head. "Are you out of your mind? I'm an escaped convict, wanted by the law. It's not safe for you even to be having dinner with me."

"Then why did you ask me?"

He dragged his hand over his jaw. How could he tell her that he didn't want to leave her, that there was no room in his life for a woman, especially now, when he was on the run. "Listen, Catharine . . ."

"I won't be any trouble."

"Honey, you were born to be trouble." He swore softly as tears welled in her eyes. "Hey, I didn't mean it in a bad way, but you've got to understand that I . . ."

He broke off as their dinner arrived.

Catharine lowered her head lest the serving woman see her tears.

Chasing Elk nodded at the Mexican woman. "*Gracias.*"

When they were alone at the table again, Chasing Elk leaned forward. "Catharine . . . I'm not staying in Tombstone. When I get my daughter back, I'm heading up to the Dakotas to look for my mother."

"I don't care. I don't have anywhere else to go. There's nothing for me back east. And I . . . I . . ." A rosy flush climbed up her neck.

"Go on."

She looked at him, mute, her cheeks flushed and damp with tears.

"Nothing."

He frowned, and then as realization dawned, he swore again. She was definitely going to be trouble.

Later that night, after he had walked Catharine back to her room, Chasing Elk sat in one of the rockers on the boardwalk in front of the hotel, staring absently into the distance. She thought she was in love with him. Didn't that take the hide off the buffalo. Even worse, he was afraid he was falling in love with her. Dammit, he didn't have time for a woman in his life. Not now. Not until he got his daughter back. Not until he found out if his mother was dead or alive. Not until he found Jim Buckner and cleared his name. . . .

But Catharine was here now.

He took a deep drag on the cigarette he had bummed from the desk clerk. Could he really put Catharine on a train headed east and let her go, perhaps never to see her again? And yet, how could he ask her to stay? He had nothing to offer her. He had no home and no hope of having one until he could prove his innocence and clear his name. He took another drag on the cigarette, enjoying the sharp taste of the tobacco. Tomorrow, he would see about getting a ticket on the next train to Tombstone. He hated leaving Catharine behind. It wasn't what he wanted, but it was for the best.

Catharine was remarkably quiet at breakfast the following morning. She spoke only when spoken to, and refused to meet his gaze, probably hoping he wouldn't notice that her eyes were red and swollen.

"Catharine, what do you want from me?"

"You know what I want."

"I told you last night, it isn't safe for you to stay with me."

"It wasn't safe for me to stay on the farm alone either, but I did it." She looked across the table at him. "My father left me. Mark left me. And now you want to leave me."

Chasing Elk swore under his breath. "Do you think I like leaving without you?"

"You must, or you wouldn't do it."

"Dammit, woman . . ." He lowered his voice when diners at nearby tables turned to stare in their direction. "Haven't you noticed that I can't keep my hands off you? I'm not leaving you here because I want to: I'm doing it because it's best for you."

"I'm a big girl, Mr. Elk. I can make my own decisions." She squared her shoulders and lifted her chin. "And do you know what?" she asked, her eyes blazing defiantly. "I just made one."

Chasing Elk regarded her warily, wondering if he dared ask just what that decision was.

She smiled sweetly as she pushed away from the table, stood, and left the restaurant.

Reaching into his pocket, Chasing Elk dropped a dollar on the table and hurried after her.

He followed her down the street to the ticket office, listened in amazement as she bought a one-way ticket to Tombstone.

Chasing Elk grinned inwardly. She had more spunk than he had bargained for.

"When does the train leave?" Catharine asked as she tucked her ticket into her reticule.

"Tomorrow afternoon right around two o'clock," the ticket agent replied. "The good Lord willin', that is."

"Thank you. Good day to you, sir." She moved away from the window, careful not to meet Chasing Elk's gaze.

The ticket agent looked at Chasing Elk. "Can I help you, sir?"

"I reckon so," he muttered, and reaching into his pocket, he withdrew his bankroll and counted out the price of a ticket to Tombstone.

Chapter 10

Catharine had never ridden on a train before. The railroad had come to Tucson earlier that year, linking the city to the outside world. It was only right, she supposed, since Tucson, with a population of more than seven thousand, was the largest city between California and San Antonio.

She stared out the window, watching the landscape fly by. The train was noisy, what with the sound of the wheels running over the tracks and the occasional blast of the whistle. The cars seemed to sway precariously when going around curves, and when the windows were down, there was the very real danger of cinders blowing inside. But, for all that, it was exhilarating. She had never ridden in anything that went so fast.

They reached Tombstone late in the afternoon. Before leaving Tucson, Catharine had purchased two carpetbags to hold their belongings. Chasing Elk retrieved their bags and his rifle, and they left the depot.

Walking down the street, Chasing Elk thought of what he knew of the place, things he had read in the infrequent newspapers that had come his way in prison, things he had overheard the guards talking about.

It was said that Tombstone was a wild and woolly town that owed its existence to Ed Schieffelin, who had founded the town in 1877. Schieffelin had staked claims to the Toughnut, the Lucky Cuss, and the Contention mines. Other mining camps had quickly sprung up throughout the area. They had colorful names like the Tiptop, the Big Bug, and Auga Fria. Then there were the Bumblebee, Gillett, Black Canyon, Cottonwoods, and the Humbug.

A few years later, the Tombstone Mill and Mining Company was established, and J. B. Allen had built the first house on the corner of Fourth and Allen streets. In that same year, the Earp brothers left their homes in Prescott and Dodge City and moved to Tombstone, where Wyatt was appointed deputy sheriff and Virgil Earp deputy marshal. Doc Holliday and Big Nose Kate arrived sometime thereafter.

The town had grown quickly, and three years after it was founded, Tombstone boasted a population of more than two thousand people, twelve general stores, nine restaurants, two drug stores, ten cigar stores, a candy factory, two watchmakers, two saddle and harness makers, two bakeries, two furniture stores, five assay offices, two stores that sold stoves and tinware, and four hotels, as well as a couple of shoe stores.

Chasing Elk stopped in front of the Russ House Hotel, said to be the best transient hotel in Tombstone. He glanced at a sign in the window. Meals and rooms were only fifty cents each; board was eight dollars a week.

With a nod, he held the door open for Catharine, then followed her inside and across the lobby.

When Chasing Elk asked for two rooms, the man at the desk informed them that there was only one available, and asked if they wanted it.

Chasing Elk didn't hesitate. "We'll take it," he said. He glanced at Catharine, whose cheeks had turned scarlet.

After signing the register, Chasing Elk walked Catharine to the room and opened the door for her. Setting down their bags, he glanced around. The room was clean and neat, with a big brass bed and a window that faced east. There was a zinc tub behind a screen in one corner.

"I'm going out to see if I can find the Watkins' place," he said. "Will you be all right while I'm gone?"

She nodded.

"If you need anything, tell the clerk. I'll be back as soon as I can. Lock the door after me."

He winked at her, then closed the door. Hefting the rifle, he left the hotel.

He walked up and down the streets. Those running east and west had names like Toughnut, Allen, and Fremont. The streets running north and south were numbered one to twenty-eight.

He passed the O.K. Corral, the office of the Tombstone *Epitaph*, the Occidental Saloon, and the Golden Eagle Brewery.

On Fifth Street, he paused to read a number of handbills and circulars on a large bulletin board. One sign offered water for three cents a gallon, another advertised a shanty for rent for fifteen dollars a month, a third offered a lot for sale on Allen Street between Fifth and Sixth streets. The asking price was five thousand dollars. He perused a few Help Wanted signs, noting that the going rate for carpenters, masons, engineers, and blacksmiths was six dollars a day, while a faro dealer earned six dollars for a four-hour shift. Houses were renting for forty dollars a month.

Whistling softly, Chasing Elk moved on.

Turning down Sixth Street, he found himself in the red-light district. There were a few madams in the West whose names were well-known, among them Madame Moustache, Dutch Annie, and Blond Mary. Business in the District was apparently pretty good, since new whorehouses were going up on both sides of the street. He grinned as a flame-haired girl standing out on a second-story balcony whistled at him.

"Hey, honey," she called, leaning over so he could see her rouged cleavage, "why don't you come on up? Just ask for Nell. I can show you a real good time."

"Forget Nell, cowboy," called a heavily painted woman from the doorway of the same establishment. "You don't want what she's got to offer, if you know what I mean."

Chasing Elk tipped his hat to both women. "Thanks, ladies, maybe some other time."

"There's no time like the present," Nell retorted.

With a shake of his head, Chasing Elk continued on down the street. He passed a number of saloons, but that was to be expected. He recalled reading in an old newspaper that Tombstone had four breweries, a winery, and sixty saloons and sampling houses.

He found saloons and whorehouses aplenty, but no sign of the Watkins bakery.

Turning, he retraced his steps. When he reached the Occidental Saloon, he went inside and ordered a whiskey. He was standing at the bar, enjoying his drink, when he heard someone mention the name Wyatt Earp.

Glancing over his shoulder, Chasing Elk saw a tall, slender man with light brown hair and a sweeping mustache. Chasing Elk was somewhat surprised to see Earp in his shirtsleeves. As far as he could tell, the lawman wasn't packing any iron, but then, maybe he didn't need to. His name alone carried a good deal of weight. Earp carried himself erect, his bearing almost military. It was said that as a young man Wyatt had been a buffalo hunter and a stagecoach driver. More recently, he had been a deputy marshal in Wichita, Kansas. He had been married twice. His first wife had died; the second marriage didn't last. Some said the Earp brothers worked both sides of the law. He had quite a reputation in these parts as a man to be reckoned with, Wyatt did. Looking at the man's piercing blue eyes, Chasing Elk believed every word.

Finishing his drink, he left the saloon. Pausing outside, he considered what to do. Under other circumstances, he would have gone to the sheriff for information on the Watkins' whereabouts. Unfortunately, he was in no position to do that.

But Catharine could.

Whistling softly, he headed back to the hotel.

"You want me to do what?"

"You heard me. I want you to go to the sheriff's office and ask if they know what happened to the Watkins woman and her husband."

Catharine shook her head. The idea of walking unescorted down any street in Tombstone sent an uneasy chill down her spine, but how could she refuse him?

Chasing Elk dug around in one of the carpetbags and pulled out the pistol. "Here, tuck this into your skirt pocket."

Reluctantly, she did as he asked.

"You do know how to fire a pistol, don't you?"

She nodded. Her father had insisted that she, Mark, and their mother all learn how to shoot. Mark had been eager to learn but rarely hit what he was aiming at. Her mother closed her eyes when she squeezed the trigger. Surprisingly, Catharine had proved to be the best shot in the family, better, even, than her father.

Chasing Elk blew out a sigh. "Be careful."

With a nod, Catharine left the hotel.

The street was crowded with men, and they all seemed to be in a hurry. Picking up her skirts so the hem didn't drag on the rough boards of the sidewalk, she hurried, too, anxious to accomplish her task and return to the relative safety of the hotel.

When she reached the sheriff's office, she paused to take a deep, calming breath, then opened the door and stepped inside. The man seated behind the desk looked up when she entered the room. He was a good-looking man, with slicked-back brown hair and penetrating blue eyes. He didn't wear a coat; his shirtsleeves were rolled up, revealing muscular forearms.

"Hello," she said. "I . . . are you the sheriff?"

"Deputy Sheriff Earp, ma'am. How can I help you?"

"I don't know if you can. I'm trying to find Mr. and Mrs. Watkins. The last I heard, they had opened a bakery here in town."

The lawman stroked his moustache thoughtfully. "Watkins. Watkins . . . Oh, yes, I remember now. Are you a relative?"

"No, just a . . . a friend of the family."

"I seem to recall one of the deputies telling me that the Watkins were both killed in a holdup not long after they arrived."

"They had a little girl. . . . Do you know what happened to her? She wasn't . . . ?"

"No. No, she wasn't in the shop at the time. The sheriff couldn't find anyone willing to look after her. Indian blood, you know. As it happened, there were a couple of nuns passing through at the time. They offered to take the child to an orphanage run by their order."

"Do you know where that might be?"

The lawman looked thoughtful a moment. "Prescott?" He drummed his fingers on the top of his desk. "No, Phoenix. Yes, that was it, Phoenix."

"Thank you very much."

"Glad to be of help."

Leaving the sheriff's office, Catharine walked slowly back to the hotel, wondering how Chasing Elk would take this latest news about his daughter.

He was waiting for her at the door. "Well? Are they here?"

Catharine moved past him. "Not exactly."

"What the hell does that mean?" he asked impatiently. "Are they here or aren't they?"

She turned to face him. "Mr. and Mrs. Watkins are dead."

"What?" Chasing Elk stared at her. "When? How?"

"They were killed in a robbery not long after they arrived."

"Where's Leah? Where's my daughter?"

"She's in an orphanage, in Phoenix."

Chasing Elk stared at her a moment more, then sank down on the edge of the bed, his head cradled in his hands.

Catharine sat down beside him. "I'm sorry."

"An orphanage." He muttered an oath, his hands clenching into tight fists as he contemplated what that meant.

Filled with fury and impotent anger, he began to pace the floor, but the room was too small to contain his anger. "I'm going out," he said, and left the hotel.

Outside, night had fallen. Chasing Elk stalked the dark streets, cursing Jim Buckner, cursing himself. It wasn't fair! Leah was only eight years old. She was innocent of any crime, yet she had suffered more than he had. She had lost her mother, seen her father sent to prison, then lost the only other family she had. Thinking of his daughter locked in an orphanage cut like a knife. He knew only too well what it was like to be locked up.

"Hang on, sweetheart," he muttered. "I'm coming. Daddy's . . ." He swallowed hard. "Daddy's coming."

They caught the next stage to Phoenix.

Catharine sat on the front-facing seat of the coach, squeezed between Chasing Elk and a portly corset salesman who introduced himself as Mr. Ernest Leroy Van Sant from New York City. An elderly priest and a nun sat across from them, both dozing. Mr. Van

Sant was a verbose man, and after introducing himself to Catharine, he rambled on and on, telling her about his business and his family.

"One wife and ten kids," he boasted, slapping his thigh. "Not bad for a traveling salesman!"

It was all Catharine could do to keep from laughing out loud when Chasing Elk leaned over and said, in a whisper, "I'll bet more than one of those ten kids aren't his."

"That's a terrible thing to say!" she admonished, poking him in the ribs with her elbow.

Chasing Elk grinned at her, then pulled his hat down over his eyes.

Not caring whether he had an audience of one or two, Van Sant rambled on. Catharine wished she had the nerve to pretend that she was asleep, like everyone else.

"Anyway, I says to the wife, no matter what Nicholas thinks—he's our oldest—anyway, I says, he's nowhere near old enough to . . . Good Lord, is that . . . Indians!"

"What?" Leaning forward so she could see past Chasing Elk, Catharine followed Van Sant's frightened gaze.

Beside her, Chasing Elk swore under his breath as he pushed his hat back and looked out the window.

Catharine heard the driver's panicked shout followed by the sharp crack of the whip. The coach lurched forward as the horses broke into a gallop.

Catharine clutched Chasing Elk's arm as dozens of painted Indians seemed to appear out of nowhere.

"Do you think it's Marteen?" she asked.

"I don't know," Chasing Elk replied. "Most likely."

She wasn't sure if that made her feel better or worse.

Thick yellow dust rose up around the coach and blew in through the windows. The air was filled with the hissing of arrows, the harsh ululating cries of the Apache, the sharp report of a rifle as the shotgun guard fired at the Indians.

The priest and the nun, both abruptly awakened by the sudden lurching of the coach, reached for their rosary beads, their faces pale as they sent silent prayers to heaven.

Catharine tried to pray, too, but she couldn't seem to concentrate, could only murmur "please, please, please" over and over again as the Indians drew ever closer. She didn't want to die, not now, not like this. Visions of being captured, of being raped and tortured or forced into a life of slavery flooded her mind. She thought about Chasing Elk and how much she wanted to be with him. She thought about his daughter and how awful it would be for the child if her father was killed now, just when he had discovered where she was.

"Please," she murmured, "oh, please. I'll be so good, please don't let them catch us." And even as she prayed, she remembered her mother's oft-repeated admonition that a body couldn't bargain with God.

The inside of the coach filled with the stink of gunpowder as Chasing Elk began firing his rifle. Leaning back against the seat, Catharine put her hands over her ears, shut her eyes, and prayed that the coach wouldn't tip over, that the Indians would soon tire of the chase and give up, that the coach horses wouldn't stumble.

She opened her eyes as a harsh cry erupted from inside the coach, gasped when she saw an arrow protruding from the old priest's shoulder.

There was a sharp crack as Chasing Elk fired at the warrior outside the window. Catharine had a quick glimpse of the warrior's face before he tumbled over the back of his horse.

It was a face she had seen in her nightmares. Marteen.

She looked at Chasing Elk. "Did you . . . is he . . . dead?"

"Yes, ma'am," Chasing Elk replied, a note of satisfaction in his voice. "He surely is."

Catharine stared at him, surprised by an unexpected feeling of regret. Not that she'd had any feelings for Marteen. And yet, because he had wanted her to be his woman, she had been allowed to live in peace on the farm after her father died.

A howl went up from the Apaches when their leader fell. And suddenly, as quickly as the attack had begun, it was over.

"What happened?" Van Sant asked. "Why did they quit?"

"Their leader's dead," Chasing Elk explained. "They won't fight anymore today. They'll pick up their dead and head home."

Catharine looked over at the priest. The nun had opened his coat and was examining the wound. The arrow was still embedded in his shoulder. Surprisingly, there was very little blood.

The priest groaned when the nun gave a tentative pull on the shaft.

"I wouldn't do that, Sister," Chasing Elk said. "Easier to just push it on through."

He had no sooner finished speaking than the coach came to a halt. Moments later, the door opened and the driver peered inside. "Everyone all right in . . ." His words trailed off when he saw the arrow sticking out of the priest's shoulder.

Catharine and Van Sant exited the stage, leaving the nun and Chasing Elk to look after the priest's injury.

Catharine paced back and forth across the dry ground, trying not to listen to what was going on inside the coach. She winced when the priest cried out.

A short time later, Chasing Elk emerged from the stage coach.

"Is he going to be all right?" Catharine asked.

"I reckon so. Turned out Sister Mary Margaret has some nursing experience. Once I pushed the arrow through, she took care of the rest. He'll need to see a doctor as soon as we get to town, but he should heal up just fine."

"I'm glad."

"All right, folks, climb aboard," the driver called. "We're losing time here."

The rest of the trip passed uneventfully. They made brief stops at way stations along the way to eat and change the horses. The priest, whose name was Father Michael, was a hearty soul. In spite of his injury, he seemed quite chipper. The incident with the Apaches had left Van Sant uncharacteristically silent, for which Catharine was grateful.

During a lull, Catharine asked Sister Mary Margaret if she knew of an orphanage in Phoenix.

"Why, yes, *Casa de la Esperanza*," the nun replied, smiling. "That is where we are headed. Father Michael is the founder."

"Really?" Catharine felt Chasing Elk tense beside her.

"Yes. We have perhaps two dozen children there, poor dears. Most of them have lost their parents. A few have been abandoned."

Chasing Elk leaned forward. "Do you have a girl there, eight years old, named Leah?"

"Why, yes, we do," Sister Mary Margaret said. "How did you know?"

"I'm her father."

Sister Mary Margaret clutched her rosary. "Saints be praised!"

"Is she all right?"

"Yes, she is quite well, Mr . . . ?"

"Nathan Chasing Elk."

The nun extended her hand. "I am pleased to meet you, Mr. Elk. As I was saying, your daughter is quite well, physically. She is a bright child, far ahead of others her age."

Chasing Elk nodded. Leah had always been a smart kid. She had walked at nine months, could count to ten when she was a year old, had talked in sentences before she was two. She could read simple words when she was four. She seemed to remember everything she saw and heard.

"Even so," Sister Mary Margaret went on, "there are days when she refuses to play with any of the other children, days when she refuses to speak to anyone except the rag doll that she carries everywhere she goes."

Chasing Elk nodded again. He remembered that doll. He had given it to Leah on her third birthday. She had named it Gretchen.

"The Lord is merciful indeed, to bring us together." Sister Mary Margaret smiled at Chasing Elk, obviously contemplating a happy reunion. "I simply cannot wait to see the look on Leah's face when she sees you."

Chasing Elk grunted softly. He was sorely afraid that Sister Mary Margaret was in for a big disappointment.

Phoenix owed its being to Jack Swilling. On a day back in 1867, Mr. Swilling stopped to rest his horse and noticed the rich brown earth that had been turned up by his horse's hooves. He decided at that moment that the land would be good for farming and organized an irrigation company to provide water for the valley.

Now, some fourteen years later, the population was more than two thousand and growing, and the town boasted a school house, a Methodist church, an ice factory, sixteen saloons, four dance halls, a telegraph office, and a brick sidewalk in front of the Tiger Saloon. The town newspaper, the *Phoenix Herald*, was published twice weekly.

The stage pulled up in front of a small white house on Third Street. A sign proclaimed it was the office of Dr. J. J. Farnsworth, MD.

The driver opened the coach door and helped Father Michael alight, then and the guard helped the priest into the doctor's office.

"Why don't you come to the *Casa* later this afternoon, Mr. Elk?" Sister Mary Margaret suggested. "It will give us time to prepare Leah for your arrival."

Chasing Elk nodded.

"Shall we say around five o'clock?" the nun suggested. Alighting from the coach, she hurried into the doctor's office.

"No sense hanging around here," Chasing Elk said. "Let's go find a room."

After bidding Van Sant a good day, Catharine followed Chasing Elk out of the coach. She stood to one side while he retrieved their luggage from the boot.

The streets were crowded with farmers and miners. Turning down Center Street, they passed a large schoolhouse. Catharine glanced in the window of one of the classrooms. A woman wearing a severe black dress and holding a ruler in one hand stood at the head of the room. She was lecturing to perhaps thirty students. One boy stood in the corner, his expression sullen.

They reached the hotel a short time later. Chasing Elk secured two adjoining rooms and requested hot water for bathing.

"The bathing rooms are upstairs at the end of the hall," the clerk said. "I believe both are vacant at this time."

"Obliged." Chasing Elk picked up their baggage and started up the stairs.

Catharine trailed behind him. The hotel was quite impressive. The walls were papered in a dark red and gold print, there were carpets on the floors, paintings graced the walls.

She opened the door to the first room and stepped inside. It, too, was nicely appointed, with a brass bed, a walnut dresser with an oval mirror, a square table, and two matching chairs.

Chasing Elk dropped their baggage on one of the chairs. Crossing the floor, he opened the connecting door to the second room. It was much the same as the first one save that the dresser was rosewood.

"We've got a few hours," he said. "Why don't you get cleaned up, and then we'll go find something to eat?"

Catharine nodded, eager to wash the dust and grit from her hair and don fresh undergarments and a clean dress. It was the last clean dress she had. Perhaps, while they were here, she could have the other two washed and pressed. Her underwear, as well.

She was ready when Chasing Elk returned. "You've been shopping again," she said, noticing he was wearing a new blue shirt.

"Yeah."

"And made a trip to the barbershop."

He ran a hand over his jaw. "Right again."

"Do you think we'll be in town long enough to take our clothes to the laundry?"

"I reckon we can make time," he said. Going to her carpetbag, he withdrew her pistol and tucked it into the waistband of his trousers.

"Do you have to take that?" she asked.

With a curt nod, he opened the door.

They ate in the hotel dining room, which was quite elegant for a town this far west. It reminded Catharine of Boston, and she felt a pang of regret for all that had been left behind when her family moved West. Had her family stayed in the East, her parents might still be alive and Mark would not be missing.

She glanced at Chasing Elk. Had her family stayed in the East, she would never have met him. It was obvious that his mind was on his daughter. Catharine studied him surreptitiously while she ate, noting the fine lines etched at the corners of his eyes, the width of his shoulders beneath the new blue shirt, the coppery hue of his skin, the way his gaze moved restlessly around the room. He sat with his back to a wall, and she noticed that he watched everyone who entered the door. She wondered if he was even aware that he was doing it. His watchfulness reminded her that he was a man on the run. The sheriff from Tucson had known that Chasing Elk had escaped from prison; no doubt the sheriff here in Phoenix had also been notified of his escape.

From somewhere in the distance, a clock chimed the hour.

Chasing Elk's head jerked up. "It's time to go." He tossed his napkin on the table, along with a few dollars. "Are you through?"

She would have liked a bit of dessert and a cup of coffee, but she didn't say so. He was, after all, understandably anxious to see his daughter. She placed her napkin on the table and stood, surprised to find that she was more than a little nervous at the thought of meeting Chasing Elk's daughter. What if the girl didn't like her?

The orphanage was a small, whitewashed adobe building surrounded by a high wooden fence. A few scraggly flowers and some cactus plants grew along the fence. Smoke curled from the chimney. A nun was hanging laundry on a clothesline on one side of the house.

After a moment's hesitation, Chasing Elk knocked on the front door.

It was opened almost immediately by a tall boy with black hair and brown eyes. "May I help you, señor?" he asked.

"We're here to see Sister Mary Margaret."

"Come in." The boy stepped back so they could cross the threshold. He led them into a small white-washed room. A carved wooden cross hung on one wall. A worn sofa and a small table were the room's only furnishings.

The boy gestured toward the sofa. "Please, sit down."

Chasing Elk followed Catharine into the room. She sat down, but he was too nervous to sit still. At last, after more than four years, he was going to see his daughter. Did she remember him? Would she speak to him? Would she refuse to go with him?

He whirled around at the sound of footsteps.

"Mr. Elk, how good to see you again."

"Sister."

The nun smiled at Catharine as she sat down beside her.

"How is Father Michael?" Catharine asked.

"The doctor insisted that he spend the night in the hospital," Sister Mary Margaret said with a grin. "Father was not happy with the doctor's decision, but—"

"My daughter," Chasing Elk said. "When can I see her?"

"In a moment."

Chasing Elk clenched his jaw. He had already waited more than four years.

"Leah did not react as I had expected when I told

her you were here," Sister Mary Margaret began. "At first, I thought she misunderstood me but then . . . I do not know of any delicate way to ask this, Mr. Elk, but is your daughter afraid of you?"

"Possibly."

"Might I ask why?"

"It's not a pretty story, Sister, and not one I care to go into."

The nun glanced at Catharine, obviously wondering what part she played in the story.

"I appreciate everything you've done for my daughter," Chasing Elk said. "If you'll bring her to me, we'll be leaving."

"That is your decision to make, of course, but I must tell you, I am reluctant to let Leah go with you when she does not wish to."

"Did she tell you that?"

"Not in words, no."

"Listen, Sister, she's my daughter, and I love her. She has no reason to be afraid of me."

"But she is afraid."

"Yes," he said impatiently, "and I know why. But it's a mistake, and I intend to tell her so. I want to see her, now."

Stung by the harshness of his tone, Sister Mary Margaret gained her feet.

"Very well," she said with asperity. "Wait here, and I will bring her to you."

Chasing Elk resumed pacing the floor, his hands clenching and unclenching. In all the years that he had thought about this moment, he'd never expected to be so apprehensive. Leah was his daughter. He had loved her from the first moment that he'd held her in his arms, a tiny scrap of humanity with a thatch of thick black hair, loved her more than his own life.

He came to an abrupt halt when he heard two sets of footsteps approaching. Slowly, he turned and went to the doorway. Looking down the corridor, he saw Sister Mary Margaret walking toward him. She held a small brown valise in one hand, but it was the girl holding her other hand who commanded Chasing Elk's full attention. His daughter wore a white pinafore over a dark blue dress. Her black hair, once long and thick, had been cut short, making her dark brown eyes seem even larger than they were. She clutched a well-worn Gretchen to her chest.

Sister Mary Margaret came to a stop in front of Chasing Elk. Leah clutched the nun's hand tightly.

"Leah, this is your father," Sister Mary Margaret said gently. "He has come to take you home."

"Hi, sweetheart," Chasing Elk said. "Remember me?"

Leah stared up at him for a full minute, her eyes slowly growing wide as recognition set in. When she spoke, her voice was barely audible, but her words cut through Chasing Elk's heart like an Apache skinning knife.

"Yes, I remember you," she said. "You killed my mother."

Chapter 11

At his daughter's words, Chasing Elk dropped to his knees. "No," he said, his voice hoarse, as though the word had been torn from the deepest part of his being. "No, Leah."

"I saw you. The knife . . ." She dropped the nun's hand and backed away from him. "The blood."

"I didn't kill your mother," Chasing Elk said. "You have to believe me. I loved her. I love you."

She stared at him, her face pale.

When he reached for her, she backed away still more.

Chasing Elk glanced at Catharine, his eyes filled with a depth of pain she could only imagine.

Rising, she walked toward Leah. "I'm Catharine," she said, holding out her hand. "Will you come with me?"

Leah stared up at her. And then, to everyone's surprise, she put her hand in Catharine's.

"I'm sorry to say this, Mr. Elk," Sister Mary Margaret said quietly, "but after what I have heard, I am somewhat reluctant to release your daughter into your care."

"I can understand that, Sister," he replied, keeping

a tight rein on his temper. "But you know how kids are. Sometimes they hear things that aren't true repeated so many times they start to believe them." He took a deep breath. "I don't know what Leah told you. I don't know what you've heard. But I swear to you on my daughter's life that I didn't kill her mother."

The nun regarded him for stretched seconds, her gaze seeming to pierce his very soul.

Chasing Elk met her probing gaze head on, his nerves taut as he waited for the nun to make her decision. His was already made, because, one way or another, he was taking Leah with him when he left.

The nun closed her eyes for a moment, as if seeking Divine guidance.

Chasing Elk glanced from Leah to the door, ready to grab his daughter and run if need be.

Sister Mary Margaret opened her eyes and looked directly at Chasing Elk. "I believe you. These are Leah's belongings," she said, handing the small valise to Catharine. "Mr. Elk, if you will follow me, there are papers that you need to sign."

With a nod, he gained his feet and followed the nun down the hall.

Leah stared after her father until he was out of sight, and then she looked up at Catharine. "Did you know my mother?"

"No. Was she as pretty as you?"

"I don't remember what she looked like," Leah said, her voice filled with such sadness it brought tears to Catharine's eyes. "Where are you taking me?"

"We're going to go and find your grandmother," Catharine said.

"She's Indian."

"Yes, I know."

"Is *he* going with us?"

"Yes."

Leah jerked her hand from Catharine's. "Then I don't want to go."

Catharine was trying to think of a suitable reply when she heard footsteps behind her. Turning, she saw Chasing Elk walking toward them. She had little doubt that he had overheard what Leah had said. He took a step toward his daughter, then flinched as though he'd been struck when Leah pressed closer to Catharine's side.

Without saying a word, he turned and left the building.

Taking a firm hold of Leah's hand, Catharine followed Chasing Elk outside. Hurrying, she managed to catch up with him in spite of Leah's attempts to hang back.

They were across the street from the hotel when Chasing Elk heard a man call his name. Turning, he saw the sheriff and two deputies striding toward him, their guns drawn.

Chasing Elk's first instinct was to make a run for it, but he couldn't risk it, couldn't take a chance on Leah or Catharine getting hit by a bullet meant for him.

And then it was too late to run.

"Get those hands up," the sheriff ordered brusquely. "Hoffman, get his gun. Redding, put the cuffs on him."

Chasing Elk offered no resistance as his hands were cuffed behind his back.

The sheriff gestured toward the jail with the barrel of his Colt. "Let's go."

Chasing Elk glanced at Catharine over his shoulder. "Take care of her for me, will you?"

"Of course."

With a curt nod, Chasing Elk turned and started walking toward the jail. Now was the time to run for it, he thought. He wasn't going back to Yuma. At least a bullet in the back would be quick. He thrust the idea aside. Leah had seen enough violence in her life. Even though she hated him, she didn't need to see her father shot down in the street like a mad dog.

A sense of hopelessness engulfed him as one of the deputies opened the door to the sheriff's office and motioned Chasing Elk inside.

The sheriff searched him, then ushered him through a narrow doorway into the cell block.

"In here," the sheriff said, jerking his chin toward an empty cell.

Chasing Elk stared at the iron bars, took a deep breath, and stepped inside. The sheriff removed the handcuffs, then closed the cell door and locked it with a flourish.

"Dinner's at six," the lawman said as he left the cell block and closed the door behind him.

Chasing Elk glanced around. There were six cells. Four of them were empty. A man lay on one of the bunks in the other occupied cell, one arm thrown across his forehead.

"How long you in for?" the man asked.

"As long as they want me," Chasing Elk replied bitterly.

"That's rough." Sitting up, the man swung his legs over the edge of the narrow iron cot.

He was a young man in his early twenties, with unruly auburn hair and light brown eyes. He wore a rumpled pinstripe city suit.

Chasing Elk frowned, thinking the kid looked vaguely familiar. "So, what are you in for?" he asked, though he really didn't give a damn.

"Drunk and disorderly," the young man said. "I broke a mirror over at the Dusty Deuce and I can't afford to pay for it. Sheriff said I have to do sixty days if I can't come up with the cash." He ran a hand through his hair. "Sixty days," he said, moaning. "It's a lifetime."

Chasing Elk grunted softly. He could do sixty days standing on his head if he had to. It was doing sixty years that made him break out in a cold sweat.

"I never should have left the farm," the boy muttered. "But I was so sick of the work. I just wanted to have a little fun." He looked at Chasing Elk. "Is that so wrong? I never meant to stay away so long, but I got on a winning streak and . . ." He shrugged. "I was having such a high old time, I sort of forgot about what I'd left behind until I broke that blasted mirror last week. Cathy must think I'm dead."

"Cathy?" Chasing Elk's hands fisted around the bars.

"My sister," the boy explained.

It couldn't be, Chasing Elk thought. The odds were too great and yet . . . He took a good look at the boy. His hair was the same color as Catharine's; there was a similarity in the slant of their eyes. "What's your name?"

"Lyons. Mark Lyons."

Chasing Elk shook his head in disbelief, and then he burst out laughing.

Leah sat on the edge of the bed, holding Gretchen in her arms. Her father had given her the doll for her third birthday. It had been her favorite present. She remembered how surprised she had been and how Mama and Daddy had looked at each other and smiled. They had all been so happy then.

Why had everything changed? Why had her father killed Mama? She was glad that he was back in jail. Mrs. Watkins had told her she would never have to see her father again, but then Mr. and Mrs. Watkins had gone away without even telling her good-bye. She had spent a few days with the sheriff's wife, and then they had told her that Sister Mary Margaret was taking her away.

Leah kissed Gretchen's cheek. She hadn't wanted to believe Sister Mary Margaret when the nun had told her that her father had come for her. Sometimes she still had nightmares about that day in the barn when she had seen her father leaning over her mother's body, a bloody knife in his hand. Mrs. Watkins had screamed and then she had run out of the barn, dragging Leah behind her. But Leah had seen it all. She had thrown Gretchen away that night, but later, lying alone in Mrs. Watkins' spare bedroom, Leah had snuck out of the house and rescued Gretchen from the trash pile. The doll had been the only familiar thing she had left.

It had been a terrible time. For weeks, her mother's death was all that the people in town had talked

about. Sometimes they forgot she was in the room.
She had been so young at the time, maybe they didn't
think she could understand what they were saying.
They called her father a murderer and a dirty half-
breed and other, worse names. They looked sad when
they looked at her. The women all hugged her and
said everything would be all right. She hadn't been
allowed to go to the trial, but she had overheard Mrs.
Watkins and her husband talking about it. Her father
had been found guilty and sentenced to life in prison.
A lot of people thought he should have been hanged
instead of locked up. Even though Leah never wanted
to see her father again, deep down inside she was glad
they hadn't hanged him.

But today she was glad to be away from the orphanage. She had never liked it there. They made her go
to Mass every Sunday, and she wasn't allowed to leave
the grounds. The nuns and Father Michael had treated
her nicely enough, but when there weren't any grown-
ups in the room, the boys and girls in the orphanage
had called her names like "dirty squaw" and "red-
skin" and "Sioux baby."

Leah glanced at Catharine, who was rummaging
through a large carpetbag. She had liked Catharine
immediately, though she didn't know why. Maybe it
was because Catharine smelled of sunshine and lavender. That's how Mama had smelled, too.

Leah clutched Gretchen tighter as a new thought
occurred to her. Everyone she had ever cared about
had been taken from her. First her mama had been
killed, and then Mr. and Mrs. Watkins had gone away.
Would Catharine go away, too?

"Leah, is something wrong?"

"You're not going to go away, are you?"

"Of course not." Catharine went to sit beside the child. "What's wrong, honey?"

"Nothing," Leah said, blinking rapidly.

Catharine frowned, then slid her arm around Leah's shoulders. The child had lost her mother and then Mrs. Watkins; it was understandable that she would be feeling insecure.

"I'll stay with you as long as I can," Catharine said. "I promise."

"Do you think my grandmother will be glad to see me?"

"I'm sure she will. And I know your father would love to see you. Wouldn't you like to go and visit him?"

"No!"

"Leah, no matter what you think, your father didn't kill your mother. He told me what happened. . . ."

"I saw him! I saw the knife in his hand!"

"But you didn't see him stab her, did you?"

Leah hesitated, as though thinking it over. "No," she said at last.

"There was another man at your house that day, wasn't there?"

"I don't remember," Leah said, and then frowned. "Mr. Buckner, he was there. He used to come visit Mama sometimes when Daddy was gone. He always sent me away."

"Your daddy thinks your mother and Mr. Buckner had a fight and that Mr. Buckner accidentally killed your mother."

Leah looked up at Catharine, hope shining brightly in her eyes. "Is that what you think?"

"That's what your father told me, and I believe him."

"Maybe he's lying."

"Has he ever lied to you before?"

Leah looked thoughtful for a moment. "No." She cocked her head to one side, her eyes narrowing. "You like my daddy, don't you?"

"Yes, very much."

"Does he like you?"

"I think so."

Leah sighed heavily. "If he didn't kill my mama, why did they send him to jail?"

"Because they didn't believe him when he said he didn't do it."

"Neither did I," Leah said, her voice barely audible. "I should have believed him, shouldn't I?"

Catharine squeezed Leah's shoulder. "Honey, you were only four years old."

"You don't think he's mad at me, do you, because I didn't believe him?"

"No," Catharine said, smiling, "I don't think he's mad at you."

"Can we go see him? Can we go see my daddy?"

"Of course we can."

"Now?"

"Right now."

Muttering under his breath, Chasing Elk paced the narrow confines of his cell, wondering who had turned him in. Damn, damn, damn, of all the rotten luck! A few more minutes and he would have been on his way out of town with Catharine and Leah.

"All the pacing in the world isn't gonna get you out

of here," Mark Lyons remarked. He was stretched out on his bunk once more, staring up at the ceiling.

"Leaving home didn't get you very far either, did it?" Chasing Elk retorted irritably.

"What do you know about it?"

"I know you left your sister home alone on a patch of ground that's not worth a plug nickel. And that if I hadn't come along when I did, she'd be warming an Apache buck's blankets right about now."

Mark Lyons bolted upright. "What the hell are you talking about? What do you know about anything?"

"I know a damn sight more than you do. For one thing, she thinks you're dead."

"How do you know that?"

"I've been living with her for the last few weeks."

"What?" Lyons sprang off the cot, his face mottled with rage, his hands clenched into tight fists. "You're lucky I can't get my hands on you!"

Chasing Elk snorted softly. "One of us is lucky."

Lyons backed away from the bars when the door to the cell block swung open. "You've got a couple of visitors, Elk," the sheriff called.

"This should be good," Chasing Elk muttered, wondering what Catharine would say when she saw her brother locked in the next cell.

He moved to the door, his hands curling around the bars as Catharine walked down the aisle. Leah trailed behind her, Gretchen tucked under one arm.

Catharine stopped in front of him. "Are you all right?"

"What do you think?" He looked past Catharine to his daughter. She had grown so much since he had last seen her. Regret washed through him when he thought of all the years he had missed, years he could never get back. "Hi, Lee."

She moved up beside Catharine. "Hi, Daddy."

He dropped to his knees so that she didn't have to look up at him. "I missed you, sweetheart. Every hour of every day."

She stared at him for stretched seconds, her eyes glistening, and then two huge teardrops rolled down her cheeks. "I missed you, too."

"Don't cry, darlin'." He reached through the bars, his thumbs swiping at her tears.

"How long are they going to keep you in here?" she asked, sniffling.

"I don't know." He caught her hand in his and gave it a squeeze. "I didn't kill your mama, Lee, you've got to believe that."

"I . . ." She drew in a deep, shuddering breath. "I do."

Tears burned the backs of his eyes as he gazed at his daughter. He felt as if the weight of the world had been lifted from his shoulders. She believed him. It was the greatest gift he had ever been given.

Pressing against the bars, Leah reached for him and he put his arms around her. For a moment, nothing else mattered in all the world but the fact that his daughter believed in him again.

The moment was shattered when Lyons coughed loudly. "Hey, Cath! Think you could throw a little of that attention my way?"

Catharine's eyes widened as she turned her head and stared at the man in the next cell. "Mark! I don't believe it! What are you doing here? I thought you were dead!"

"I . . . that is . . ." He shrugged, a faint blush washing into his cheeks.

"Do you know how worried I've been?" Catharine exclaimed. "Do you know what I've been through since you left? How could you run off and leave me with all the work?"

"I'm sorry, Cath. I intended to come back, I really did. But once I got to the Crossing, I don't know, I just kept going."

She glared at him, her hands on her hips, her eyes flashing fire. "It's a good thing you're behind bars," she said. "If I could get my hands on you, I'd . . . I'd . . ." She stamped her foot. "I don't know what I'd do, Mark Lyons, but you'd be sorry."

Lyons tried to look properly abashed, but he burst out laughing instead.

Catharine wasn't amused. "Why are you in here, anyway? What did you do?"

"Nothing, really," Lyons said with a placating gesture. "I broke a mirror, that's all, and when I couldn't pay for it, they locked me up."

"Daddy, who's that man?" Leah whispered.

"Catharine's wayward brother."

Chasing Elk grinned as Catharine turned to glare at him in turn.

"I can't believe it," she murmured with a shake of her head. "I just can't believe you're *both* locked up in here." Exasperated, she glanced from one man to the other. "The question is, how are we going to get you out?"

Chapter 12

How indeed, Chasing Elk mused later that night. Stretched out on the cot, he stared up at the ceiling, wondering how long it would be before they sent him back to Yuma. The thought made his stomach clench. He couldn't go back there, couldn't face the high gray walls, the loss of his freedom, the cruelty of the guards. Even worse, he couldn't face the thought of being separated from his daughter again.

Leah. In spite of the bleak future that awaited him, thinking of his daughter brought a smile to his face. She didn't hate him anymore. Remembering how she had come to him and told him that she believed him would be a sweet memory to hang onto when despair threatened to overwhelm him.

Mark Lyons stirred restlessly in the next cell. "Nights can sure be long, can't they?"

"You have no idea."

Lyons rolled onto his side. "Are you in love with my sister?"

Chasing Elk grunted softly. "Where I'm going, it really doesn't make a bit of difference, does it?"

"True enough," Lyons agreed. He sighed heavily.

"When I get out of here, I'm going to take Cathy and head back to Boston, where we belong. I don't know about my sister, but I've had enough of the West."

Chasing Elk swore softly. He had been so relieved that his daughter didn't hate him anymore, he hadn't given any thought to who was going to take care of her when he was gone. He didn't want to send her back to the orphanage. One of them in jail was bad enough! Leah seemed taken with Catharine, and Catharine seemed fond enough of Leah, but would Catharine be willing to look after his daughter until she was old enough to look after herself? He had no money with which to make it worth Catharine's while, nothing to offer her.

"You asleep?" Lyons called.

"No." How could he sleep when his daughter's future was so uncertain?

"How long were you in Yuma?"

"A lifetime."

"I couldn't help overhearing what you were saying to the kid. Must have been rough on her, thinking you killed her mother."

"Yeah."

"Maybe you could get a new trial?"

"What for? I still can't prove I didn't do it."

"Well, it could have been worse. They could have sentenced you to hang."

"There were plenty of days when I'd wished they had."

Lyons whistled softly. "That bad, uh?"

"Until you've been there, you have no idea." Chasing Elk swung his legs over the side of the cot and sat up. "Dammit, I can't go back to that hellhole!"

Rising, he began to pace the floor, his agitation mounting with every step. He had to get out of here. But how?

"How long is my daddy going to be in jail?"

Catharine had been looking through a rack of ready-made dresses, hoping to find a new frock for Leah. Now she paused to look down at Chasing Elk's daughter. "I don't know. A very long time, I'm afraid."

"But he said he didn't do it."

"I know, honey, but . . ." Catharine paused. How could she explain about laws and courts to an eight-year-old when she didn't fully understand it herself?

"I don't want him to be in jail. I don't want to go live with the nuns again."

"You don't have to," Catharine said. "You can stay with me."

"I can? Really?"

"Really." Catharine plucked a pink and green striped dress off the rack and held it up in front of Leah. "Do you like this one?"

"Oh, yes!"

"Good. We'll take it. And how about this one?" She held up a dark blue print.

Leah nodded excitedly. "I haven't had a new dress in a long time. Is your brother going to prison with my daddy?"

"No." She hated to leave Mark in jail, but after buying a ticket on the train to Tombstone and the stage to get here, she just didn't have enough money left to bail him out and still have the funds necessary to carry out the plan that was taking shape in the back of her mind.

"Is he a bad man?" Leah asked.

"No, just a foolish one. Come on, let's go pay for these things."

"Can we go visit my daddy again?"

"Sure."

Chasing Elk's spirits rose considerably when Catharine and Leah came to visit that afternoon. Leah was wearing a new dress, and there was a pretty bow in her hair. As always, she clutched Gretchen in one arm.

Leah smiled brightly when she saw him. "Catharine took me shopping."

"So I see. You look right pretty, sweetheart."

Leah beamed at him. "She bought me another dress, too. And look, new shoes!"

Chasing Elk smiled, then looked at Catharine. "I appreciate what you're doing."

"It's nothing. We had a good time, didn't we, Leah?"

Leah nodded enthusiastically. "She bought me a peppermint stick, too."

"So, Cath," Lyons called, "what did you buy me?"

"Just what you deserve. Nothing."

"Come on, Cath, at least bring me a change of clothes. These are getting ripe."

"I'll think about it." She turned her attention to Chasing Elk, her expression softening. "Are you all right?"

"It doesn't matter. Listen, I need to ask you something."

"So ask."

"Leah, why don't you go talk to Mark for a few minutes?"

She looked uncertain for a moment; then, with a shrug, she walked down to Mark's cell.

"So, what is it you don't want her to hear?" Catharine asked.

Chasing Elk gripped the bars in his hands. "I don't want Leah to go back to that place. Is there any chance she could stay with you? I can't pay you, and I won't blame you if you say no, but . . ."

"Of course she can stay with me. I already told her she could."

"Catharine, I . . ." Words failed him. How could he tell her how much it meant to him to know that his daughter would be taken care of?

"It's all right," she said, smiling. "I understand."

"Dammit, I wish . . ." He blew out a sigh. Wishes were for fools.

"Do you know how much longer you'll be here?"

"Sheriff says the wagon from Yuma will be here sometime tomorrow afternoon."

"So soon?"

"Listen, Catharine, I appreciate all you've done for me and for Leah. The sheriff took my belongings and my cash. I've still got a few dollars left from selling the horses. Take it, it's yours."

She started to protest, but he spoke again before she could refuse. "Take it. It's all I've got to give you for looking after my daughter."

"All right, I'll take it. For Leah."

"Did I ever tell you how beautiful you are?"

"Yes, once," she said, and flushed as the memory

of that moment rose to the forefront of her mind. He had been kissing her at the time.

"I'm sorry now that I stopped," he said quietly.

"So am I. Isn't there something we can do to get you out of here?"

"Not unless you've got another gun stashed somewhere. The sheriff's got your pistol."

Before she could reply, the cell block door swung open and the lawman poked his head in. "Time's up."

"I'll bring Leah by to see you tomorrow morning."

"Thanks."

"And we'll write you, every day, and . . ."

"Bye, Daddy."

Bending down, Chasing Elk hugged his daughter through the bars. "Be a good girl. Do what Catharine tells you."

"I will."

He gave her one more hug, then reluctantly let her go. His gaze met Catharine's. She leaned closer, and he slipped his arm around her waist.

"Kiss me," she whispered.

Murmuring her name, he drew her closer. Her eyelids fluttered down as he claimed her lips. Sweet, he thought, even sweeter than he remembered. He deepened the kiss, wanting to imprint the moment in his memory, the honey of her lips, the flowery fragrance of her hair, the softness of her skin, the warmth of her breath against his cheek.

"All right," the sheriff said impatiently, "let's break it up."

Catharine kissed him again, quickly. "I love you," she whispered, and taking Leah by the hand, she left the cell block.

Chasing Elk stared after them as they walked away—the woman he wanted to know better and the daughter he hardly knew.

One more day, and then he would never see either one of them again.

Chapter 13

"Come on, Leah, hurry," Catharine said, tugging gently on the girl's hand.

"Where are we going?"

"To buy a gun."

"A gun!" Leah stared up at her, her eyes wide. "Why do we need a gun?"

"Because we don't have one."

Leah frowned at her. "Sister Mary Margaret said guns were bad."

"She was probably right," Catharine said, "but we still need one."

"Are you going to . . . to shoot somebody?" Leah asked, wide-eyed.

"No, of course not. I just want to scare someone." Catharine paused outside the gun shop. If things went awry, she might find herself locked up alongside Mark and Chasing Elk. If that happened, Leah would undoubtedly be sent back to the orphanage. Catharine was certain that Chasing Elk would never forgive her if that happened. But it was a risk she had to take. She couldn't let them send him back to prison for the rest of his life. He deserved to be with his daughter, and Leah deserved to be with her father. And Catharine wanted to be with both of them.

"We need to buy some horses, too," Catharine said. "Do you know how to ride?"

It was after ten o'clock that same night when Catharine knocked on the door of the sheriff's office. When there was no immediate answer, she knocked again, harder.

She heard a muffled curse, heavy footsteps, and then the door opened.

"Yeah, what do you want?"

"Is the sheriff here?" Catharine asked politely.

"Not right now," the man said, rubbing his eyes. "Kin I help you?"

"We'd like to see one of the prisoners."

"At this time of night?" He shook his head. "Come back tomorrow afternoon."

"We can't, we're leaving town. This is Mr. Elk's daughter," Catharine said, hurrying on before he could refuse her again. "She wanted to tell her daddy good-bye. She hasn't seen him in four years, and after tomorrow, she'll never see him again." Catharine stroked the top of Leah's head. "Poor child. Her mother's dead and her father's going back to prison."

The deputy scratched his head. He was tall and fair-skinned, with a smattering of freckles across his nose. He was the most unlikely-looking lawman Catharine had ever seen. She didn't think he was more than twenty-two or twenty-three.

"I don't know, ma'am," he said with real regret. "I really shouldn't let you in this late. . . ."

Catharine smiled at him. "Couldn't you make an exception, just this once? For the child?"

"I don't think I'd . . ."

A loud sob from Leah drew the man's attention. "Please, mister lawman," she said plaintively. "I just want to see my daddy one last time," she wailed, and burst into tears.

"There, there," Catharine said, giving Leah's shoulder a sympathetic squeeze. "You see how upset she is? It would be a real act of Christian charity to let the child see her father."

"Well . . ." The deputy took a step back and opened the door wider. "I reckon it will be all right, just this once."

"Bless you, kind sir." Taking Leah by the hand, Catharine stepped into the office.

The deputy closed the door behind them. "I'll . . . uh, have to look inside your bag, ma'am," he said apologetically. "I mean, well, it's the rules, you know."

"Of course." She handed him her reticule.

He looked through it quickly, then handed it back to her. "This way."

Holding Leah's hand, Catharine followed the deputy to the cell block door, waited while he unlocked it.

"I can't let ya stay more'n five minutes."

"I understand. God bless you, sir, for your kindness to this poor, heartbroken child."

The deputy cleared his throat. "I reckon you can stay for ten minutes. Just knock on the door if you need me afore that."

"Thank you so much, Deputy. You've been very kind."

A flush stained his cheeks as he turned and left the cellblock, locking them inside.

"Come, Leah," Catharine said. "We don't have much time."

They hurried down the aisle to Chasing Elk's cell.

"What the devil are you two doing here so late?" he asked, rising from his cot.

"We came to break you out of here," Catharine said, smiling.

"What?"

"You heard me. Leah, give me Gretchen."

"Hi, Daddy," Leah said cheerfully. She handed her doll to Catharine, who quickly turned the doll upside down, exposing Gretchen's ruffled pantalets and a small derringer that was securely taped to the doll's legs.

Removing the tape, Catharine passed the weapon to Chasing Elk.

"Is it loaded?" he asked.

"Of course. What good is an empty gun?"

"Hey," Mark called sleepily, "what's going on?"

"Put your boots on," Chasing Elk said. "We're getting out of here."

Mark sat up. "What? How?"

"No time for questions," Chasing Elk said. "Catharine, take Leah and move down by Mark, then call for the deputy. We need him inside the cell block."

"Come on, Leah." Taking the child by the hand, Catharine went to stand in front of Mark's cell. And then, with a scream loud enough to wake the dead, she fell to the floor.

Chasing Elk bit back a grin as the cell block door

swung open and the deputy stepped across the threshold, the key ring dangling from his hand.

"What's wrong?" the lawman asked.

"I don't know," Chasing Elk said, keeping the derringer out of sight behind his back. "One minute we were talking and the next . . ." He shrugged. "I think she's fainted."

"Fainted!" The deputy hurried down the aisle and knelt beside Catharine. "Ma'am?" He dropped the key ring on the floor, took one of Catharine's hands in his, and began patting it. "Ma'am, are you all right?"

"She'll be fine as soon as you open this door," Chasing Elk said.

"What?" The deputy looked up, his face draining of color when he saw the gun in Chasing Elk's hand.

"You heard me," Chasing Elk said. "Open the damn door."

"I can't do that."

Chasing Elk thumbed back the hammer. "You'd better do it, right quick."

The deputy looked longingly at the cell block door.

"Don't even think about it," Chasing Elk warned.

"Oh, this is ridiculous," Catharine said. Grabbing the key ring, she scrambled to her feet and unlocked the door to Chasing Elk's cell, then Mark's.

Grabbing his hat, Chasing Elk stepped outside.

The deputy groaned loudly. "Sheriff Linderman is gonna whup me good."

"Reckon so," Chasing Elk agreed. "Catharine, give me your sash."

She quickly untied it and handed it to Chasing Elk, who used it to tie the deputy's hands behind his back.

Removing the kerchief from the deputy's neck, Chasing Elk used it to gag the lawman, then motioned the man into the cell.

"That ought to do it," Chasing Elk said as he closed and locked the cell door, then tossed the keys into the cell across the aisle. Settling his hat on his head, he pulled Catharine into his arms and gave her a quick kiss. "Let's go."

He led the way out of the cell block with Leah, Catharine, and Mark following. He found Catharine's pistol in the bottom drawer of the sheriff's desk and tossed it to Mark.

"Don't shoot me by mistake," Chasing Elk muttered, and then, pistol in hand, he opened the door to the sheriff's office and peered outside. The streets were dark and mostly quiet, though noise could be heard coming from a nearby saloon.

"Behind the jail," Catharine said. "I've got horses waiting."

"Good girl!"

Pulling his hat low over his eyes, Chasing Elk glanced up and down the street. "Don't be in a hurry," he warned. "Don't look behind you. Mark, close the door after us." And so saying, he stepped out into the street.

There were three horses waiting for them behind the jail: a flea-bitten gray, a lineback dun, and a white-faced chestnut. Catharine's carpetbags were draped over the saddlehorn of the gray. Chasing Elk noted there were bedrolls and bulging saddlebags behind the cantles of all three horses. Canteens hung from the pommels.

Chasing Elk helped Catharine onto the back of the

gray, lifted Leah onto the back of the dun and then swung up behind her. He grunted with satisfaction when he saw that his rifle was tucked into the saddle boot. Bless the girl. She'd thought of everything.

Mark climbed onto the back of the chestnut.

Taking up the reins, Chasing Elk clucked softly to his mount and rode down the street as if he was in no itching hurry at all.

Catharine and Mark followed him.

Once they were well clear of the town, Chasing Elk slipped his arm around Leah's waist and then urged his horse into a lope. He grinned as the wind stung his cheeks. It felt remarkably like freedom.

They rode for several hours, until Chasing Elk felt it was safe to stop for what was left of the night.

Leah was asleep by then. Catharine lifted her from the saddle and held her while Chasing Elk spread a blanket on the ground. The child made an incoherent sound, then curled up on the blanket, Gretchen held tight in her arm.

Chasing Elk covered his daughter, then stood looking down at her for several moments.

"She's beautiful," Catharine said, coming to stand beside him.

He nodded. "Thanks for getting me out of there," he said, and then grinned. "You're really something, you know that?"

"I couldn't leave you in jail, could I?"

"Sure you could."

"Well, that's true," she said, returning his grin, "but I couldn't leave Mark there." She shrugged. "It was just as easy to break both of you out. Besides," she said with a toss of her head, "it was exciting."

"Exciting!" Lyons exclaimed, joining them. "If we'd been caught, you'd have found yourself in one of those cells right along with us."

"Well, we weren't caught," Catharine retorted.

"I think we'd all best turn in," Chasing Elk suggested. "I want to get an early start in the morning. We've got a long way to go."

"Darn right," Mark said. "How long do you think it will take us to get to Boston?"

"I have no idea," Chasing Elk said. "I'm headed for the Dakotas."

"Not me," Lyons said. "Like I told you before, I've had enough of the West and everything in it."

Chasing Elk and Lyons unsaddled the horses while Catharine spread her bedroll next to Leah's. She spread Chasing Elk's blankets on the other side of the girl's and put Mark's beside her own.

In no time at all, the three of them were rolled up in their blankets. Mark's soft snores soon filled the air.

Catharine lay awake, wondering what Mark would say when she told him she wasn't going back to Boston with him.

Chasing Elk woke just before sunup, aware that he was no longer alone in his blankets. Leah had climbed in beside him sometime during the night and her back was pressed close to his. Rolling over onto his other side, he rose up on his elbow so he could see her face. How pretty she was, and how like her mother. It was a miracle, having her with him at last. He only hoped he could make her happy, keep her safe. She had been through so much heartache in her young life. He was determined to protect her from any more pain.

Lightly, he ran his fingertips over her hair, a rush of anger engulfing him. The last time he had seen her, her hair had been much longer. Why had the nuns cut it? Had it been a punishment of some kind, or had they done it in hopes of making her look less Indian?

Leah stirred, rolled over, and snuggled close to him. Chasing Elk closed his eyes, his heart swelling with love for his daughter and gratitude that he had found her.

Looking up, he saw that Catharine was awake and watching him. She smiled at him, her face filled with warmth and understanding. Did she still want to go with him to the Dakotas, or would she decide to go to Boston now that she had found her brother? If she decided on the latter, he wondered how he would ever let her go.

"Good morning," Catharine murmured.

"Morning."

"You said you wanted to get an early start," Catharine said, "but I didn't think you meant in the middle of the night."

"It'll be daylight in a few minutes, and we've got a long way to go."

She sat up, wincing as she did so. "I'm not sure I'll ever get used to sleeping on the ground."

"It's a lot softer than my cot at Yuma."

"I don't believe you."

He grinned at her. "Mother Earth is the best bed there is. If you listen to her late at night, she'll sing you a lullaby."

"You're making that up."

He shrugged. "I'd rather have a rock and free air than a feather mattress and iron bars."

"It must be awful to be locked up. I can't imagine such a thing."

"It's worse than awful," Mark said, jackknifing to a sitting position. "What are you two doing awake so early, anyway?" He yawned hugely. "I'm hungry."

"You're always hungry," Catharine retorted.

Mark shrugged. "I'm a growing boy. I need nourishment. And then we'd best be on our way. The sooner we get going, the sooner we'll get to Boston."

"I'm not going to Boston," Catharine said.

"Of course you are. Where else would you go?"

"I'm going with Chasing Elk."

"I don't think so."

"Oh? And why not?"

"Because I'm the man of the family. I'm responsible for you, and I'll decide where we're going."

"Is that right?" Catharine demanded, her hands fisted on her hips. "Fat lot of help you've been lately, Mr. Head of the House. You ran off and left me alone, remember? If it wasn't for Chasing Elk, I'd be living in Marteen's lodge now."

A dark flush stained Mark's cheeks. "All right, so I made a few mistakes. But you can't travel cross-country with him, just the two of you."

"No? Well, that's exactly what I've been doing! And if I wasn't, you'd still be in jail!"

"Listen," Chasing Elk said, rising. "You two can hash this out when we get to Prescott."

"How far is that?" Lyons asked.

"Seventy-five miles or so. We should get there day after tomorrow. . . ." His words trailed off as Leah sat up, rubbing the sleep from her eyes. Bending down, he ruffled her hair. "Morning, sweetheart."

"Morning, Daddy."

He smiled at her. "All right, it's time to get a move on. Lee, can you help Catharine fix us some breakfast while Mark and I look after the horses?"

"Sure, Daddy," Leah said, smiling at Catharine. "I'm a good cook."

"I'll bet you are."

In less than an hour, they were on the trail again. Chasing Elk rode ahead with Leah. He could hear Mark and Catharine bickering behind him, with Mark insisting that Catharine was going to Boston, and Catharine just as adamantly refusing. He had to admire her spunk and her quick wit: For every good reason Mark came up with for why Catharine should go to Boston, she came up with an equally good reason for why she wasn't. Apparently growing tired of the subject, Catharine changed it by asking Mark what he thought they should do about the house they had left behind.

To keep Leah from getting bored, Chasing Elk told her the story of Coyote and the fire, and how, long ago, only the yellow jackets had fire to keep them warm. Old Coyote decided that all the animals should have fire, so one night he stole a burning stick from the yellow jackets' fire. When the yellow jackets chased Coyote, he handed the stick to Eagle, who handed it to Mountain Lion, who passed it on to Bear, until, finally, Frog put a hot coal in his mouth and dove into the river, where the yellow jackets couldn't follow. After the yellow jackets flew away, Frog spit the coal out onto the bank, and Willow Tree swallowed it. Old Coyote showed the other animals how to retrieve the fire by rubbing two sticks together.

Thus the animals had fire to warm themselves at night while they told stories to one another.

Leah clapped her hands when he finished the story. "Tell me another."

"Yes," Catharine said as she rode up alongside Chasing Elk's horse. "Tell us another."

"Later," he said. "There's a stream ahead. We need to rest and water the horses."

Catharine groaned softly as she dismounted. Sleeping on the ground and riding for hours on end had made her aware of muscles she'd never known she had. Mark seemed to be moving a little slower, too. Whatever he had been doing since he left the farm, it apparently hadn't included sleeping on the ground or long hours in the saddle.

Leah was exploring along the banks of the stream. Chasing Elk stood with the horses while they drank.

They hadn't had any time alone since he had been arrested. She needed to talk to him, needed to make sure he hadn't changed his mind about wanting her to accompany him and his daughter to the Dakotas.

"Now is as good a time as any," she murmured, and made her way down to the water.

He looked at her and smiled when she stopped beside him.

"How you holding up?" he asked.

"I'm sore all over," she confessed.

He grinned. "You'll get used to it."

"Will I?"

"Sure. By the time we reach the Dakotas, you'll turn up your nose at a soft mattress."

"I doubt that," she said, laughing. And then she

grew serious once more. "I told Mark I was going with you."

"Several times, as I recall."

She took a deep breath, and then dived in. "You've never really asked me to go with you. Would you rather I didn't?"

"I never asked you to go to Tombstone, either, but you went."

He didn't want her. It was as simple as that. "I'm sorry I've been such a burden." She fought back the urge to cry. "Mark will be glad to know that . . ."

"Don't put words in my mouth, woman. I never said you were a burden, and I told you why I didn't want you to go to Tombstone with me." He put his hand over her mouth to keep her still. "I know, you got me out of jail, and I'm grateful, but it was a damn fool stunt. You might have been hurt. If things had turned out differently, you'd be in jail now."

"I know. Everything you say is true, but . . ."

"But what?"

"I want to be with you, no matter where you go."

Chasing Elk blew out a sigh. "And I want you with me, no matter where I go."

"Do you? Truly?"

"Truly."

She smiled up at him, her eyes shining. "Nathan."

"What?"

"Nothing. I've just never called you by your Christian name before. Do you mind?"

"No, but it's been so long since anyone called me that, I might not answer." He slid his arm around her waist and drew her up against him. "I knew you were going to be trouble."

"Did you?"

"Uh huh." He glanced over his shoulder to see what Leah and Mark were doing. Leah was plucking the petals from a wildflower. Mark was sitting on his haunches nearby, tossing pebbles into the water. "But a nice kind of trouble." He kissed her lightly. "That's for busting me out of jail." His hands slid down her back and settled on her hips to draw her closer, and then he kissed her again, longer, deeper. "And that's for knowing what I wanted even before I did."

"I'm in love with you," she said quietly. "Do you mind?"

"I'm thinking I must love you, too," he replied, "because I can't think of anything else when you're around."

She looked up at him through the veil of her lashes, a saucy grin on her face. "And when I'm not around?"

"Then, too," he confessed with a smile.

"Are you going to kiss her again, Daddy?"

Chasing Elk glanced over Catharine's head to see his daughter staring up at him.

Lyons was standing behind Leah, his arms crossed over his chest. "I sure as hell hope you're planning to marry my sister," he drawled. " 'Cause I'd hate to have to call you out."

Chasing Elk started to laugh at the idea of Mark Lyons taking him on, then thought better of it when he saw that Lyons was dead serious.

"Well?" Lyons demanded.

Chasing Elk looked at Catharine. "I guess it all depends on the lady."

"Are you going to get married, Daddy?" Leah asked excitedly.

"I don't know, sweetheart. It's up to Catharine."

The lady in question blinked up at him. "Are you asking me to marry you?"

"Reckon so," he said soberly. "Unless you want your brother to call me out."

"I wouldn't want that to happen," she said, merriment dancing in her eyes. "He's the only brother I have."

"I heard that!" Mark said. "Don't you think I could take him?"

"I don't think you could take *me*," Catharine replied, glancing at her brother.

"I let you win all those mud fights we used to have," Lyons muttered, red-faced.

"Sure you did."

"Hey." Chasing Elk put his finger under her chin and turned her head so she was facing him again. "You owe me an answer. Will you marry me, Catharine?"

"Of course I will."

Leah ran forward and tugged on Catharine's arm. "Does that mean you'll be my new mother?"

"Yes, I guess it does. Would you like that?"

"Oh, yes!" Leah said. "I haven't had a mother in a very long time."

Chasing Elk slipped his arm around Catharine's waist and gave her a squeeze. "I guess it's settled then." He looked over at Lyons. "Satisfied?"

Mark nodded. "But I think she could do a whole lot better!"

Chapter 14

The trip to Prescott went by much more quickly than Catharine would have imagined. They passed through several small towns along the way, where they stopped to spend the night and replenish their supplies. Catharine paid little attention to most of them, her mind preoccupied with more important things, like thoughts of marrying Nathan Chasing Elk. It occurred to her that before agreeing to marry him she should have asked him a few pertinent questions, like where he intended for them to live. She was certain he wouldn't want to live in the East, and just as certain that she didn't want to make her home on an Indian reservation in the wilds of the Dakotas. She didn't know how he planned to support her and Leah. She also realized that as much as she knew about Nathan's past, she really didn't know very much about him. She didn't know what his favorite foods were, or his favorite color, or even how old he was. She didn't know if he believed in God, or if he wanted more children. And what about Leah? Catharine was already fond of the child, but was she ready to be a mother to an eight-year-old?

Suddenly beset by doubts, she glanced over at the man who would soon be her husband. He had given her his hat to shade her face, and she studied him from beneath its brim. His long black hair gleamed in the sunlight; his profile was strong and clean and masculine. He rode like one born to the saddle, his body moving in perfect rhythm with his horse. He had one muscular arm wrapped around Leah's waist, a half-smile on his face as he listened to something his daughter was saying. It made Catharine's heart ache in a good way to see the two of them together.

Just then, Chasing Elk looked over at her and smiled. His gaze rested on her face, the love in his eyes filling her with a warmth that rivaled that of the sun as it melted her doubts away. She returned his smile, and for a moment she lost herself in the almost palpable attraction that hummed between them.

They rode all that day, stopping now and then to stretch their legs and rest the horses. Late in the afternoon, Leah fell asleep in her father's arms.

Catharine looked at the child with a touch of envy, wishing she were the one resting in Chasing Elk's arms, that it was her head comfortably pillowed on his broad chest. If she were riding with him, she could reach up and stroke his cheek, draw his head down and press her lips to his, feel the heat of his body against her own. . . .

Her cheeks grew hot when she realized he was looking at her again. No doubt he would be scandalized if he could read her mind! She had been taught that virtuous women did not entertain such titillating thoughts. It was quite improper. But she couldn't help it, couldn't stop thinking about how wonderful it would be to feel his hands on her body, to have him touch her and to touch him in return.

They reached Prescott as the sun was setting. Like so many of the towns in Arizona, Prescott had its beginnings when gold was discovered in the 1860s.

Chasing Elk dismounted in front of the Hollister Hotel, then lifted Leah from the saddle. Yawning, she leaned against him, hugging Gretchen to her chest.

"Lyons, why don't you take the horses over to the livery and get them settled," Chasing Elk suggested. "We'll go inside and see about getting a place to bed down for the night."

Mark nodded, though it was obvious that he resented taking orders from the other man.

Chasing Elk lifted Catharine from the back of her horse. Taking Leah by the hand, Catharine stepped up onto the boardwalk.

Chasing Elk handed the reins of both his own horse and Catharine's to Mark. He lifted the carpetbags from the saddlehorn, then removed the saddlebags from behind the cantles and slung the heavy packs over his shoulder. "Tell the hostler to give the horses an extra ration of oats," he said, pulling his rifle from the boot. "They've earned it."

With a nod, Mark rode down the street. It galled him to be taking orders from a man who was no better than he ought to be. A man who intended to marry his sister. A man who wasn't nearly good enough for her. What did Catharine see in Nathan Chasing Elk anyway? The man was an escaped convict, and for all that he claimed he was innocent—was there ever a man who had been sent to jail who *didn't* claim to be innocent?—Chasing Elk had nothing to offer Catharine. No home, no prospects, and he was wanted by the law. He could be arrested again at any time, and then where would Catharine be? Stuck in some backwater town with a kid who wasn't even hers.

Mark shook his head in exasperation. Women! Was there ever a man born who could understand them?

After leaving the horses at the livery with orders to give them an extra ration of oats, Mark strolled down the boardwalk, his hands shoved in his pants' pockets. Life out West sure hadn't turned out the way he had planned!

Feeling a sudden need for a drink, he crossed the street and went into the saloon. Ordering a beer, he stood with his back to the bar, glass in hand. Well, Catharine was on her own now. He had tried to convince her to go back to Boston with him, but she had always been a stubborn female and . . . Thoughts of Catharine fled his mind as a vision loomed before him. A vision in a ruffled red skirt that stopped just above her knees, and black net stockings that showed off a pair of gorgeous legs. His gaze moved up. She wore a white off-the-shoulder blouse that displayed a remarkable amount of cleavage.

Mark drained his glass in a long swallow just so he could ask her to bring him another drink.

"Coming right up, honey." Her voice was as husky as sin, her smile that of an angel. It was the smile that was his undoing. Who needed Boston, he thought as he watched her walk away. Everything he had ever wanted was right here.

Catharine looked out the window for the fifth time in as many minutes. "Where can he be?"

Chasing Elk shrugged. "He's a grown man, Catharine. He can take care of himself."

"Oh, sure. That's why he was in jail! He should have been here hours ago."

At least six hours ago, she thought anxiously. Chasing Elk had secured three rooms at the hotel, one for her and Leah, an adjoining one for himself, and one for Mark across the hall. She and Leah had bathed and changed their clothes. Chasing Elk had washed up as well, and then the three of them had gone out to dinner. And still Mark hadn't returned. Leah had gone to bed two hours ago. Catharine and Chasing Elk had gone to his room so they wouldn't disturb his daughter, though they had left the door ajar so they could hear her if she woke in the night.

Catharine paced to the window and stared out into the dark street again, then turned and paced toward the opposite end of the room.

Chasing Elk grabbed her hand when she moved past the bed and pulled her down onto his lap. "Calm down, darlin'. I'm sure he's fine."

"What if he isn't? He doesn't belong out here; he never did."

"Do you want me to go look for him?"

"Would you?"

"Sure, if you don't mind watching Leah."

"I don't mind."

He kissed the tip of Catharine's nose, then set her on her feet and reached for his hat. "I won't be gone long."

He found Mark in a saloon some twenty minutes later. The kid was at a table in a back corner playing cards. It looked like he was doing pretty well judging from the cash and chips stacked in front of him. But it was the blonde sitting on the kid's lap that caught Chasing Elk's attention. She was a remarkably pretty young woman for a saloon girl. Her skin was smooth and clear. Her eyes were still bright and alive, not yet dulled by despair, nor did she wear the world-weary expression he'd seen on the faces of so many other soiled doves.

Coming up behind Lyons, Chasing Elk tapped him on the shoulder.

Mark looked up, the smile on his face fading when he saw his future brother-in-law. "What are you doing here?" he asked irritably.

"Looking for you. Catharine's worried about you."

"Nothing to worry about." Mark gestured at the table with his chin. "I'm better than three hundred dollars ahead and just about to win another pot."

Chasing Elk glanced at the other men seated at the table. Hardcases, all of them, and none too happy about the kid's winning streak. "I think you'd best come with me."

"I think you'd best mind your own business," Lyons retorted. He looked at the girl on his lap and smiled. "I've decided to stick around for awhile."

"Uh-huh."

"Lyons, you in or out?"

"I'm in." He tossed a silver dollar into the pot.

Muttering under his breath, Chasing Elk turned away from the table and made his way to the bar, where he ordered a whiskey. He remained there for the next hour, keeping an eye on Lyons until the kid picked up his winnings. He whispered something in the girl's ear. She smiled a smile as old as time as she took him by the hand and led him up the stairs.

With a shake of his head, Chasing Elk left the saloon.

Returning to the hotel, he found Catharine asleep beside Leah. Well, there was no point in waking her. He was pretty sure she wouldn't approve of where her brother was spending the night, nor was he looking forward to telling her about it in the morning.

Putting out the lamp, Chasing Elk went into his own room and closed the door. He undressed in the dark, pulled off his boots, and crawled under the covers, only to lie there, wide awake and staring up at the ceiling, wishing that Catharine was curled up beside him.

He'd been right in thinking that Catharine would be upset in the morning, although "upset" was putting it mildly.

"So, you just left him there?" Catharine asked, her eyes narrowed, her hands on her hips.

"What did you want me to do, throw him over my shoulder and carry him home?"

"Yes. No. I don't know." She glanced over at Leah, who was sitting in the middle of the bed, playing with Gretchen. Lowering her voice, Catharine said, "He wasn't in his room this morning. Where do you suppose he is?"

"Yeah. Well, about that . . ."

She looked up at him, her eyes narrowed suspiciously. "What aren't you telling me?"

"He spent the night at the saloon."

"How do you know? You said you left around eleven."

"He took a girl upstairs."

Catharine frowned. "A girl? What girl?" And then her eyes grew wide. "Not a . . . a saloon girl?"

Chasing Elk nodded.

She stared at him. "How could he? Oh! He was upset because he saw you kissing me and now he's . . ."

Remembering that Leah was in the room, Catharine stopped in mid-tirade.

"He's a grown man, darlin'," Chasing Elk said matter-of-factly, "and he's got a man's needs."

"So, it's okay for him to . . . to . . ." She glanced at Leah again. "Well, you know, but it's not all right for you to kiss me?"

"Something like that."

"Oh! That is so unfair! I'll bet if he knew I was . . . you know . . . with a man, he wouldn't hesitate to throw me over his shoulder and take *me* home."

Chasing Elk had to laugh at that, partly because she was so incensed and partly because it was true. In fact, if she was doing *you know* with another man, Chasing Elk knew he would drag her outside himself, right after he beat the holy hell out of the man.

"I've never understood why it's all right for a man to sow his wild oats but it's not all right for a woman."

He shrugged. "That's just the way it is, the way it's always been."

She tilted her head to one side. "Have you sown a lot of oats?"

"One or two."

Before Catharine could pursue that line of thought, Leah slid off the bed.

"I'm hungry, Daddy."

Chasing Elk smiled at her, thinking that she had interrupted his conversation with Catharine at just the right time. "Me, too. Let's go downstairs and get something to eat. You coming, Catharine?"

They were just finishing breakfast when Mark swaggered into the hotel dining room, his arm around the pretty blond girl Chasing Elk had seen him with the night before. This morning, the girl was clad in a short-sleeved, low-cut gingham dress that outlined every voluptuous curve. It wasn't the most modest outfit Chasing Elk had ever seen, but it was a lot less revealing than what she had been wearing the last time he had seen her.

"Hey, Cath, Nathan," Mark said cheerfully. "This is Bonnie Lee Brisco." He held out a chair for Bonnie Lee, then pulled a vacant chair from a nearby table and sat down. "Bonnie Lee, this is my sister, Catharine, and her intended, Nathan, and his daughter, Leah. Bonnie Lee and I got married this morning."

"Is that right?" Chasing Elk said. "I guess congratulations are in order."

Bonnie Lee blushed prettily. "Thank you."

Catharine stared at her brother as if she had never seen him before.

"Aren't you going to congratulate us, Cath?"

"You got married? This morning?"

Mark nodded.

He looked mighty pleased with himself, and with life in general, Chasing Elk thought, but who could blame him? Bonnie Lee was a pretty girl with a bright smile and a figure to drive a man wild. He'd bet his stolen horse and rifle that she hadn't been a saloon girl very long.

"But . . . you just met her last night," Catharine said.

"Yeah, well." Mark shrugged, then smiled at his bride. "I knew she was the one for me as soon as I saw her."

Catharine shook her head in disbelief. How could Mark have married a girl he had known less than a day? It was unthinkable.

"I was hoping you'd be happy for me, Cath," Mark said quietly.

Catharine stared at him. Happy that he had married a girl who earned her living selling her favors to men? Was he kidding?

Rising, Mark took his bride's hands in his and pulled her to her feet. Leaning down, he kissed Catharine on the cheek. "If you ever get to Boston, look us up. Let's go, Bonnie Lee," he said, and turned away from the table.

"I'm sorry you don't approve," Bonnie Lee said over her shoulder, and followed Mark out of the dining room.

Catharine stared after the two of them, too stunned to speak. Her baby brother had married a soiled dove.

"Well," Chasing Elk drawled. "You could have handled that a little better."

"Better! What was I supposed to do, congratulate him on marrying a . . . a strumpet?"

"What's a strumpet?" Leah asked.

"I'll tell you when you're older," Chasing Elk replied. "And yes," he said to Catharine, "you should have wished them well. No sense crying over spilt milk."

"I should have known you'd take his side. You men always stick together."

"You're judging her without even knowing her."

"She's a . . . a trollop. What else do I need to know?"

"What's a trollop?" Leah asked.

"She looked like a nice girl," Chasing Elk said, ignoring his daughter.

"Nice!"

Leah tugged on her father's sleeve. "What's a trollop?"

"She hasn't been in the business very long," Chasing Elk said. "You can tell that by looking at her."

"You can?"

"Sure."

"Daddy . . ."

"Leah, not now. Catharine, are you ready to go?"

She nodded.

Her brother was married. It was all she could think about as she packed up Leah's belongings and then her own. He hadn't even invited her to the wedding. Of course, judging by the way she had reacted to the news, who could blame him? He had probably known she wouldn't approve. A saloon girl! A "nice girl," Chasing Elk had called her. And maybe she was, Catharine mused. If she hadn't been so judgmental, she might have gotten to know a little more about her new sister-in-law. Now that the initial shock was wearing off, Catharine was ashamed of the way she had behaved. Mark was the only family she had left, after all. She should have put her own feelings aside and made Bonnie Lee feel welcome for Mark's sake.

Chasing Elk knocked on her door a few minutes later. "Are you ready to go?"

"Yes, but I need to find Mark first. I owe him an apology. And Bonnie Lee, too."

He smiled at her. "That's my girl."

"Where do you think they are?"

"I don't know. You might try Mark's room here at the hotel."

"I'll be right back."

Moments later, Catharine stood in front of Mark's hotel room. She took a deep breath, then rapped lightly on the door. No one answered. Maybe they weren't there, she thought, then felt her cheeks grow hot. Or maybe they were in bed and hadn't heard her knock.

She was about to turn away when the door opened and her brother stood before her. He was shirtless, his hair mussed.

"What do you want?" he asked.

"I came to apologize to the two of you."

He stepped back. "Come on in."

Bonnie Lee was sitting on the edge of the bed, brushing her hair. Catharine noticed the covers were rumpled and hoped she hadn't interrupted anything.

She smiled tentatively at Bonnie Lee. "I'm sorry for the way I behaved earlier," she said. "I was just so surprised. And a little hurt that I wasn't invited to the wedding." She glanced at Mark, then back to Bonnie Lee. "I hope the two of you will be very happy."

"Thank you," Bonnie Lee replied with a shy smile. "I know what you must think of me, but Mark's the first man I ever took upstairs."

"You don't have to explain anything to me," Catharine said quickly.

"I know, but I don't want you to think badly of me. My mama passed on a few months back. She didn't leave me anything to get by on. Working in the saloon was the only job I could find." Bonnie Lee looked at Mark. "I knew your brother was something special the minute I saw him."

"Now that Bonnie Lee's my wife, she won't be working at the saloon anymore," Mark said. "We're both going to find jobs and save some money, and then we're heading East, like I said."

"I'm happy for you, Mark, really," Catharine said. Impulsively, she hugged her sister-in-law. "I've got to go. Nathan is waiting for me. Mark, when you get back to Boston, let Mrs. Montgomery know where you're staying." Mrs. Montgomery had been their neighbor back East, and their mother's best friend. "When I get a chance, I'll write and let you know where we are."

"Will do, Cath." He put his arm around her and gave her a squeeze. "Make sure he marries you, hear?"

"Don't worry about me," she said, blinking back her tears. "Take care of yourself. You're the only brother I've got."

She hugged him tight, then left the room.

Chapter 15

Catharine looked out the window of the stage coach, wondering how many more days it would be until they reached the reservation and how Chasing Elk would find his mother once they arrived. She was heartily sick of traveling, both by train and by stage. Truth be told, she was just sick of traveling! The constant jouncing over ruts, the fine yellow dust that worked its way through her clothing and into her underwear, the layovers at way stations along the road where the accommodations were crude at best. She didn't like sleeping on the floor, not that she got much sleep. One of their traveling companions, a Mr. Jonathan Norris from New York City, snored so loudly she wouldn't have been surprised if he brought the ceiling crashing down on top of them. There were two other passengers in the coach, Mr. and Mrs. Alistair Shayne, who were on their way to Chicago to visit their son, daughter-in-law and new grandchild. The Shaynes were a quiet, middle-aged couple. Mrs. Shayne spent most of her time knitting a blanket for the baby.

The only good thing Catharine could say about the journey was that it gave her a chance to get better acquainted with Chasing Elk's daughter. Leah continued to charm her. In spite of her tumultuous past, she seemed to be a bright child who was eager to learn. Much of the sadness had left her eyes. She smiled more easily. And she rarely let her father out of her sight, as if she were afraid that he might be taken from her again.

Catharine grabbed hold of the leather strap by her head as the coach started down a long, sloping hill.

"We're only a few miles from the next town," Chasing Elk said. "Think you can hold out until then?"

Before she could answer, she was thrown back against the seat as the coach suddenly careened down the hill. She heard the driver holler "whoa," but the coach's speed didn't lessen.

"What's happening?" she asked.

"Something must have spooked the horses," he replied. "Hang on." He slipped his arm around Leah and drew her up against him.

Mrs. Shayne began to wail that they were all going to die and she would never get to see her new granddaughter. Her husband tried to calm her, but he looked even more frightened than his wife.

Catharine didn't blame either of them for being scared. Her heart was pounding a mile a minute as the coach continued to career down the hill and then, slowly, began to slide sideways. Leah scrambled into her father's lap, her arms wrapping around his neck. A scream rose in Catharine's throat as the coach toppled over onto its side, tossing the passengers around like drops of cold water hitting a hot skillet as it skidded down the hill, gradually coming to rest at the bottom.

When the dust settled, Catharine found herself pressed up against Mr. Norris's back. His bulk had provided a soft place to land, and she was relieved that nothing seemed to be broken.

There was movement outside and then the driver opened the coach door, which was now above their heads. "Anybody hurt?" he asked, peering down at them.

There was a barrage of voices as everyone started talking at once. Reaching inside, the driver gripped Mrs. Shayne under her arms and lifted her outside. She had hit her head on the side of the coach, and her cheek and one eye were already turning black and blue. Her husband climbed out of the coach after her. The driver assisted Catharine out next. After much grunting and a boost from Chasing Elk, Mr. Norris heaved himself out of the coach.

The driver peered into the coach again. "You all right in there?"

"I think my daughter's leg is broken," Chasing Elk said. "Be careful with her."

Catharine stood to one side, her hand pressed to her heart, as the driver lifted Leah out of the coach. The girl's face was pale, her eyes wide, her cheeks wet with tears.

Chasing Elk pulled himself out of the coach, then took his daughter from the driver. "Hush, sweetheart," he murmured. "You'll be all right."

"It hurts."

He smoothed a lock of hair from her brow. "I know." He carried her to a place in the shade. "Just rest easy. I'm going to find something to wrap your leg with."

"Stay with me!" Leah cried.

"I won't be gone long. Catharine will sit with you."

Catharine smiled. "Of course I will." Sitting down beside Leah, she took the girl's hand in hers.

"Where's Gretchen?" Leah said fretfully. "I want Gretchen."

"I'll get her," Chasing Elk said.

While the driver and the guard unhitched the team, Chasing Elk pulled a blanket from the boot. He searched inside the coach until he found Gretchen and his rifle. Tucking the doll under one arm, he gathered a couple of sturdy sticks, then cut a length of leather from the reins.

"Here you go, sweetheart," he said, handing Leah her doll. "I'm going to splint your leg now. It might hurt a little, but it'll feel better when I'm done."

Leah clutched Gretchen to her chest with one hand and clung to Catharine's hand with the other. "Her dress is torn," Leah said, sniffling.

"I'll make her a new one," Catharine said. "Would you like that?"

Setting his rifle aside, Chasing Elk splinted his daughter's leg, carefully wrapped the blanket around it, and tied it in place with the strip of leather he had cut from one of the reins.

By the time he finished, the driver and the guard, both of whom were miraculously unhurt, had unhitched the horses from the stagecoach.

"The axle and one wheel are busted," the driver said. "We'll have to ride into town. There's eight of us and only six horses, so a couple of you will have to double up."

"My daughter will ride with me," Chasing Elk said.

The driver nodded. "Mr. and Mrs. Shayne, you'll have to double up, too."

"But . . . but I've never ridden a horse," Mrs. Shayne sputtered, obviously appalled at the very idea.

"Well," the guard said matter-of-factly, "it's high time you learned."

"But what about our baggage?" Mrs. Shayne asked. "You can't mean to leave it out here?"

"If you've got any valuables, you might want to dig them out, but I suggest you hurry. If we leave now, we can make it to town before dark. We'll send someone out to collect your things."

They reached the stagecoach depot a little over two hours later. By then, Leah had a fever and Mrs. Shayne had finally stopped complaining.

Chasing Elk didn't stop at the depot but rode on down the main street until he came to a small white house with a sign in the front yard that proclaimed that Doctor Elias Whitcomb practiced medicine there.

Dismounting, he lifted Leah from the back of the horse and carried her through the arched gate in the white picket fence.

Following him, Catharine quickly rang the bell beside the front door.

An elderly woman in a dove-gray dress and crisp white apron answered their summons. She took one look at Leah and motioned them into the house.

"Come in, come in. Elias, we need you!"

A tall man with short brown hair and a graying goatee entered the room. "Afternoon, folks," he said, tossing aside the towel he had been drying his hands on. His gaze ran over Leah and settled on her leg. "Is it broken?"

Chasing Elk nodded.

"How long ago?"

"About two hours."

The doctor nodded curtly. "Martha, we'll need to operate right away."

"Yes, Doctor," the woman replied and hurried from the room.

The doctor stepped forward, his arms outstretched. "I'll take her."

Chasing Elk shook his head. "No. I'm going to stay with her."

The doctor looked Chasing Elk up and down. "Are you the girl's father?"

"Yeah."

Elias Whitcomb shook his head. "It's usually better if parents wait out here."

"Daddy . . ." Leah clutched her father's shirt.

"I'm not leaving her," Chasing Elk said firmly.

"All right," the doctor said dubiously. "Bring her on back." Turning, he went through the same doorway Martha had gone through earlier.

Chasing Elk glanced over his shoulder at Catharine. "Why don't you go get us a couple of rooms at the hotel?"

"All right." She squeezed his shoulder. "She'll be fine."

He nodded. Going through the door the doctor had used, Chasing Elk found himself in a fair-sized room. Martha and the doctor had both donned masks, and the doctor was washing his hands again.

"Just put her there, on the table," Whitcomb directed.

Chasing Elk laid his daughter on a long narrow table covered with a white sheet, then took her hand in his. "Don't be afraid, sweetheart."

She clung to his hand, her nails digging into his skin. Her face was almost as white as the sheet. Perspiration beaded her brow.

She flinched when the doctor began to remove the binding that held the blanket in place.

"Close your eyes, sweetheart," Chasing Elk said. "I'm right here beside you."

His own heart was pounding as he watched the doctor and his assistant spread out the necessary equipment. Taking a deep breath, he glanced around the room. There was a large, glass-fronted cabinet that held bottles of quinine, ipecac, ether, spirits of ammonia, alcohol, oil of turpentine, black tea, and morphine, as well as a mortar and pestle and a variety of bandages. In an open drawer, Chasing Elk saw a number of knives and forceps. A table on the far side of the room held a wash basin and pitcher and a set of scales.

Whitcomb touched Leah's shoulder, and she opened her eyes. The doctor smiled at her. "I'm going to give you something to make you sleep," he said. "When you wake up, your leg won't hurt anymore. Are you ready?"

Leah looked at her father. "You won't leave me? Promise?"

"I promise I'll be here the whole time."

Squeezing her father's hand, she said, "I'm ready."

The quiver in her voice tore at Chasing Elk's heart.

He stroked the back of her hand as the doctor measured a small dose of ether.

"Take slow, deep breaths," the doctor told her as he placed the cone over her face. "That's right, nice and slow. Nothing to be afraid of."

In minutes, she was sound asleep.

Whitcomb looked across the operating table at Chasing Elk. "Are you sure you want to stay?"

"I promised her I would."

"Very well. Martha, are you ready? Let's begin."

Stepping out of the doctor's house an hour later, Chasing Elk took a deep breath. If there was anything worse than seeing your child in pain, he didn't know what it was. But she was resting comfortably now. Whitcomb had assured him that Leah wouldn't wake for several hours, and had advised him to find something to eat and try to get some rest. Martha had promised to sit with Leah and to send for him immediately if she woke up sooner than expected. Chasing Elk didn't want to leave, but he needed to make sure Catharine was settled at the hotel, and then he needed a good stiff shot of whiskey to calm his nerves.

There was only one hotel in town. When he inquired after Catharine, he was told that the hotel was full.

"I sent Miss Lyons to see Mrs. Littlefield," the clerk said. "She runs a boardinghouse. You'll find it at the south end of town, not far from the blacksmith's shop."

"Obliged," Chasing Elk said, and left the hotel.

Chasing Elk's first thought when he saw Mrs. Littlefield's boardinghouse was that it was in bad need

of a coat of paint and repair. The front gate was off
its hinges, some of the pickets in the fence were missing, there was a hole in the roof, and the chimney was
leaning perilously to one side. Climbing the porch
stairs, he noticed that there was a step missing.

When he knocked on the front door, a tiny little
woman with graying red hair and sharp blue eyes answered it.

"If you're here about the room," she said, "I just
rented it."

"I'm looking for Catharine Lyons. Is she here?"

"Why, yes, she is. Are you her young man?" Mrs.
Littlefield opened the door and stood back so he could
enter. "She told me you'd be coming around sooner
or later. How's the little girl?"

"She's gonna be fine."

"I'm Emma Littlefield," the woman said. She patted
her hair in place as her gaze moved over him from
head to foot. "You're not going to scalp me, are you?"

"No, ma'am."

She smiled at him. "Catharine's in room three, just
down the hall on the left."

"Thank you, ma'am."

She beamed at him. "I do so like a young man with
good manners."

With a nod, he walked down the hall to number
three and opened the door.

Catharine was standing at the window. She turned
as he entered the room. "How's Leah? Is she going
to be all right?"

"She's sleeping. Whitcomb said her leg should heal
up just fine, but that I probably shouldn't move her
for awhile. I need to get back there right quick. I want

to be with her when she wakes up. I just wanted to make sure you were settled in."

"Why don't you rest a minute while I see about getting you something to eat and some hot water so you can wash up."

"Thanks."

Catharine cleared her throat. "There's just one thing . . ."

"What's that?"

"Mrs. Littlefield thinks we're married."

"Oh?" He lifted one brow. "Why does she think that?"

"She only had one room. I had to tell her we were married, you know, because, well, because. So, if she calls you Mr. Lyons, remember to answer."

"Lyons, right," he said with a wry grin.

"She put a cot in here for Leah. I thought . . ."

He nodded. "I'll take the extra bed."

"I won't be long." Obviously relieved that he wasn't angry, she left the room.

He sat down on the edge of the double bed, only then realizing how exhausted he was. Worry sure as hell took a lot out of a man.

Chapter 16

"How's that?" Chasing Elk asked as he settled Leah on one of the porch chairs with her injured leg propped up on an empty crate.

"Fine, Daddy."

"You sure?"

She nodded. "Where's Gretchen?"

"I don't know, but she can't have gone far. You rest here for awhile. I'm going to fix the hinges on Mrs. Littlefield's gate. It shouldn't take too long."

"But I want Gretchen."

"I'll find her for you, don't worry." Kissing his daughter on the cheek, he went down the stairs to where he had left the tools he had found in a dilapidated shed behind the house.

A week had passed since the accident. Leah spent the first night at the doctor's office. Chasing Elk had stayed with her, sleeping in a chair beside the bed. She had slept most of the second day as well. By the fifth day, she was fretting because she had to stay in bed. Chasing Elk had brought her out onto the porch, hoping that being outside for awhile would improve her spirits.

It took him only a few minutes to repair the gate. It felt good to be working with his hands, to be out of doors with no one watching his every move or waiting to tell him what to do next.

He waved at Leah. As soon as she was fit to travel, they would again be on their way to the Dakotas.

Catharine looked out the parlor window, the new dress she was making for Leah's doll momentarily forgotten as she watched Chasing Elk repair the broken hinge on the front gate. She never tired of watching him. She loved the effortless way he moved, the latent strength that emanated from him, the tenderness in his eyes when he looked at his daughter.

Picking up the doll's dress, she began to sew the hem. Chasing Elk hadn't mentioned their getting married again. She wondered if he intended to go through with it, or if he had proposed to her merely to satisfy her brother.

She didn't think it was her imagination that the tension between herself and Chasing Elk seemed to grow a little stronger every day. Leah fell asleep early each night, leaving the two of them to fill the remaining hours until they went to bed. Catharine was acutely conscious of his every move, his every look. Excitement fluttered in the pit of her stomach whenever he touched her, whether by accident or design. Lying in the big double bed next to Leah, Catharine was ever aware of Chasing Elk lying in the cot only a few feet away. Her insides quivered tremulously every time he stirred, hoping that he would carry her to his bed and hold her close. She yearned for his touch, ached for his kisses.

Finishing the hem on the doll's dress, she cut the

thread and laid her needle aside. She quickly removed Gretchen's old dress and put on the new one, as well as the pantalets she had made earlier, and then she picked up the doll and went outside, eager for Leah's reaction.

Leah looked up as Catharine joined her on the porch. Seeing her doll, she held out her arms. "Gretchen! You found her!"

Catharine handed Leah the doll, watched as the child's eyes sparkled with delight. "You did it," she said. "You made her a new dress."

"Do you like it?"

"Oh, yes. How did you know pink was my favorite color?"

Catharine smiled at Chasing Elk, who was standing at the bottom of the porch stairs. "A little bird told me."

Chasing Elk looked at his daughter. "What do you say to Catharine, sweetheart?"

"Oh. Thank you," Leah said.

"You're welcome. I'll ask Mrs. Littlefield if she has any more scraps. Maybe we could make Gretchen a whole new wardrobe. Would you like that?"

"Could you teach me how to sew?"

"If you like."

Leah turned the doll this way and that, then squealed, "You made her new bloomers, too!"

Listening to Catharine and his daughter filled Chasing Elk's heart with a warmth he had never expected to feel again. He didn't know what he had done to deserve a woman like Catharine in his life, but he intended to do everything he could to make sure she stayed.

He was sitting on the front porch swing later that night when Catharine came to sit beside him. She looked young and vulnerable in a pale blue robe with her toes peeking out from under the hem.

"I thought you'd gone to bed," he remarked.

"I couldn't sleep."

"Something wrong?"

"No."

He grunted softly. "I was thinking of taking a walk. Wanna come along?"

She looked down at her robe and frowned. "Like this?"

He shrugged. "Why not?"

Rising, he took her hand. Descending the porch steps, they turned right and walked away from the house and away from the town.

"It's so dark out here," Catharine said. "I don't remember it being this dark back East. Or this quiet."

"Or this beautiful," he murmured, and drew her into his arms.

She let out a little sigh and snuggled against him. What with one thing and another, it had been a long time since they were alone. He nuzzled the top of her head with his chin, then tipped her face up with his forefinger and kissed her. One taste of her lips and he wanted more, wanted it all. He ran his hands up and down her back, then drew her up against him once more. They were going to have to get married soon, he thought, before he went mad with desire. Lately his dreams had been filled with images of Catharine lying beneath him, her legs wrapped around his waist, her voice crying his name.

With a low groan, he broke the kiss.

"Don't stop," she whispered.

"Darlin', if I don't stop, I'm going to take you right here, right now."

His words sent a thrill of excitement and anticipation rushing through her. "If we were married . . ."

"I know." He ran his knuckles along her cheek. "I saw a flyer tacked to the bulletin board near the sheriff's office. It's got my name on it." And a helluva lot more than his name, he thought grimly. It had a description that was so thorough a blind man could recognize him in the dark.

Catharine understood what he was saying. They couldn't get married here, not now, not when there was a chance that the minister might recognize Chasing Elk's name and turn him in to the sheriff. It had happened before. She still couldn't believe that Sister Mary Margaret had turned him in, but if it hadn't been the nun, then who? The priest, perhaps?

"We should leave town," she said. "Right away."

"No. I don't want Leah bouncing around inside a stage just yet."

"But . . ."

He brushed a kiss over her lips. "Don't worry. As long as I stay out of town, we should be all right. There was no picture on the flyer, just my name and description."

She slid her arms around his waist. "I'm scared, Nathan."

"Don't be."

"I can't help it. I don't want to lose you, not now."

His arms tightened around her. "Catharine, worrying won't help."

"I know," she said with a sigh, and then she looked

up at him, a faint smile curving her lips. "Kiss me again, Nathan. I can't think of anything else when you kiss me."

He lowered his head, his lips capturing hers in a searing kiss that stole the breath from her lungs and made her toes curl. She felt his need rise as he deepened the kiss, felt her own quick response as his tongue slid along her lower lip. She leaned into him, moaned softly as her breasts were crushed against his chest.

"Dammit, Catharine," he muttered, his voice gruff, "do you know what you're doing to me?"

She knew. Oh, yes, she knew. She could feel the heat of his desire pressing against her belly.

Blowing out a long, shuddering sigh, he released her. "We'd better go back," he said, his voice ragged, "before I drag you into the bushes."

With a nod, she ran a hand through her hair, then straightened her robe. But all the while they were walking back to the boarding house, she wondered if it would have been so bad to have been dragged off into the bushes.

Catharine sat on the front porch, watching Chasing Elk replace the broken slats in the fence. Leah was napping inside the house, and Mrs. Littlefield had gone into town. The other boarders, a school teacher and a women's wear salesman, had gone off earlier in the day.

Catharine rocked gently, content to sit in the shade and admire Chasing Elk. From time to time, he looked up and smiled at her, and each time it made her heart skip a beat. He was a joy to watch, she thought, whether he was sawing a board in half or driving a nail. He worked with a kind of effortless grace, his muscles bunching and relaxing beneath his shirt.

She was about to go into the house and fix him a glass of lemonade when Mrs. Littlefield came hurrying down the road. Catharine grinned, surprised to see how spry the older woman was, and then she noticed the grim expression on the woman's face.

Mrs. Littlefield stopped outside the fence to talk to Chasing Elk. Curious to know what she was saying, Catharine descended the stairs and walked quickly toward them.

". . . posters all over town," Mrs. Littlefield was saying, her voice indignant. "I simply cannot believe you didn't tell me you were wanted by the law."

"I'm sorry, ma'am," Chasing Elk said, "but I needed a place for my little girl to stay."

Mrs. Littlefield's gaze narrowed suspiciously as she lifted Catharine's left hand, then let it fall. "No ring. She's not your wife, is she?"

"No, ma'am."

The woman made a tsking sound. "Disgraceful! I'm afraid you'll have to leave right away."

A muscle twitched in Chasing Elk's jaw. "Did you tell the sheriff that I'm here?"

"No. I don't want that dreadful man snooping around here, upsetting my boarders and causing a lot of talk." She drew herself up to her full four feet, seven inches. "But I will, if you don't leave immediately."

Chasing Elk dropped the hammer he'd been holding, opened the gate he had fixed, and caught Catharine by the hand. "Come on."

Inside their room, with the door closed, Catharine muttered a very unladylike curse. "I don't believe the gall of that woman! After all you've done for her, fixing the gate and the hole in the roof, and now she has the nerve to throw us out!"

Chasing Elk shrugged. He had hoped to let Leah's leg heal up a few more days but that couldn't be helped now. They had to get out of town before the Littlefield woman changed her mind or someone else realized who he was.

"Let's get packed before we wake Leah," he said quietly.

"Aren't you upset, even a little?" Catharine asked.

"I'd be more upset if she'd gone to the sheriff. Come on, let's get the hell out of here before she changes her mind."

Catharine was heartily sick of traveling by the time they reached Tequila Springs. It was a small town, yet it looked extremely prosperous. The buildings were all well kept; the streets were wide and hard-packed, which kept the dust down considerably.

She glanced up and down the street as Chasing Elk assisted her from the coach. It was Saturday afternoon and the boardwalk was crowded with men and women. She saw several men in Cavalry blue, stared at a Chinese man as he crossed the street.

She waited on the boardwalk while Chasing Elk lifted Leah from the coach. Carrying her around to the boot, he pulled out the crutches the doctor had given her. She had practiced using them at every stop along the way. Settling them under her arm, she looked up at her father and smiled.

"How long until we find my grandma?"

"I'm not sure, sweetheart. We'll have to wait until you can ride, and then we'll get some horses and light out for the reservation."

"But I want to go now. I want to see the Lakota and sleep in a tepee."

Chasing Elk grinned at her. "That's what I want, too, but I don't think you're up to spending long hours on the back of a horse just yet."

"But . . ."

"And I need to earn some money," he said. "We spent most of what we had to get here."

Leah sighed dramatically, then frowned. "Where's Gretchen?"

Chasing Elk muttered an oath under his breath, then ducked inside the coach. He emerged a moment later with Gretchen in hand. "Good thing you remembered her before the stage took off again," he said.

"Will you carry her for me?" Leah asked.

Chasing Elk had a mental image of himself walking down the street with a rag doll tucked under his arm. "I think we'll let Catharine carry Gretchen," he said with a wry grin. "I'll carry our bags."

The Darlington Hotel was one of the loveliest hotels Catharine had ever seen. There were patterned carpets on the floor of the lobby; a delicate crystal chandelier hung from the ceiling. Chairs and settees covered in crisp damask were placed at intervals along the walls or grouped around highly polished mahogany tables. The desk clerk wore a natty city suit and a black bow tie.

"Welcome to the Darlington," he said with a polite smile. "Will you be staying . . ." His voice trailed off as he glanced from Leah to Chasing Elk. "I'm sorry, sir," he said quietly, "but the hotel doesn't allow Indians."

Catharine glanced at Chasing Elk. A muscle twitched in his jaw.

She placed her hand on his arm. "Let's go," she said.

"Dammit . . ."

She squeezed his arm. "Please?"

Without a word, he turned and stalked out of the hotel.

"What's wrong?" Leah asked, frowning. "Why is my daddy so mad?"

"I'll tell you later," Catharine said.

He was waiting for them outside, his face a mask of barely suppressed anger. "I saw a sign for a boardinghouse. It's located around the corner on Cottonwood Street."

Realizing this wasn't the time for questions or conversation, Catharine held her silence as they walked down the boardwalk to the corner and turned right on Cottonwood Street. Simpson's boardinghouse was a far cry from the one owned by Mrs. Littlefield. Simpson's place was a large white two-story house with dark gray shutters. White lace curtains fluttered at the open front windows. Flowers grew along the walkway leading up to the house and on either side of the front porch. A large black cat slept in the shade of a weeping willow tree.

Catharine breathed a sigh of relief when she saw the vacancy sign in the window; then, remembering what had just happened at the hotel, she wondered if her relief was premature.

A tall, austere-looking woman answered Chasing Elk's knock. She looked him up and down, noting the baggage he carried and the rifle snugged under his arm.

"You're Injun, ain't ya?" Her voice was low and gruff. Had Catharine not seen her face, she might have thought it was a man speaking.

Chasing Elk nodded.

"That yer little girl?"

He nodded again.

"You got names?"

"I'm Nathan Rossiter. This is my daughter, Leah."

"Rossiter?" the woman asked skeptically.

Chasing Elk nodded curtly.

The woman looked at Catharine. "And you'd be?"

Catharine hardly dared breathe as the woman turned her hard blue gaze in her direction. "Catharine."

"You two hitched?"

"No, ma'am." Catharine sent a quick look at Chasing Elk. She had intended to lie and say yes, but something in the woman's forthright gaze demanded the truth.

The woman grunted. "I reckon you'll be wantin' two rooms."

"Yes, ma'am," Catharine said meekly.

The woman looked at Chasing Elk again. "I don't allow no smokin' or chewin' in my place," she said, holding the screen door open for them. "Your rooms are this way."

She walked through a parlor that looked as though it had never seen a speck of dust in its life and down a long hallway papered in a dark green stripe.

She paused outside a door marked with a gold num-

ber eight and looked over her shoulder at Chasing
Elk. "I don't allow no drinkin' in my place, neither."

"Yes, ma'am," he said between clenched teeth.

"You can have this room and the one adjoining."
She glanced at Leah, then looked at Chasing Elk and
Catharine. "I run a respectable place here, but I know
how it is with young people, so if you two are of a
mind to cohabit, be discreet about it."

Catharine knew she was blushing, but she couldn't
help it.

"Breakfast is at six sharp. I serve dinner at noon.
Supper's at six-thirty. Don't be late. I'm Mrs. Simpson.
You can pay me when you get settled." And with
that, she turned and walked back to the main part of
the house.

Chasing Elk stared after her, his expression so vitri-
olic Catharine was surprised Mrs. Simpson didn't go
up in flames.

Leah tugged on her father's hand. "Daddy, what
does co . . . cohabit mean?"

They quickly settled into their rooms and into the
routine at Mrs. Simpson's boardinghouse. There were
four other boarders. Mr. Bartholomew was the town's
schoolteacher. They didn't see much of him other than
at breakfast. Miss Brashear was a middle-aged maiden
lady who worked at the millinery shop. She was intimi-
dated by Chasing Elk and rarely spoke in his presence.
Regina and Rae Ann Whiddon were sisters, though
they looked nothing alike. Regina was rather buxom
and leaned toward bright colors that complemented
her black hair and brown eyes. Her sister, Rae Ann,
was tall and flat-chested. She wore drab colors that

did nothing to enhance her mousy-brown hair and pale blue eyes. Regina made no secret of the fact that she found Chasing Elk attractive, and rarely missed an opportunity to gain his attention.

Chasing Elk and Catharine had decided that Leah should sleep in Catharine's room because it wasn't seemly for an eight-year-old girl to share a bed with her father. Chasing Elk sat with her each night until she fell asleep. Sometimes they talked. Sometimes he told her Coyote stories or stories of his childhood with the Lakota. Those were Leah's favorite, and Catharine's, too.

He was telling her one now, about how he had killed his first buffalo.

"It was my first time to go on a hunt with the warriors," he said. "I rode with my uncle. He was a mighty hunter, the best in our village. I had painted my horse and tied up his tail. My heart was pounding as I swung onto his back. My quiver was over my shoulder, my bow in my hand.

"We rode in silence until we came to the place where the herd had been seen. It was only a small herd, nothing like the herds that had once roamed our land. My uncle told me that the great herds had once been so big, you could not ride around them in a day, but those days were gone.

"And then we crested a hill and there was the herd, grazing in the valley below. I drew an arrow from my quiver as we rode down the hill. Several of the warriors began shooting at the animals on the edge of the herd. At first, none of the other animals paid us any attention, and then, in less than a heartbeat, the herd took off running.

"My pony gave chase and we flew over the ground. When my pony dodged to the left, I found that we were surrounded on all sides by huge shaggy bodies."

Leah's eyes grew wide. "Were you scared?"

Chasing Elk nodded. "But my excitement was greater than my fear. I put my arrow to my bow, sighted down the shaft, and let the arrow fly."

"Did you get one?" Leah asked, her voice high with excitement.

"Yes. A cry of victory rose in my throat as the buffalo fell. When the hunt was over, the women came to skin and butcher the carcasses. My mother made me a blanket from the hide of the buffalo I had killed. My uncle cut out its heart and gave it to me."

"What did you do with it?" Leah asked, her eyes still wide.

"I ate it."

Leah wrinkled her nose. "I don't believe you!"

"I didn't eat all of it," Chasing Elk said, "just a few bites. Our people believe that eating the heart of your enemy gives you his power."

Clutching her stomach, Leah made a gagging sound deep in her throat.

Chasing Elk grinned at her. "Wouldn't you like to be as strong and fast as a buffalo?"

"Not if I had to eat its heart!" She looked at him speculatively. "Are *you* as strong and fast as a buffalo, Daddy?"

He nodded solemnly. "Of course."

Leah looked at Catharine, her expression skeptical. "Do you believe what he said?"

Catharine met Chasing Elk's gaze. "Of course," she replied solemnly.

Leah looked at her father, then at Catharine and shook her head. "I'm still not eating any buffalo heart."

Late the next afternoon, Chasing Elk took a walk through the town. He was relieved to see that there were no flyers bearing his name or his likeness, no posters offering a reward for his capture, but then, Tequila Springs was such a small town, it probably wasn't even on the map. He figured they would be safe here until Leah's leg mended and they could head out for the reservation.

He made two stops on his way back to the boarding-house. The first was at a gun shop, where he purchased a used Colt, a holster, and a box of ammunition.

His second stop was at the Lucky Strike Saloon, to see if he could get a job dealing for the house. The owner, Frank Quincannon, seemed a little leery about hiring a half-breed, but after he watched Chasing Elk deal a few hands, he agreed to give him a chance. After extending his thanks, Chasing Elk left the saloon. Spending time in prison hadn't been a total waste of time, he mused as he sauntered down the street. One of the inmates had taught him all the tricks of the trade where poker and blackjack were concerned. Having nothing better to do at night, Frank "Three-Finger" Cain had spent long hours teaching Chasing Elk everything he knew about the game, declaring that Chasing Elk was a natural-born cardsharp.

He returned to the boardinghouse a few minutes

after six. Catharine, Leah, and the other boarders were already at the table.

Mrs. Simpson lifted one eyebrow when he entered the dining room. "I do not allow guns at the table," she said.

Grunting softly, he hung his holster on the hall tree, then went back to the dining room and took his seat between Catharine and Leah.

"You're late, Mr. Rossiter," Mrs. Simpson noted.

"Yes, ma'am."

The words *don't let it happen again* hung unspoken in the air between them. She handed him a large bowl of beef stew, her disapproval evident in her expression.

There was very little conversation at the dinner table other than requests to pass this dish or that. Regina Whiddon glanced frequently in Chasing Elk's direction. There was no mistaking either her interest or her curiosity.

That evening, her curiosity got the best of her. "You're Indian, are you not?" she asked.

All heads turned in Chasing Elk's direction.

"Yes, ma'am."

"I've never met an Indian before. What tribe do you belong to?"

"Lakota. The whites call us the Sioux."

Her eyes widened. "Sioux! Like the ones who killed Custer?"

He nodded.

"Were you there?"

He shook his head. He would rather have been there, fighting at the Greasy Grass, than locked up in Yuma, but he saw no need to tell her that.

"I've heard that Indian men take more than one wife," Regina remarked. "Is that true?"

"Yes, ma'am."

Regina glanced at Catharine, then leaned across the table toward Chasing Elk. "Do you?" she asked. "Have more than one wife, that is?"

He didn't like where this conversation was headed, he thought, not one damn bit. Hoping to shock her or at least shut her up, he said, "Not yet."

"Not ever," Catharine said. Flashing Regina Whiddon a smile that was decidedly smug, Catharine laid a proprietary hand on Chasing Elk's forearm.

Regina shrugged. "You can't blame a girl for trying."

"Yes, you can," Catharine said. She looked at Chasing Elk. "Shall we go for a walk, dear?"

Biting back the urge to laugh out loud, Chasing Elk pushed away from the table and offered Catharine his hand. "Come along, Leah," he said as he led Catharine from the dining room. "We're going for a walk."

Chasing Elk burst out laughing once they left the house. "Well," he said, "that was subtle."

"Oh, she makes me so mad!"

"You're mighty pretty when you're mad," he said, noting the high color in her cheeks and the way her eyes flashed with blue fire. She wore a white skirt and a pale pink shirt with white cuffs and a white collar. The outfit made her look every bit as young and innocent as she was.

Leah tugged on Catharine's hand. "Why are you mad at Miss Regina?"

"Because I . . . that is, because she . . ." Catharine looked to Chasing Elk for help.

"Catharine's jealous," he said with a wicked grin.

Leah frowned. "Why?"

"I'll tell you when you're older."

"Is it because of the way Miss Whiddon smiles at you?"

Catharine and Chasing Elk exchanged startled glances.

"I think she likes you, Daddy," Leah said. "Can I have some candy?"

"I think she likes you, too," Catharine said later that night, after they had put Leah to bed.

"Is that right?"

"Don't tease me, Nathan. I don't like the way she looks at you."

"I can't help how she looks at me. Anyway, you don't have to worry about her. You don't see me looking back, do you?"

"No."

"Come here."

Still pouting, she let him draw her into his arms.

"Don't be mad, darlin'." He kissed his way up the curve of her throat to the soft spot behind her ear.

Catharine shivered. "Do you think she's pretty?"

"Not as pretty as you." Chasing Elk leaned back against the porch rail and pulled her into the cradle of his thighs. "Let's not waste time talking about her."

"Do Indian men really have more than one wife?"

"Some do."

"And no one says anything about it?"

"It makes sense, if you think about it. Most camps have more women than men. Sometimes a man will marry sisters. If a man has a brother and his brother dies, he's expected to marry his brother's widow, or widows if he had more than one wife, so that they'll have someone to protect them and to provide for them. Sometimes an older woman will tell her husband to take a younger wife. . . ."

"I don't believe you! You're making that up."

He shrugged. "Having another woman in the lodge means sharing the work."

"You won't ever take another wife, will you?"

"You're all the woman I need." His hand slid around her nape, drawing her head toward his. With a little sigh of capitulation, she closed her eyes as his lips claimed hers, driving all thought of Regina Whiddon and everything else right out of her mind.

"Nathan." Her voice was ragged with the same need and desire that pulsed through him.

"I know, darlin'," he whispered. "I can't take much more of this. What do you say we get married the day after tomorrow?"

"Sunday?" She looked up at him. "Do you mean it?"

"Damn right."

Catharine smiled. He wanted to marry her. On Sunday.

Her smile widened as she imagined breaking the news to Miss Regina Whiddon.

"So," he said, taking her hand, "where would you like to be married?"

"Where?" Catharine frowned. "I don't know. A church, I suppose, if that's all right with you?"

"Wherever you want is fine with me. We won't be able to have much of a honeymoon, I'm afraid, at least not right now."

"That's all right." She slipped her arms around his waist. "I'll try to be the best wife I can," she murmured, and even as she said the words, she found herself thinking of his first wife. How would she measure up to Ellenora? Would he be disappointed in her? Would he compare everything she did to the way Ellenora had done it?

She frowned. When they kissed, did he compare her kisses to those of his first wife? She suddenly felt sick to her stomach as she imagined their wedding night. Would Nathan be remembering what it had been like with Ellenora?

"Catharine?"

"What?"

"You're frowning. Is something wrong?"

"No." She slipped out of his embrace. "Yes."

He lifted one brow. "Which is it, yes or no?"

"Were you and Ellenora happy together?"

He looked surprised by her question. "Yes, very. Why do you ask?"

"Because . . . I . . . what if . . . ?" She blew out a sigh. How could she explain how she was feeling, what she was thinking? It wasn't right to be jealous of a dead woman.

"Something's bothering you, sweetheart. You can tell me what it is."

"What if I don't make you as happy as she did? What if I . . . what if you don't . . ."

"I don't what?"

"Never mind."

"Oh no you don't." He feathered kisses over her cheeks. " 'Fess up. What's got you so riled up?"

"What if you don't like me as much as you did her?"

He stared at her. "What the devil are you talking about? I love you, Catharine."

"Oh, I don't mean that!" She looked away, wishing she had never brought up the subject.

"What do you mean? Look at me, Cate, and tell me what's wrong."

"No one's ever called me Cate before," she said with a smile. "I like it."

"Good. Now, what's wrong?"

"Can't we just forget I said anything?"

" 'Fraid not, darlin'."

"I'm just afraid you'll be disappointed in me. When we . . . you know. In bed."

She said the last two words very quietly.

"Is that what this is all about?" he asked, stifling the urge to grin.

Feeling miserable, she nodded, her cheeks burning. "No matter what we do, you'll have already done it with someone else. What if . . ."

Chasing Elk drew her into his arms again and hugged her tight. "Sweetheart, I loved Ellenora. She was my wife and the mother of my daughter. But that's got nothing to do with you and me. I love you for you. When we're together, you're the only one I'm thinking of. When we get married, there's only going to be the two of us in our bed, you got that? Just you and me, no one else."

She nodded. "I feel so foolish."

"No need to feel that way." He brushed a lock of hair from her brow. "I was thinking maybe we could ask Mrs. Simpson to keep an eye on Leah Sunday night."

"Why? Where are we going?"

"You'll see."

"Tell me."

He shook his head. "I want it to be a surprise. I want us to be alone on our wedding night, and since we can't go to the hotel as I'd like, I thought of another way. What do you say?"

Filled with curiosity, she could only nod.

Chapter 17

Saturday night was Chasing Elk's first night at work. Catharine had been pleased when he told her he had a job, until he mentioned that his shift was from eight to midnight.

"I hate those hours," she had muttered under her breath.

"It's only for a few weeks," he had assured her. "You know that."

"I know. And I don't mean to complain."

"Go ahead and complain," he'd told her good-naturedly. "You've had reason enough the last few months."

"What's that supposed to mean?"

"You've been through a lot since we met. I've never heard you complain once."

"Well, there have been times when I wanted to," she had admitted.

He had tweaked her nose and then kissed her.

He thought of that now as he shuffled the cards and dealt a new hand. Another hour and he'd be finished here. As much as he enjoyed playing cards and spending a few hours in a smelly saloon, he couldn't wait to get back to Catharine.

He left the table at a quarter after twelve, stopping by the bar when the owner motioned him over. He had noticed Quincannon watching him from time to time throughout the night.

"Have a drink?" Quincannon asked. "It's on the house."

"Whiskey."

The bartender handed him a shot glass and refilled his own beer mug.

"I like the way you handled yourself tonight," Quincannon said. "There could have been trouble when old man Douglas tried to buy his way into the game, him being drunk and all."

Chasing Elk shrugged. "I just told him to go home and sober up."

Quincannon grunted. "I'll see you Monday night."

With a nod, Chasing Elk tossed back his drink, then left the saloon.

Whistling softly, he made his way back to the boardinghouse. He was climbing the stairs when he saw movement out of the corner of his eye. Turning, he saw a woman gliding toward him from the shadows on the porch. At first he thought Catharine had waited up for him. And then he realized it was Regina Whiddon.

She floated toward him, ethereal in a gown of gossamer silk. "Good evening, Mr. Rossiter," she purred.

"Evenin'." His gaze moved over her. "Aren't you a little chilly in that getup?"

"Don't you like it?" She smiled at him. "I had you in mind when I bought it this afternoon."

He cleared his throat. Damn! He'd never done anything to encourage her, never given her any reason to
think he was the least bit interested in her.

"Listen, Miss Whiddon . . ."

"Regina."

"I think you'd best go inside before you catch
your death."

She closed the distance between them. "You could
warm me." Her fingertips slid down his arm.

"It's a mighty tempting offer," he said, "but . . ."

She put her hand over his mouth. "No buts," she
said, her eyes glittering as she pressed herself against
him. "I've wanted you since the first time I saw you."

He understood then. She was looking for a little
excitement, something titillating that she could talk
about with her friends. He had known other women
like her, women who liked to play with fire, who
sought out men they thought were beneath them, or
men who, for one reason or another, were forbidden
to them.

Gently, he removed her hand from his mouth. "I'm
flattered, but I'm getting married tomorrow."

She blinked up at him. For a moment, Chasing Elk
thought she would admit defeat. But then she put her
hand on his arm and gave it a squeeze. "I guess we'd
better not waste any more time."

He laughed softly, amused by her boldness. "Honey,
I don't have any time to waste."

A faint footfall caught Chasing Elk's attention.
Glancing over his shoulder, he saw Catharine standing
in the doorway. She stared at the two of them for a
moment, her expression hidden in the shadows, and
then she marched across the porch.

"Excuse me, Miss Whiddon," she said, her voice like satin over steel as she removed Regina Whiddon's hand from Chasing Elk's arm, "but I believe this is mine, and I hate to share."

Even in the dark, Chasing Elk could see the flush of embarrassment that crept up Regina Whiddon's neck and into her cheeks.

"Are you ready to go in, Nathan, dear?" Catharine asked sweetly.

"Reckon so, darlin'."

Looking just a trifle smug, Catharine slipped her arm through Nathan's. "Goodnight, Miss Whiddon."

Once inside his room, Chasing Elk loosed the laughter he had been holding back.

Catharine glared at him. "I fail to see what's so amusing. If I hadn't come out when I did, she would have been all over you."

"Now, Cate," he said, drawing her into his arms, "why would I want her when I've got you?"

"Are you sure you didn't encourage her just a little?"

"Did I ever tell you how pretty you are when you're jealous?"

"Nathan . . ."

He drew her closer. "Hush, Cate. I can't see anyone but you."

When he looked at her like that, his eyes hot, how could she doubt him?

Catharine stood in front of the mirror in her room. It was her wedding day. Gazing at her reflection, she wondered what Nathan would think when he saw her.

She and Leah had gone shopping the day before, and Catharine had bought them both new dresses. Catharine's was pale pink with a square bodice, long fitted sleeves, and a slim skirt. It was the prettiest dress she had ever owned. It made her feel beautiful inside and out. Leah's dress was a robin's-egg-blue organdy with a wide dark blue satin sash.

Catharine glanced over her shoulder at Nathan's daughter. "What do you think? Will he like it?"

Leah nodded enthusiastically. "You look very pretty."

"So do you."

Leah twirled around the room, then threw her arms around Catharine's waist. "I'm so glad you're going to be my mother."

"And I'm glad you're going to be my daughter," Catharine replied, dropping a kiss on the top of Leah's head.

"Daddy's lucky to have us, isn't he?"

"Yes, he is. And we're very lucky to have him." Catharine grinned inwardly, remembering how she had snatched Chasing Elk out from under Regina Whiddon's nose the night before. And then she frowned, wondering where he was. He hadn't been at breakfast this morning. She wondered fleetingly if he had changed his mind and left town, then thrust the unwelcome thought aside. He loved her, and she had no reason to doubt it.

Catharine took a last look in the mirror. It was time to leave for the church. She handed Leah a small bouquet of wildflowers. "Are you ready?"

Leah nodded, her cheeks pink with excitement.

"Let's go, then." Catharine picked up her own bouquet. They left the house and walked to the small, white-washed church down the street.

Upon entering the church, Catherine saw Mrs. Simpson seated at the organ. She began to play when Leah entered the chapel.

Catharine took it all in in a single glance: Mr. Bartholomew and Miss Brashear sat on one side of the aisle. Regina and Rae Ann sat across from them. Regina had a decidedly pinched look on her face. The minister stood in front of the altar, Bible in hand.

Chasing Elk stood beside the minister. He had been shopping, too, Catharine thought, noting that he wore a new pair of black wool trousers, a crisp white shirt, and a long black coat. He smiled when he saw her.

She smiled back, her heart pounding like thunder. This was it. Her wedding day. She wished that Mark and her mother could be there to see how happy she was, that her father was walking her down the aisle.

Mrs. Simpson played the last note, and the room fell silent.

Chasing Elk took Catharine's hand in his and gave it a squeeze.

The minister glanced at the others in the room before focusing his attention on the couple before him. "Dearly beloved, we are gathered here this day to join this man and this woman in holy matrimony, which is an honorable estate, and not to be entered into lightly. . . ."

Chasing Elk kept his gaze on Catharine's face as he listened to the minister's words. She had never looked more beautiful to him than she did at that moment, her eyes shining with love and trust, her voice soft yet fervent as she vowed to love him for as long as she lived.

His own voice sounded thick in his ears as he repeated his own vows.

"You may now kiss the bride."

Chasing Elk smiled faintly as he drew Catharine into his arms. His bride. His wife. "I'll love you as long as I live," he murmured, and then, unmindful of the others in the room, he drew her close to his chest and kissed her. No mere peck, this. It was a kiss of love and longing, of possession and promise.

She was breathless when he released her. Cheeks pink, eyes glistening with tears of happiness, she looked up at her new husband and knew all her doubts and fears had been foolish indeed.

Their guests came forward to offer their congratulations, and then Mrs. Simpson announced that there was cake and champagne back at the boardinghouse. Chasing Elk paid the minister, who politely declined an invitation to join them for cake, saying he had a parishioner who was ill and in need of comfort.

"So, Mrs. Rossiter," Chasing Elk said, "and Miss Rossiter," he added, including his daughter, "shall we go and have some cake?"

Catharine frowned. "Nathan . . ." She glanced around, making sure they were alone. "Are we really married? I mean, we aren't really Mr. and Mrs. Rossiter. Is it legal?"

He laughed softly. "Not to worry, darlin'. Rossiter was my father's name."

"So, is your full name Nathan Chasing Elk Rossiter?"

He nodded. It was his legal name, though only a handful of people knew it.

When they returned to the boardinghouse Catharine stayed close to Nathan's side, ever aware of Regina Whiddon's envious glances. Knowing it was childish, Catharine nevertheless felt an almost overpowering urge to look at the other woman and stick out her tongue.

Later, Chasing Elk took Catharine and Leah out to dinner at a restaurant that had just opened. It was all Chasing Elk could do to be patient as Leah asked for seconds and then wanted dessert. All he could think about was later that night, when he and Catharine would be alone, and what she would think of the place he had chosen for them to spend their first night together as man and wife.

Finally, his daughter was ready to go. Hand in hand, Chasing Elk and Catharine walked her back to the boardinghouse. Catharine helped Leah get ready for bed and tucked Gretchen in beside her. Chasing Elk told his daughter a story, then held her hand until she fell asleep.

They stopped in the front parlor to speak with Mrs. Simpson, who assured them that Leah would be fine, then shooed them out of the house. In spite of her austere ways and blunt manners, it seemed that Mrs. Simpson was a romantic at heart.

Catharine's curiosity grew as they strolled to the end of the boardwalk. She had expected Chasing Elk to turn back toward town. Instead, he turned left at the corner.

"Come on," he said with a mysterious smile.

She peered into the darkness. "Where are we going?"

"You'll see. You're not afraid, are you?" he asked as they moved deeper into the darkness.

"Not when I'm with you."

They walked for perhaps another fifteen minutes. For the life of her, Catharine couldn't imagine where they were going.

"We're almost there," Chasing Elk said. "It's right around that bend."

"What's right around the . . . ?" Her voice trailed off. "Is that . . . is that a tepee?"

"Yes."

"Where on earth did it come from?"

"I'll tell you later." Opening the door flap, he swung her into his arms and carried her inside. "It's not the bridal suite at the Palace," he said, nuzzling her cheek, "but at least we're alone."

"It's so dark."

"Not for long." Setting her feet on the floor, he struck a match and lit the tinder in the fire pit in the center of the lodge. Next, he closed the door flap, then he sprinkled white sage into the fire. Soon the air was filled with a sweet fragrance.

Catharine glanced around. The floor was covered with furs. There was a bottle of Champagne chilling in a bucket of ice; a covered basket stood beside it. More furs made up the bed located against the back wall of the tepee. A white box tied with a white bow sat at the foot of the bed.

Chasing Elk came up behind her, his lips pressing butterfly kisses along her neck. She shivered as he began to unfasten her gown.

"Are you cold?" he asked.

"Oh, no. Just a little nervous."

"Me too."

She turned in his arms. "I don't believe you."

"It's true." He slid her gown over her shoulders and down her arms and let it fall. It pooled at her feet, a puddle of pale pink silk and lace.

She removed his coat, slid her hands under his shirt, loving the feel of his skin, the sudden tensing of his muscles as her fingers glided up and down his back.

His hands were warm as he helped her out of her undergarments, taking off her shoes and peeling away her stockings until she stood naked before him, a blush warming her from head to foot.

His gaze slid over her body, as hot as the fire in the pit. "Beautiful," he murmured. "More beautiful than I imagined."

With fingers that trembled, she unbuttoned his shirt and slid it over his shoulders, unfastened his belt and his trousers, her cheeks growing hotter as more and more of her husband's body was laid bare to her eyes.

She couldn't help staring.

"Honey, if you keep looking at me like that, I'm going to blush," he muttered.

His words made her laugh, as he had hoped they would, easing the tension between them.

"I love you, Catharine," he whispered, drawing her down into the nest of soft furs. "Let me show you how much."

"Nathan . . ." The furs were warm and soft beneath her bare back, his hand warm and gentle as he caressed her. She was surprised and pleased to see that his hands were trembling almost as much as hers.

"I'll try not to hurt you," he promised.

"No one told me it would hurt."

"Only for a minute, I promise." And then he was kissing her, caressing her, whispering that he loved her. Any fears she'd had were swept away as, for the first time, she explored her husband's form. His skin was hot, smooth save for the spiderweb of scars on his back and the puckered ones on his thigh. She discovered a few older ones, as well. One on his shoulder, another on his chest. He was long and lean and well-muscled. And he wanted her. There could be no doubt of that.

She was ready for him when he rose over her, his eyes dark with desire, his body trembling with need.

She gazed up at him, her whole body pulsing with feelings and emotions that were new and strange and wonderful. He claimed her mouth in a long, searing kiss as he joined his body with hers. She gasped with pain and then with pleasure as he moved deep inside her.

Whispering his name, she gave herself up to the wonder of the moment, the sheer ecstasy of truly being part of the man she loved.

Later, they shared a glass of Champagne. Chasing Elk lifted the cover of the basket, revealing a bowl of apples and cheese and a box of chocolates. They took turns feeding each other, laughing when Catharine spilled her Champagne. A few drops fell on her breasts and belly. She was astonished when Chasing Elk leaned forward and lapped them from her skin. The touch of his tongue made her insides melt, and before she knew it, she was on her back again and he was rising over her.

There was no pain this time, nothing but pure delight as his body meshed with hers. Pleasure, she knew nothing but pleasure. The unbelievable silkiness of the furs beneath her, the heat of his skin, the flexing of his muscles beneath her fingertips as she clung to his arms, the wiry feel of the hair on his chest brushing against her breasts, his breath on her face as he urged her on, the sheer unadulterated sense of peace and fulfillment as pleasure unlike anything she had ever known exploded deep within her.

Breathless, she lay beneath him, her eyes closed, the weight of his body warm and welcome. She wrapped her arms around him when he made as if to move.

"No, don't."

"I must be heavy."

"Yes, but I like it." She paused, summoning her courage. "You're not disappointed?"

Resting on his elbows, he grinned down at her. "Do I look disappointed?"

"No." She smiled at him. "Can we do it again?"

Catharine stretched her arms over her head. Feeling sated and languorous, she rolled onto her side and looked at her husband. Husband, she thought, what a wonderful word. She glanced up at the narrow patch of sky visible through the smoke hole.

"So," she said, "where did you find a tepee?"

Chasing Elk laughed softly. "I was wandering around the outskirts of town, trying to figure out how we could spend some time alone, when I saw it. Seems it belongs to an old Cheyenne Indian. His house is about a half a mile from here. I asked him if I could borrow it for the night. He said no, but when I told him why

I wanted it, he changed his mind, said he'd have his granddaughter clean it up." He glanced around the lodge. "She did a nice job, don't you think?"

"Yes." She ran her fingertips over his chest, stopping over a scar.

"How did you get this one?" she asked.

"Knife fight with a Crow."

"And this one?" Her finger traced the scar on his shoulder.

"Bullet wound."

"You've led a dangerous life, haven't you?"

He shrugged. "From time to time."

"You won't take any chances from now on, will you? I couldn't bear to lose you."

His arm curled around her, pulling her closer. "You're not gonna lose me, darlin'. I've got too much to live for now."

"I love you, Nathan, so much. I'm so happy, it scares me."

"Don't be afraid, Cate."

"Do you . . . We never talked about having children. Do you want more?"

"Sure. Another daughter, one that looks like you."

"And a son that looks like you." She looked thoughtful a moment. "What do you suppose Leah will think of having a little brother or sister?"

He shrugged. "She might be a mite jealous at first, but I'm sure she'll get over it."

Catharine snuggled against him. It would be so wonderful to have a baby boy with Nathan's dusky skin and black hair.

She slid her hand down Nathan's chest, slowly going lower, lower.

He groaned softly, his body reacting instantly to the touch of her hand. "You're going to get into trouble if you're not careful," he warned, his voice husky.

"Well, there's only one way to make a baby."

"In a hurry, are you?"

"No, but . . ." She felt her cheeks grow hot.

"But?"

"Making a baby is . . ." Her cheeks grew hotter, her voice softer. "You know."

"Pleasurable?"

She nodded. "We don't have to, if you don't want to."

He laughed softly. "Honey, you'll never see the day when I don't want to."

It was much later when Chasing Elk handed Catharine the white box with the pretty bow. "You never opened your present."

"Oh! I forgot all about it." She shook the box. "What is it?"

"Open it and see."

She slid the bow off and lifted the lid. There, wrapped inside layers of white tissue paper, she found a nightgown.

"Oh, Nathan," she murmured, lifting it out of the box. "It's beautiful."

It was indeed beautiful, though it was little more than a whisper of gossamer white silk and lace. Cupping his face in her hands, she kissed him. "Thank you." She ran her hand over the soft silk. "Shall I put it on?"

Taking the gown from her hand, he tossed it aside. "Later," he said, his voice husky as he wrapped her in his arms once more. "Later."

Chapter 18

It was late the next morning when Chasing Elk and Catharine returned to the boardinghouse. They found Leah playing checkers in the parlor with Mrs. Simpson.

Leah smiled at her father. "Look, Daddy, I'm winning!" she crowed.

"Good for you, sweetheart." Crossing the floor, Chasing Elk knelt in front of his daughter and gave her a hug.

Leah looked over his shoulder at Catharine. "Are you truly my momma now?"

"If you want me to be."

"Oh, I do. Can I call you Momma?"

"I'd like that very much."

"How's your leg feeling, sweetheart?" Chasing Elk asked.

"Better."

Mrs. Simpson rose gracefully. "Perhaps your father would like to finish the game," she suggested. "I must go see about fixing dinner."

"Do you know how to play, Daddy?"

"Sure do, sweetheart." Chasing Elk sat down in the chair that Mrs. Simpson vacated.

"It's your move," Leah said, gesturing at the board. "You're red. What did you and momma do last night?"

Chasing Elk glanced at Catharine.

"Well," Catharine said, biting back a grin, "I think I'll just go freshen up so the two of you can talk."

"Coward," Chasing Elk said.

Catharine kissed Chasing Elk, then gave Leah a hug. "I'll see you two later," she said, and left the room.

"Daddy?"

He cleared his throat. "Well, we went for a walk and then we, ah, talked for awhile."

"What did you talk about?"

"Catharine wondered what you'd think about having a little brother or sister."

"Really?" Leah's eyes lit up. "When?"

"Well, not for awhile. You wouldn't mind, then?"

"Oh, no, Daddy. I hope it's a girl."

"I'll do my best. Did you have a good time with Mrs. Simpson?" he asked, effectively changing the subject.

Leah nodded. "We made sugar cookies and gingerbread men. Do you want one?"

"Sure."

He spent the next half hour playing checkers and sampling Leah's gingerbread men, and then they went into the dining room for dinner.

The next few weeks passed peaceably enough. Chasing Elk continued working at the saloon. Catharine and Leah and Mrs. Simpson got quite chummy. It seemed to Chasing Elk that there was some new dessert for him to try at supper every night. The doctor examined Leah's leg and declared that it was healing nicely and that she could put her crutches away as long as she didn't do any running or climbing for another week or two.

With that in mind, Chasing Elk told his boss at the saloon that he would be leaving the following week.

"I'm sorry to see you go," Quincannon said, shaking his hand. "If you ever get back this way and need a job, look me up."

"I will, thanks."

Mrs. Simpson also expressed her sadness that they would be leaving, though Chasing Elk knew it was Leah that the woman was going to miss the most. Catharine had told him that Mrs. Simpson had three granddaughters, ages thirteen, nine, and six. They all lived back East, and she had never seen any of them.

A week later, they caught a stage headed north, toward the Dakotas. Once again, Chasing Elk found himself thinking of his mother, the reservation, and what he would find when he got there.

They stopped in Yankton for supplies. Fifteen years ago, back in 1861, Yankton had been designated as the capital of the Dakota Territory. Bordered on the south by the Missouri River, Yankton had seen an influx of miners during the gold rush days, and it became a stopping-off place for settlers heading west into the Dakotas.

It was in Yankton that Wild Bill Hickock's killer, Jack McCall, had been tried and hanged. Chasing Elk recalled reading about the incident back in Yuma. One of the guards had gotten hold of a copy of the *Black Hills Pioneer*. The newspaper reported

that Wild Bill had been killed in Saloon #10 in Deadwood on the second day of August. As practically everyone knew by now, Hickock had been holding aces
and eights, a hand soon to be known as the dead
man's hand. Some said that McCall had killed Hickock
to avenge his brother's death, others believed it was
to enhance his own reputation, while still others believed it was over a previous disagreement about a
game of poker.

Chasing Elk's first stop was the livery, where he
bought three riding horses, tack, and a pack mule.
From there, they headed for the mercantile to stock
up on supplies. They spent the night in a hotel.

For Chasing Elk, renting a room was a waste of
money. Sleep eluded him, but maybe that wasn't so
surprising. After thirteen years, he was finally going
home.

They headed for the reservation early the following morning.

As they traveled deeper into the land of the Sioux
and the Cheyenne, Catharine could see why the Indians had loved the Black Hills and fought so hard to
keep them. The country was beautiful, with vast
stretches of rolling prairie and stands of tall timber.
The Hills themselves were impressive. They rose up
in the midst of the great plains, lofty and majestic.
From a distance, they did indeed look black due to
the profusion of ponderosa pines, spruce, and juniper
that grew on the slopes. Nathan had told her that the
Hills were teeming with wildlife, including white-tail
deer, bighorn sheep, mountain goats, mule deer, buffalo, elk, goshawks, and osprey.

Nathan had told her that the Lakota people considered the Hills to be sacred, a place for physical and spiritual renewal.

Bear Butte, an ancient volcano known as *Mato Paha* to the Lakota, was located in the Hills. It was another site the Lakota considered to be sacred, a place his people and the Cheyenne had often used for sweat lodges and vision quests.

"Can we climb Bear Butte, Daddy?" Leah asked. "Is there a bear at the top?"

"Perhaps one day," he replied. "It's a long climb, at least two hours. And there aren't any bears on top," he said, grinning. "At least there weren't the last time I was there. Maybe we'll get a chance to see the Devil's Tower, too."

"Devil's Tower?" Leah said, her eyes growing wide. "Does the devil live there?"

"No, it's another place that's holy to our people. The Lakota call it *Mateo Teepee*."

"What does *Mateo Teepee* mean?" Catharine asked.

"Grizzly Bear Lodge."

"How much farther is the reservation, Daddy?" Leah asked.

"We'll be there tomorrow. Does your leg hurt?"

"No, I'm just tired of riding."

"Would you like to hear a story?"

Leah nodded. "Oh, yes."

"My mother told me this story when I was about your age," he said. "In the long ago time, there were seven brothers. One day the wife of the oldest brother went out to fix the smoke wings on her lodge. While she was outside, a big bear carried her away to his cave. Her husband was very sad. He went out every day to scream and cry at the bear.

"The youngest brother was a medicine man who had great powers. He told the oldest brother to make a bow and four blunt arrows. He was to paint two of the arrows red and fletch them with eagle feathers. The other two arrows were to be painted black and fletched with the feathers of a buzzard.

"The youngest brother then took the bow and arrows, and they set out to find the big bear. When they reached the entrance to the cave, the youngest brother told the others to wait for him. He then turned himself into a gopher and dug his way into the cave. Inside, he found the bear lying with his head in the woman's lap. Using his magic, the young man put the bear to sleep and then changed back into his own form. He told the woman to crawl out of the cave, where the brothers were waiting for her.

"The bear woke shortly thereafter. He called all the other bears, and they started after the woman and her rescuers. Soon the Indians came to the place where the Devil's Tower now stands. They all stood on the rock.

"The youngest brother told the woman and his older brothers to close their eyes, and when they did so, he sang a song. When he finished the song, the rock had grown. He sang the song four times, and each time the rock grew higher, until it was as high as it is today.

"The brothers killed all the bears except the one who had taken the woman. The big bear kept trying to climb the rock to get to the brothers. You can still see his claw marks on the side of the Tower. The youngest brother shot the red arrow and two of the black arrows at the bear, but they had no effect. The last arrow killed the bear."

"How did they get down off the tower?" Leah asked.

"The youngest brother made a noise like a bald eagle. Soon, four eagles came. The Indians took hold of the legs of the eagles, and the eagles carried them to the ground."

Leah smiled. "That's a good story, Daddy."

"Maybe someday you'll tell it to your children," he said with a smile. "I think we'll camp here for tonight."

Later, after Leah was tucked into bed, Chasing Elk picked up one of the blankets and then, taking Catharine by the hand, walked a short distance away so they could be alone.

He spread the blanket on the ground and they sat side by side, looking at the stars and listening to the sounds of the night.

Catharine shivered.

Chasing Elk put his arm around her shoulder. "You cold?"

"No."

"You're shivering. Not afraid are you?"

"A little," she admitted. It was disconcerting, being so far from civilization, so far from anything that was familiar. They were in the heart of Indian country now, and even though most of the Sioux and Cheyenne were on reservations, she couldn't help being a little fearful.

"There's nothing to be afraid of."

"What will you do if your mother is . . . if you can't find her?"

"I don't know. I haven't thought that far ahead. I would like to stay on here for awhile. Leah needs to know where she came from and who her people are. You don't mind, do you?"

She hesitated a moment, then shook her head.

"I could take you to Deadwood. You could stay there." But even as he suggested it, he knew he wouldn't do it. Deadwood was no place for a decent woman. The town was crawling with gamblers and con men and prostitutes.

"No," she said quickly. "I don't want to leave you. I'm just afraid your people won't like me."

He blew out a breath. "I guess we'll just have to wait and see." He wanted to tell her she had nothing to worry about, but the truth was, he didn't know if his people would accept her or not. Back in the old days, in the shining times, the Indians had welcomed the whites into their land. They had traded with the *wasichu*. But those days were long gone, destroyed by the white man's lies and his greed for land and yellow iron.

He shook off his dismal thoughts. He didn't want to think about that now. All he wanted to do was make love to his wife, here in the heart of the Dakotas.

His fingertips trailed down her arm and she shivered again. He knew without asking that it wasn't fear making her shiver this time. Claiming her lips with his, he gently lowered her to the blanket, his mouth never leaving hers.

She moaned softly, her need for him rising as quickly as his for her. He loved the way she responded to his touch, the little purring noises she made deep in her throat as he caressed her. Her skin was smooth and warm, her hair like silk beneath his hand, the recesses of her mouth like the sweetest honey. She was bold yet shy as she caressed him in return, eager to learn the contours of his body, to explore the differences between them. He basked in her touch, the pleasure so exquisite it was almost painful. He inhaled her scent, a tantalizing blend of sun and soap and woman. His woman.

He didn't know what he had ever done in his life to deserve her, but as his body melded with hers, he sent a silent prayer of thanks to *Wakan Tanka* for bringing Catharine into his life.

"*Sunke*." Chasing Elk said. "Dog."

"*Sunke*," Leah and Catharine repeated.

It was late afternoon and they were crossing a stretch of grass-covered prairie. To pass the time, Chasing Elk was teaching them a few words of Lakota.

"*Ate*," he said. "Father."

"*Ate*."

"*Pilamaya*. Thank you."

"*Pilamaya*."

Chasing Elk pointed at the red-tailed hawk circling above them. "*Cetan*."

"*Cetan*."

Pointing at the sun, he said, "*Anpetu-wi*."

Leah frowned. "Does that mean sky?"

"No, it means the sun," Chasing Elk said. "The sky is *skan*; *hanhepi-wi* means moon, or night sun."

"It's a pretty language, isn't it?" Catharine said. "But I don't think I'll ever be able to learn it. I don't suppose your mother speaks English."

"She used to. She may have forgotten it by now."

"How do you say horse?" Leah asked.

"*Tashunka.*"

"*Tashunka,*" Leah repeated. "I like that." Leaning forward, she stroked her pony's neck. "I'm going to name him *Tashunka.*"

Catharine wasn't sure how Chasing Elk knew when they had crossed into the reservation, but he did. She didn't know what she had expected, but this part of the countryside didn't look much different from what they had been traveling through.

"How will we find your mother?"

"Beats the hell out of me." He urged his horse into a lope, heading north.

An hour or so later, they reached a flat stretch of ground dotted with tepees. As they drew nearer, Catharine saw a number of children gathered together, obviously playing a game of some kind. A small horse herd grazed in the distance. A group of men sat together in front of one of the larger tepees.

She felt a sudden apprehension as they approached the camp. The Lakota had been treated badly by her people. The government had stolen thousands of acres of land that the Lakota people had lived on for centuries, land they held sacred. Would they look at her with hatred and disdain? Would they shun her? She wasn't sure she could live among people who hated her.

Everyone in the camp stopped and stared at them when Chasing Elk reined his horse to a halt in the midst of the village.

A group of men quickly surrounded the three of them.

Catharine was keenly aware of the hostile glances sent in her direction. She urged her horse closer to Chasing Elk's, wishing she could understand what was being said. Even if she could speak the language, she doubted she could have understood what they were saying because they were all speaking so rapidly.

She forced a smile when Chasing Elk pointed in her direction.

Moments later, he dismounted. He lifted her from the back of her horse and then Leah from the saddle.

"Catharine, Leah, this is Kangi Wiyaka, a friend of mine from long ago."

Catharine smiled at Kangi Wiyaka. "I'm pleased to meet you."

The warrior nodded. "It is good to meet the woman who has brought a smile to my brother's face."

Catharine looked at Chasing Elk. "Brother?"

"It's a term of affection."

"Oh." She smiled at the warrior again. He was a tall man with sloping shoulders and long, muscular arms. He wore a cotton shirt, a clout, leggings, and moccasins.

Smiling shyly, Leah dropped a curtsey, something Chasing Elk figured she must have learned in the orphanage, and something Kangi Wiyaka had certainly never seen before.

Chasing Elk spoke to the warrior, explaining what it meant, then turned to Catharine. "Kangi Wiyaka says we can sleep in his lodge tonight. He'll spend the night with his sister and her husband."

"That's very kind of him," Catharine said. "Did you ask him if your mother is here?"

Chasing Elk nodded. "She was, but she's gone now.

Apparently some of the warriors who've had a belly full of life on the reservation decided to hightail it out of here. They left a couple of weeks ago. One of them was her husband."

"She's married?"

"So it seems. We'll spend the night here. Tomorrow, I'm going to ride into the Hills and see if I can find her."

"I'm going with you!"

"We'll talk about it later."

She didn't want to make a scene in front of his friends, so Catharine bit down on her lower lip and followed Chasing Elk and Leah across the camp and into Kangi Wiyaka's lodge.

While the warrior took his leave, Catharine glanced around. The tepee was similar to the one she had shared with Chasing Elk on their wedding night, though this one was much larger. There was a single bed of furs against the far wall of the lodge, a fire pit in the center of the floor with a cleared space behind it, a few cook pots beside the door. Buckskin bags hung from a couple of the lodge poles.

Chasing Elk went outside, returning a few minutes later carrying their belongings. "Make yourselves at home," he said, dropping their saddlebags on the floor. "I'm going to go unsaddle the horses and get them settled for the night."

He kissed Catharine on the cheek, ruffled Leah's hair, and left the lodge.

"Well," Catharine said, "here we are."

Leah turned in a slow circle. "I've never seen an Indian tepee before. It's big."

Catharine nodded.

"I've never seen Indians before, either," Leah remarked, frowning. "Do you think they'll like me?"

"I'm sure they will." Not that it really mattered, Catharine thought, since they were only staying one night.

"I wonder what they eat?" Leah said.

Catharine wondered that, too. She knew the Apache ate mule meat and dog meat, but saw no reason to mention that to Leah. She just hoped something else was available for dinner. As a child, she had been taught to eat whatever was placed before her, whether she liked it or not. But, good manners notwithstanding, she didn't think she could eat dog meat.

"Do you think we could go outside?" Leah asked, pulling Gretchen from one of the saddlebags.

"I suppose it will be all right. Stay close to me, though."

"I'll have to give Gretchen an Indian name," Leah decided. She looked up at Catharine. "I have an Indian name."

"You do? What is it?"

"Winonah."

"It's very pretty. Do you know what it means?"

"Yes. It means firstborn daughter." Leah looked thoughtful for a moment. "Maybe Daddy will give you an Indian name, too."

"I'd like that."

Ducking outside, Catharine and Leah sat down in the shade. They were immediately the focus of all attention, though the Indians were careful not to stare at them.

Several girls about Leah's age seemed especially curious. They watched her surreptitiously for a quarter of an hour or so as she ran her fingers through Gretchen's hair then smoothed the wrinkles from her dress.

The girls conferred for a few moments and then, with a smile, one of the girls ran forward. Taking Leah by the hand, the girl pulled Leah to her feet and gestured for her to follow.

"Can I go?" Leah asked.

"I don't know." Catharine looked around, hoping to find Nathan. What would he do? True, these were his people so he probably wouldn't worry. Still, Leah wasn't her daughter and she didn't want to make a decision that Nathan might not approve of.

Before she could make up her mind, she saw him walking toward her. Leah saw him at the same time and ran to meet him.

"Daddy, these girls want me to play with them. Is it all right?"

"Sure, sweetheart. Just be careful."

"I will. Thanks, Daddy. I mean, *pilamaya*."

Chasing Elk grinned as she ran off with the other girls. "She's a quick study," he remarked, dropping down beside Catharine.

"You were surprised to hear that your mother had remarried, weren't you?"

"Yeah."

"Does it bother you?"

He shook his head. His mother was alive and that was all that mattered. He just hoped she would forgive him for staying away so long.

"When are we leaving?"

"I'm leaving. You and Leah are staying."

"I'm not staying here without you!"

"Listen, Cate . . ."

"No, you listen. If you're going, I'm going, and that's that!"

"Have you always been this bullheaded?"

"Always."

"You'll be safer here."

"We just got married, Nathan. Wither thou goest, I will go."

He snorted softly. "You quotin' scripture at me now?"

She shrugged. "I'm going. If you leave without me, I'll just follow you."

"Dammit, woman . . ." Biting back the rest of his words, he put his arm around her waist and drew her up against him. "All right, Cate. Have it your way."

"What about Leah?"

"She's going to stay here, with Kangi Wiyaka's sister and her family."

"Have you told her that?"

"Not yet."

Surprisingly, Leah was eager to remain behind. She was tired of riding, and in spite of the language barrier, she had struck up a friendship with the three girls she had met earlier in the day, one of whom was Kangi Wiyaka's niece.

Catharine followed Chasing Elk out of the village early the following morning. For all that she had refused to be left behind, after a couple of hours Catharine found herself wishing she had stayed with Leah. She wasn't sure why she felt so uneasy. The land was beautiful, the sky a dazzling clear blue, the air cool and crisp. A pair of bald eagles soared overhead, drifting on the warm air currents. Everything was beautiful. Peaceful. Yet she couldn't help feeling apprehensive.

She glanced at Nathan, wondering if he felt it, too.

"You all right?" he asked. "You look a little . . . worried."

She forced a smile. "I'm fine."

"Something's bothering you. What is it?"

"I don't know. I just have a bad feeling. . . ."

"About what?"

"That's what I don't know." She thought he might laugh at her; instead, he drew his rifle from the boot.

She glanced at the copse of trees to their left. "We're not going that way, are we?"

He regarded her a moment. "You ever had feelings like this before?" he asked, his gaze sweeping the countryside.

"Just once, right before Mark was run down by a runaway wagon."

The words had barely left her mouth when three horsemen rode out of the trees, their guns drawn.

Chasing Elk yelled, "Get the hell out of here!"

Without waiting to see if she obeyed or not, he brought his rifle to his shoulder as he wheeled his horse around and charged the oncoming riders.

Catharine rode off a few yards and took cover in a copse of trees. Peeking around a tree trunk, she watched Chasing Elk, her heart in her throat, a prayer for his safety on her lips. The sound of gunshots and the stink of powder smoke filled the air. One of the men screamed and tumbled over his horse's rump. Chasing Elk fired again and another man toppled from his horse.

The third man dropped his weapon and lifted his hands over his head.

"Who are you?" Nathan called, his voice carrying easily in the stillness.

"Bounty hunter."

"Not very good at it, are you? Get off your horse. And keep your hands where I can see them."

Sullen-faced, the man did as he was told.

Dismounting, Chasing Elk picked up the man's pistol and shoved it into the waistband of his trousers.

"What are you gonna do with me?" the bounty hunter asked, his tone surly.

"I haven't decided." Chasing Elk didn't turn around when Catharine rode up.

"What are you going to do with him?" she asked.

Chasing Elk shrugged. "Go get their horses and collect their weapons."

He kept one eye on the bounty hunter as he watched Catharine. She grimaced as she neared the first body and retrieved his Colt. She was turning away when the man's hand snaked out and grabbed her ankle.

Catharine screamed, then lashed out at the man. Her foot caught him high in the chest. He let her go, then rolled onto his knees and reached for her again.

And Chasing Elk shot him clean between the eyes.

The third bounty hunter backed up a step, his hand delving inside his coat.

"Stupid," Chasing Elk muttered, and fired his rifle yet again.

The man dropped dead in his tracks.

Catharine stared at the body by her feet, unable to

take her gaze from the bloody horror that had once been his face.

"Catharine? Cate?" Chasing Elk took her by the hand and pulled her away from the carnage, not stopping until the three dead men were out of their sight.

"It's all right," he said, smoothing a lock of hair from her brow. "It's over. Do you hear me, Cate? It's over."

She stared at him a moment, her expression blank, and then she fell into his arms.

"Shh," he murmured. "It's all right." He kissed the top of her head. "Good thing you listened to your feelings, Cate, or it might have turned out differently."

"You . . . you killed them."

"Damn right. Come on, let's get out of here."

"You're just going to leave them?"

He didn't bother with a reply. "Stay here."

In a matter of a few minutes, he had rounded up the dead men's horses, collected their weapons, and stowed them in one of the saddlebags. When that was done, he lifted her onto the back of her horse and handed her the reins.

"We ought to bury them," she said dully.

Chasing Elk grunted softly as he swung onto the back of his horse. "What do you suggest we use for a shovel?"

She blinked at him, then fell silent.

"Cate, I know it seems cold-blooded, but they're past caring."

"How did they find you?"

"I wish I knew." Frowning, Chasing Elk glanced back at the last bounty hunter he had shot. The man looked vaguely familiar. Had he seen the man in

Yankton? Tequila Springs? It didn't matter now. Whatever information the man could have given them had died with him.

It was near dusk when Chasing Elk found the camp he was looking for. It was located in a valley deep in the Hills.

Chasing Elk removed his hat and his shirt, hoping that the sentries on duty would realize that he was one of them.

Keeping his hands clear of his weapons, he took a deep breath and breathed in the near-forgotten scent of home. It was a beautiful wild land of vivid hues and colors, from the deep green of the pines to the rusty red shale and sandstone cliffs. He loved this place as no other, loved the rugged land, the lush grass, the valleys and foothills. As a boy, he had played here among the jagged rock formations, hunted his first deer, come face to face with a bear. He knew the sandstone canyons and gulches, had fished in the lakes and streams. Late at night, the melancholy wail of the coyotes had lulled him to sleep.

He didn't miss the sentries who watched them as they rode through the narrow opening that led into the valley.

He recognized the place immediately. It had always been one of his favorite winter camps. There were perhaps a dozen lodges spread along the banks of a narrow winding stream. A handful of boys chased one another along the shore, laughing and splashing in the shallow water. A group of girls sat in a circle, playing a game. Men sat in the shade, smoking or gambling. Women relaxed in the sunshine, nursing their babies or watching young ones take their first tentative steps.

Other women could be seen hanging meat on drying
racks or fleshing hides. It reminded him of the old
times, the good times.

An excited hum of voices rose on the wind as Chasing Elk and Catharine drew nearer the center of the
small village. All other activity stopped as men,
women, and children turned to stare at them.

Chasing Elk's attention was drawn to a woman
standing outside the nearest tepee. A boy who looked
like he was three or four years old clung to her hand.

Chasing Elk's breath caught in his throat as his gaze
moved over the woman and then the child. Dismounting, he took a tentative step toward her. "*Ina?*"

The woman stared up at him, her eyes widening
with disbelief. "*Chaska?*" Dropping the little boy's
hand, she ran forward, her arms outstretched.
"*Chaska!*"

Tears stung Chasing Elk's eyes as his mother embraced him. He wrapped his arms around her and held
her tight as a rush of memories flooded his mind: his
mother waiting for him when he returned from his
first solo hunt, her pride in his skill, the robe she had
made for him when he killed his first buffalo, her tears
when his father decided it was time for him to go and
live with the *wasichu* and learn the white man's ways.

"*Ina.*" He drew back a little so he could see her
face. In spite of the added lines around her eyes and
mouth, she looked much as he remembered. Her hair
fell to her waist like a fall of black silk. Her skin was
still smooth and firm. Sending a silent prayer of thanks
to *Wakan Tanka*, he hugged her again. "I missed
you."

"It has been many years since I saw your face. I feared you were dead."

He smiled at her, blinking back the hot tears that stung his eyes. "Not yet."

"What brings you back to us after such a long time?" she asked.

"I'll tell you all about it later. First I want you to meet someone." Turning, he lifted Catharine from her horse. "*Ina*, this is my wife, Catharine. Catharine, this is my mother, Macawi."

The two women regarded each other for a moment, then Macawi nodded at Catharine. "Welcome, my daughter."

"Thank you. I'm happy to meet you."

Chasing Elk's mother was tall and slender, with smooth copper-colored skin only a little darker than her son's. She wore an ankle-length tunic made of what looked like doeskin, and moccasins beaded in black and yellow.

Macawi looked at her son. "And I have someone for you to meet." Turning, she motioned the little boy to her. "This is your brother Kohana."

Chasing Elk stared at the boy. It had never occurred to him that his mother might have had more children.

Chasing Elk dropped to one knee. "*Hau, ciye.*" Hello, my brother.

The boy looked up at his mother. "*Ciye?*"

Macawi nodded.

Kohana looked back at Chasing Elk uncertainly.

"That's okay, *ciye*," Chasing Elk said with a grin. "I don't know what to say either."

Chapter 19

Catharine sat beside Chasing Elk in his mother's lodge, listening as he told Macawi and her husband, Ohitekah, what he had been doing for the last thirteen years. When he told Macawi that she had a granddaughter, the woman immediately swamped him with questions, asking how old her granddaughter was, what she looked like, if she spoke Lakota, and, most importantly, why he had left her behind on the reservation.

"She was hurt recently," Chasing Elk said. "She broke her leg. She says it no longer bothers her, but I think it still pains her sometimes. When we reached the reservation, she was tired of traveling." He smiled. "She met some girls her age and wanted to stay behind. I thought she could use the rest. I have told her about you and she is anxious to meet you."

"I am anxious to meet her," Macawi said. "There is much that she must learn about our people and our ways."

Chasing Elk nodded. "Yes." He took Catharine's hand in his. "And much for you to learn, as well."

Catharine nodded. She looked around the lodge as Chasing Elk and his mother talked of people they had known in years past. Macawi's lodge was warm and comfortable. There were cooking pots stacked on one side of the doorway, a small pile of firewood on the other side. Two beds were spread in the back of the lodge. Kohana slept in the smaller one.

Behind the fire pit was a small cleared space. She remembered seeing a similar space in Kangi Wiyaka's lodge and wondered what it was for. She would have to ask Nathan about it later.

A number of buckskin bags and bundles hung from the lodge poles. There was a shield on a tripod. A cloth of some kind lined the tipi; there were scenes painted on it. One depicted a man killing a buffalo with a lance; another was of a man on a bucking horse. Catharine wondered if the warrior in the drawings represented Ohitekah.

She yawned behind her hand, wondering where they were going to sleep.

Macawi saw her and smiled. "I think Catharine is tired," she remarked. "We will talk more tomorrow."

Rising, Macawi unrolled some furs, and in no time at all, had laid out a bed for Catharine and Chasing Elk beside the fire pit.

Catharine looked at her husband, uncomfortable at the thought of sharing a bed with him in the same lodge where his mother slept. However, he didn't seem at all bothered by the arrangement.

Taking her aside, he said quietly, "It's the Lakota way."

But that didn't make it any less embarrassing.

Ohitekah and Macawi slipped out of their clothes and into bed as if they were used to having company in their lodge.

Catharine removed her shoes and stockings, then turned her back and stepped out of her dress. Clad in her undergarments, she slipped under the furs.

Undressing, Chasing Elk slid in beside her and drew her into his arms.

She put her hands against his chest and pushed him away. "What are you doing?" she whispered.

"Trying to hug my wife," he whispered back.

She glanced across the lodge. In the faint light of the coals, she could see Ohitekah and Macawi lying under the covers. "Not now."

"Why not now? They're hugging."

Hearing the laughter in his voice, she made a face at him, then rolled over on her side.

Muttering under his breath, Chasing Elk snuggled up behind her, his arm sliding over her waist, drawing her back against his chest. Brushing her hair aside, he nuzzled her nape, smiling as he felt a shiver run down her spine.

"Nathan . . ."

"You want me," he whispered.

"Yes, but . . ."

"Come outside with me."

"Now?"

His hand cupped her breast. "Now."

"All right. Let me get dressed."

"No. Just wrap up in the blanket."

Unable to believe what she was doing, she stood and wrapped the blanket around her, darting glances at Macawi and Ohitekah all the while.

Her eyes widened as Chasing Elk picked up a fur and started toward the door, stark naked.

"Aren't you going to get dressed?" she whispered.

"Why? I'll just have to get undressed again."

Taking her by the hand, he led her outside, then walked behind the lodge and started up a grassy slope. The grass was damp beneath her bare feet, the air cool, heavy with the scent of pine.

Walking a little further along the flat top of the slope, they came to a thicket. Chasing Elk spread the fur on the ground, then drew her down beside him.

"Cozy?"

"Very." It was like being in their own private tepee, with the thicket surrounding them and the sky for a cover. The moon hung low in the sky.

But it was the man who held her attention. She couldn't stop staring at him. He was a sculptor's delight, she thought, from the fall of his ebony hair to the soles of his feet. His body was long and lean, every muscle well-defined.

He laughed softly as she stole a quick glance at that part of him that made him a man.

"Can you tell what I'm thinking?" he asked with a grin.

A blush warmed her cheeks. A moment later, her undergarments were scattered on the ground and she was in his arms, her body pressed to his, their legs entangled. His mouth was hot on her skin, his hands gentle yet filled with an urgency that was unmistakable. His touch, his voice whispering that he loved her enflamed her senses. He lowered her to the ground, his body a welcome weight, his kisses like fire, his words of love making her heart swell until she thought it might burst with joy and happiness. And then, as he moved deep within her, she lost herself in the wonder of his touch, all her senses alive and attuned to his until there was nothing in all the world but the two of them and the exquisite pleasure that was beyond the power of mortal words.

Later, lying in his arms, her head pillowed on his shoulder, she gazed up at the stars twinkling above.

"What are you thinking about?" Chasing Elk asked.

"I was just thinking how glad I am now that my father decided to move west."

"Is that right? I thought you hated it out here."

"I did, but if we'd stayed in the East, I never would have met you."

"Does that mean I should be glad I was sent to Yuma?" he asked with a wry grin.

"No, not glad." She ran her fingers over his chest. "But maybe it was fate."

"Do you believe in fate?"

"I didn't used to, but I think I do now. What else but fate could have brought us together?"

His hand delved into her hair. "Luck?"

She laughed softly. "Fate, luck, call it whatever you will. I think we were meant to be together."

"I think so, too."

"How long are we going to stay here?"

"I don't know. Long enough for Leah to get a sense of who she is. Long enough for her to get to know her grandmother."

"It's a beautiful place. No wonder your people love it so."

It was a wild and rugged land filled with lush grass and deep green valleys. There were gentle foothills and jagged rock formations, deep gulches and sand-stone canyons. Stands of aspen and pine, birch and oak grew along the winding streams. Bald eagles were often seen in the winter.

"The Lakota believe the Hills are sacred, the heart of the people. Our old ones are buried here. Our blood is here." He turned so they were lying face to face. "And now you're here." He caressed her cheek. "I love you, Cate."

The tremor in his voice, the look of love and desire on his face, brought tears to her eyes and she knew in that moment that if it would make him happy, she would stay there, with his people, forever.

It was near dawn when they returned to Macawi's tepee. Catharine was embarrassed to see that Chasing Elk's mother and Ohitekah were already awake. She blushed at the knowing expression in Macawi's eyes, felt her cheeks burn hotter when Chasing Elk and Ohitekah looked at each other and grinned.

"Young blood," Ohitekah said. "It always runs hot."

Chasing Elk laughed out loud as he wrapped an arm around Catharine's shoulders. "That it does. What are you two doing up so early?"

"We need meat," Macawi said.

Ohitekah looked at Chasing Elk. "I am going hunting. Will you come?"

"I don't know." Chasing Elk looked at Catharine, a question in his eyes.

"How long will you be gone?" she asked.

"We will be home by nightfall," Ohitekah assured her.

"All right," Catharine said.

"Are you sure?" Chasing Elk asked. "I won't go if you don't want me to."

But she could tell that he wanted very much to go, so she said, "No, it's all right, really. Have a good time."

Standing outside the tepee an hour later, her hand shading her eyes as she watched Chasing Elk and Ohitekah ride off, Catharine wondered if she had made the right decision. What was she going to do here all day without him?

As it turned out, there was no end of things to do. She helped Macawi gather wood and water and shake out the bedding. Later, it was all she could do not to gag as Macawi taught her how to scrape the flesh off a hide. Macawi explained that the hair had been left on because the hide was going to be used for a sleeping robe. If she intended to use the hide for clothing or moccasins, the hair would have been scraped off as well.

That afternoon, Catharine followed Macawi and Kohana down to a shallow stream. Several other women and their children were already there, splashing in the cool water.

The women looked at Catharine suspiciously, the children with wide-eyed curiosity. Catharine smiled tentatively as Macawi introduced her to the other women. Most of them smiled in return; a few turned their backs to her.

"*Wasichu* blue coats killed her husband and her sons," Macawi explained as another woman turned her back.

"I'm sorry."

Taking Kohana by the hand, Macawi walked farther

downstream. "There has been much pain on both sides," she said. "Our people have lost much. Our land. Our freedom. Our loved ones. It is a burden some cannot put aside or forget."

"Perhaps, in time, your people and my people will put their differences behind them," Catharine remarked.

"And perhaps, in time, the *wasichu* in Washington will honor their treaties and give us the Black Hills, as promised."

It was, Catharine thought, Macawi's way of telling her that friendship between their people was impossible.

Later, sitting on the bank, Catharine watched Macawi and her son play in the water. Perhaps one day she and Chasing Elk would have a son. She placed one hand over her belly. She could be pregnant even now. She spent a few minutes thinking of what it would be like to have a baby. She had no experience with babies, but the idea of being a mother, of holding a child of her own in her arms, filled her with longing.

Chasing Elk and Ohitekah returned at dusk, as promised. Macawi beamed at her husband when she saw the deer slung over his horse's withers.

Dismounting, Chasing Elk put his arm around Catharine and gave her a hug. "How was your day? Did you miss me?"

"What do you think?"

"I think I'll let you show me later."

Catharine smiled up at him, only then realizing how worried she had been while he was gone.

"I'm going back for Leah tomorrow," he told her. Loosening the cinch, he unsaddled his horse, then spread the blanket over the saddle to dry out. "Do you want to come with me or stay here?"

"I think I'll stay here, if you don't mind. It's a long ride."

He nodded. "It's probably for the best. I'll be able to travel faster alone. If I leave first thing in the morning, I should be back by tomorrow night."

Watching Chasing Elk ride away the following morning, Catharine had the sudden, unshakable feeling that she should have gone with him, but it was too late now.

The feeling persisted while she helped Macawi with breakfast and later while she went down to the stream to draw water.

She was on her way back to Macawi's lodge when a rider burst out of the trees. Startled, she stared up at him, a cold chill wending its way down her spine when she saw the red paint that covered his face.

Before she could think to scream, the rider leaned over his horse's neck, his arm snaking around her waist. Lifting her off her feet, he dropped her over his horse's withers. When she tried to lift her head, his hand pushed her back down.

Fear shot through her as the warrior wheeled his horse around and disappeared into the trees. Eyes wide, she watched the ground fly by beneath the horse's hooves.

She tried to scream, tried to pray, but fear paralyzed her. All she could think of was that she would never see Chasing Elk or Leah again.

On and on her captor rode, never slowing, never speaking. Her body ached from the constant pounding; her head throbbed. Nausea roiled in the pit of her stomach.

She was numb when she realized the horse had slowed. A short time later, her captor pulled his mount to a halt. Grabbing a handful of Catharine's hair, he jerked her head up and back. She screamed as pain lanced through her scalp. When he let go, she tumbled off the horse and landed hard on the ground.

The warrior dismounted and tossed his horse's reins over a low branch. When he took a step toward her, Catharine scrabbled backward, her heart pounding with fear.

He said something in a language she didn't understand, then reached down and grabbed her by the arm. Hauling her to her feet, he dragged her to a tree, pushed her down, and tied her wrists to the trunk.

She looked up at him, her breath coming in hard, shallow gasps. He was going to kill her. She knew it with a cold certainty that turned her blood to ice and made her sick to her stomach.

He stared at her for a long time, his black eyes glinting with hatred. Finally, when she thought he was going to stand there glaring at her forever, he turned and went to look after his horse.

As soon as his back was turned, Catharine tugged on the rope that bound her wrists. She kept tugging in spite of the pain, in spite of the skin that rubbed off, in spite of the blood she could feel dripping down her hands. But, struggle as she might, the rope held.

The warrior hobbled his horse, then sat cross-legged on the ground, gnawing on a piece of dried meat, his malicious gaze fixed on her face all the while.

She licked her lips when he took a drink, shivered as a cool evening breeze wafted across the land.

As darkness fell, the warrior wrapped up in a blanket and went to sleep, leaving her to spend the night shivering from the cold and the constant fear of what awaited her on the morrow. There was no hope of sleep that night. She was hungry and thirsty and more afraid than she had ever been in her life.

Please. Please let Chasing Elk come for me. Please let him find me before it's too late. Please, I don't want to die, not now, not when I've just found him. Please, I'll be so good. Please, please, please . . .

Even as the prayer rose in her heart, she knew she was asking for a miracle. She knew Chasing Elk would look for her when he returned to his mother's lodge, but by then it would be too late.

Chapter 20

Chasing Elk urged his weary horse toward the Hills, quietly cursing himself for leaving Catharine behind. If anything happened to her, he would never forgive himself. But how could he have known?

He had been halfway to the reservation when he had been suddenly overcome by the unmistakable feeling that Catharine needed him.

Frowning, he had reined his horse to a halt.

Go back!

The words had shouted in his mind. He hadn't stopped to question them. He had known with a cold, clear certainty that Catharine was in danger, known it in the deepest part of his soul.

He had wheeled his horse around with a sharp jerk on the reins. A rising sense of urgency and dread had him drumming his heels unmercifully into his mount's flanks.

Hurry!
Hurry!
Hurry!

The words had pounded in his mind to the beat of his horse's hooves as they flew across the prairie. Almost there. He clung to that thought as he thundered through the narrow opening that led into the valley.

It was near dusk when he drew rein in front of Macawi's tipi. His horse was covered in lather, its sides heaving.

His mother stepped out of the lodge as soon as he rode up. One look at her face sent a chill down his spine.

"Where is she?" Chasing Elk demanded. "What's happened to Catharine?"

"I do not know," Macawi replied. "We cannot find her. Ohitekah is searching for her even now."

"Where did you see her last? When?"

"This morning. She went to the river for water."

Turning on his heel, Chasing Elk ran down to the stream. He found Ohitekah there, checking the ground for sign.

"She was here." Ohitekah gestured at the footprints near the water. There was no mistaking that the prints were Catharine's. The Indians did not wear shoes with heels.

Chasing Elk read the sign quickly. She had been on her way back to the camp when someone had ridden out of the cover of the trees and carried her off.

"Why didn't you go after her sooner?" Chasing Elk asked, anxiety making his voice sharp.

"I have only just returned. I left to go hunting this morning shortly after you rode out of camp."

"I need a fresh horse," Chasing Elk said.

"I will go with you. We will leave at dawn."

"I can't wait until then," Chasing Elk said curtly. "I'm going. Now." Even though he knew it would be dark in less than two hours, he couldn't just sit there and wait. He'd go crazy.

Ohitekah regarded him solemnly for a moment, then nodded his understanding. "Macawi will pack food for our journey. I will get the horses."

Catharine stared at the back of the warrior who had captured her. She walked behind him, her hands bound by the long rope that he held in his hand, her feet dragging with every step. Her feet hurt; there was a blister on her right heel. Her throat was dry, her lips cracked, and she was hungry, so hungry. She wondered if he would grant her a last meal.

She had been walking for hours, knowing that if she fell, he wouldn't stop. He hated her. She felt it every time he looked at her. She knew he intended to kill her. The only question was when.

Please. The plea rose in her mind yet again. *Please let Chasing Elk come for me. Please let him find me before it's too late. Please . . .*

She stumbled and fell to her knees. Clinging to the rope, she pulled herself to her feet.

She was so tired, so utterly weary. She wiped the sweat from her face with the back of her hand.

He stopped at noon to rest and water his horse.

Catharine dropped to her knees, her head hanging. She ached all over. Her stomach growled loudly. The sun beat down on her head and sweat dripped down her back and gathered between her breasts. Her mouth was dry, so dry. She glanced at the water hole where the Indian was watering his horse. Just one drink . . .

She waited until the Indian led his horse away, and then she crawled toward the water hole on her hands and knees. It wasn't easy with her hands tied, but she struggled onward, her gaze fixed on the shimmering pool.

She was less than a foot away when the Indian jerked on the rope.

The force of it pulled her toward him so that she landed on her back, hard.

"No!" She screamed the word, though the sound that emerged from her throat was little more than a whisper. "Please."

He tugged on the rope, dragging her across the ground, away from the water. Away from life.

With a smirk, he swung onto his horse's back and urged it into a walk.

Sobbing, Catharine scrambled to her feet. And even as she did so, she wondered why she didn't just give up.

She turned her thoughts to Chasing Elk. He wouldn't give up, she thought. He had spent four and a half years in prison and he never gave up. He had clung to life and hope and he had escaped. And so would she!

She clung to that thought as the sun climbed higher in the sky. Feeling numb, she stumbled onward, knowing that if she fell now, she would never get up again.

Chasing Elk rode steadily onward. The evening before, he and Ohitekah had ridden until it was too dark to see the invader's trail. This morning, they had risen before dawn, stopping only when necessary to rest their horses.

Chasing Elk's gaze was focused on the ground, never leaving the tracks left by the horse they were following. An hour ago, they had found the place where their quarry had spent the night. Chasing Elk had breathed a sigh of relief when he saw Catharine's footprints. She was still alive.

He was keenly aware of each passing minute, not only because he knew how frightened Catharine must be, but because he didn't know what her captor intended to do with her. Had the warrior taken her for a slave? A wife? Or did he intend to use her in an act of revenge? The very thought sickened him.

He paused when he saw where the horse's tracks stopped, then started again. And then, seeing her footsteps trailing in the wake of the horse, he swore under his breath. The bastard who had taken her was making her walk.

Ohitekah rode up beside him. "It is cruel," he said, "but it will slow him down. We will have him before nightfall."

With a nod, Chasing Elk urged his horse into a trot, his gaze hot on the trail.

Before nightfall, the man would be praying for death.

It was late in the afternoon when Catharine stumbled and fell. She was surprised when her captor reined his horse to a halt. She had expected him to drag her to death. She watched him dismount and walk toward her.

Closing her eyes, she made no effort to get up. She was going to die and she was so hungry, so thirsty, so hellishly hot that she no longer cared. Anything, even death, seemed preferable to what she was feeling now. Her feet hurt. Her face and arms were burned by the sun. Her stomach was in knots.

Her captor spoke to her in a harsh, guttural tongue. Yanking her to her feet, he dragged her across the ground to a tree, then tied her arms to a branch above her head.

She stared at him, her breath coming in short, shallow gasps. A moment ago she had been ready to die, but no more. Fear of the pain to come congealed deep within her, stealing the strength from her legs. Added to that fear was her regret that she would never see Chasing Elk or Leah or Mark again.

She watched with growing horror as the warrior began gathering an armful of dry brush. Did he mean to burn her to death?

She shivered convulsively as he began to spread the dry brush and twigs around her feet.

Numb with fear, she stared toward the west. The sun was setting in a bright blaze of gold and orange. Splashes of crimson and scarlet cut across the sky like ribbons of blood.

She was going to die. Now. Today. How could that be when there were so many things she still wanted to do? She wasn't ready to die, not like this, not now. She wanted to have children and grandchildren. Tears leaked from her eyes. What if she was pregnant?

She shivered convulsively as her captor added more wood to the pile at her feet, then knelt on the ground, flint in hand.

She stared past him, her gaze fixed on the setting sun. The sky was ablaze now, looking like the flames that would soon take her life.

She frowned as a faint cloud of dust rose in the distance, gradually growing larger. The earth trembled beneath her feet. A long ululating cry broke the stillness of the evening, sending a chill down her spine.

And then a rider emerged out of the gathering darkness. Shirtless, his long black hair streaming behind him like a battle flag, he rode toward her captor. As he drew nearer, she saw the black paint that covered the lower half of his face, the diagonal slashes that streaked his broad chest.

Springing to his feet, her captor drew a knife from the sheath on his belt. Crouching low, arms spread wide, he waited for the rider to close the distance between them.

Another war cry filled the air as the oncoming rider advanced. He drew back on the reins and his horse reared, its forelegs pawing the air. When the horse dropped to its feet, the rider vaulted from the saddle and suddenly there was a knife in his hand, too. A ray of sunlight skittered across the blade, touching it with crimson.

Knees bent, heads lowered, chins tucked in to protect their throats, the two warriors circled each other.

They moved in a slow and deadly ballet, lunging, feinting, whirling out of harm's way, the knives in their hands hissing through the air like deadly fangs.

Her captor drew first blood. Drops of crimson dripped from a shallow gash on the other warrior's chest. Leaping back, the injured warrior dragged his fingertips through the blood and then, with a wild cry, he surged forward, all restraint gone. His knife flashed in a wide arc, and as her captor darted to one side to avoid the deadly blade, the attacking warrior deftly tossed his knife from his right hand to his left. An exultant cry rang out in the air as the warrior drove the blade deep into her captor's chest and then took a step backward, ripping the knife free. It was a killing blow.

Her captor stood there a moment looking stunned, and then he pitched forward. He twitched once then lay still.

Catharine watched, hardly daring to breathe, as the warrior walked toward her. His dark eyes glowed with savage triumph. She couldn't take her gaze from the single drop of blood that clung to the tip of the knife in his hand.

"No." The word was a prayer, a plea.

"Catharine."

She blinked at the sound of her name, drew back as his knife moved toward her.

"It's all right, Cate."

The sound of his voice penetrated her fear as he cut her hands free then drew her into his arms.

"Nathan?" She stared at him, only then recognizing his face behind the black paint. "Oh, Nathan!"

She wanted to hold him close, tell him how frightened she had been, but the world seemed to tilt and go out of focus, and then she was tumbling down a long black tunnel into nothingness.

"She will be all right," Ohitekah said. "Are you sure you do not want his scalp?"

"I'm sure," Chasing Elk said. "Take it if you want it." The Crow's scalp was the last thing on his mind.

Chasing Elk spread his bedroll on the ground and

laid Catharine on it. Kneeling at her side, he gently removed her shoes and her stockings, swore under his breath when he saw how swollen and blistered her feet were. Her face, neck, and forearms were sunburned, her lips cracked. Her knee was skinned from where she had fallen.

He clenched his fists, sorry that he had killed the bastard who had taken her so quickly. He should have dragged the man behind his horse until there was nothing left but a bloody pulp, or given him a taste of the grisly death he had planned for Catharine.

"I will go find the herbs she needs," Ohitekah said.

Chasing Elk nodded again. He tore a strip of cloth from Catharine's skirt and soaked it with water from his waterskin, then carefully wiped her face, neck, arms, and legs.

She stirred beneath his touch, a soft sound of discomfort rising in her throat. Her eyelids fluttered open. For a moment, she stared at him, her gaze unfocused, and then she whispered his name.

"Lie still," he said.

"So . . . thirsty."

Lifting her, he offered her a drink from the waterskin. "Slowly," he admonished.

She drank greedily, protesting when he drew the waterskin from her lips. "Too much will make you sick," he said. "You can have a little more later."

His gaze moved over her. If he had ignored the voice that warned him she was in danger, if he had arrived a few minutes later . . .

His arms tightened around her as he silently thanked *Wakan Tanka* for sparing her life.

"You came." Her voice was scratchy, barely audible. "How . . . did you . . . know? How did you . . . find me?"

He shook his head. "I'm not sure, darlin'. I just knew you were in trouble. As for finding you, that was no problem. His tracks were easy to follow."

"You killed him."

"Damn right. I just wish I could do it again." He had dragged the warrior's body out onto the prairie and left it for the coyotes, the birds, and the worms.

Her eyelids fluttered down. For a moment, fear clutched at Chasing Elk's heart, but then he realized she had fallen asleep.

He held her until Ohitekah returned. Using the herbs the warrior had found, Chasing Elk mixed a paste and smeared it over Catharine's sunburned skin, her knee, and the blisters on her heels. When that was done, he woke her long enough to drink a cup of the willowbark tea that Ohitekah had made.

It was full dark by the time Ohitekah finished looking after their horses and that of the dead Crow warrior. He started a small fire and prepared their evening meal.

Chasing Elk stayed at Catharine's side, giving her more tea to drink when she woke, offering her broth made from a few strips of dried meat.

"Why do you suppose he took her?" Chasing Elk asked Ohitekah later, when Catharine was sleeping again.

"Who can know for certain?" Ohitekah shrugged. "He meant to torture her to death. I would say he was seeking revenge on the *wasichu* for the death of a loved one."

Chasing Elk grunted softly. That had been his first thought, too, and the only one that made sense. Revenge. He knew all about the need for vengeance, how it could twist a man's insides. It made him think of Jim Buckner. Chasing Elk had spent his first two years in prison imagining all manner of torturous ways to kill Buckner if he ever got his hands on him. He had known it was a waste of time and energy. Jim Buckner had probably quit the territory long ago. Chasing Elk had conceded that even if he managed to escape Yuma, he would probably never find the man who had killed his wife or know for certain what had happened the day Ellenora had died. Still, his dreams of vengeance had been the only thing that had kept him going day after day.

Catharine stirred, calling his name.

"I'm here, darlin'." Drawing her into his arms, he held her close, one hand stroking her hair. "I'm here."

She wandered through a dark alien land filled with pain and images of blood and death. And then a man rode out of the darkness, a tall man with black hair and eyes that glowed with anger. Like a knight in shining armor, he rode valiantly to her rescue, slaying the dragon before carrying her off to the safety of his castle.

She sighed, snuggling closer to the warmth of the arms around her, feeling the brush of lips on her cheek, a familiar hand threading through her hair.

"Nathan?"

"I'm here."

She blinked up at him. It hadn't been a dream. He was real. He was here.

"What do you need, darlin'?" he asked quietly.

"I'm thirsty."

With a smile, he offered her the waterskin. This time, he let her drink a little more. It wasn't enough. She was certain she could drink it all and still want more.

"How are you feelin'?" he asked.

She considered that a moment. Her skin no longer burned. Her feet didn't hurt. He had eased her thirst and satisfied her hunger. "Much better," she decided.

"Thank God."

"I was so afraid. . . ."

"Shh, it's over now."

She stared up at him. He had washed the black paint from his face and chest. The fierce glow had left his eyes. He wasn't a frightening stranger anymore, but the man she had married, the man she loved. The man who had risked his life to save hers.

"You could have been killed," she said quietly.

He shrugged. "Don't think about it." He gathered her into his arms once again. "Go to sleep now."

She wanted to tell him she wasn't tired, that he should rest too, that she loved him more than life itself. But her eyelids were suddenly too heavy to keep open, and she slid into the peaceful abyss of sleep knowing there was nothing to fear.

Chasing Elk held her all through the night. Ohitekah had offered to keep watch while Chasing Elk slept, but Chasing Elk had refused. He needed to hold her, needed to know she was safe. He had lost one woman he loved; he didn't intend to lose another.

And so he sat there, cradling her in his arms, listening to the soft sound of her breathing, touching her cheek, her hair, inhaling the scent of woman. His woman.

As dawn's first gray light began to brighten the eastern sky, Chasing Elk lifted his face toward the heavens.

"Hear me, *Wakan Tanka*. I thank you for this day, for this life, for this woman. Thank you for helping me find my daughter. Give me the wisdom and the courage to do what is best for them. Give me the strength to provide for them and to protect them always."

He looked down as Catharine stirred in his arms, felt his heart turn over as her eyelids fluttered open and she smiled a sleepy smile.

"I didn't know Indians prayed."

He nodded. "A true warrior greets every day with a prayer to the Great Spirit. It's something I've neglected for far too long."

Catharine insisted she felt well enough to travel, but Chasing Elk refused to hear of it. He built a shelter to protect her from the sun, urged her to drink as much water as she could hold, refused to let her get up except for a few minutes to stretch her legs and to relieve herself.

She appealed to Ohitekah, hoping he would take her side and convince Chasing Elk that she wasn't an invalid and didn't need to be treated like one, but he just shrugged. And so she sat in the shade and enjoyed the view or took long naps or listened quietly as Chasing Elk and Ohitekah talked of the old days, when the buffalo herds roamed the prairie and the Lakota ruled the land as far as the eye could see.

It must have been a hard life, she mused, following the buffalo, living off the land. And yet it must have been a good life, too, a way of life that was forever gone. She heard the wistfulness in Ohitekah's voice as he spoke of days spent hunting for game, of battles against the Crow, of coup counted and boasted of around the campfire. He spoke of Crazy Horse, his voice almost reverent, of Red Cloud and Sitting Bull. His voice grew harsh as he recalled the tide of white men who had swarmed into the Black Hills in search of yellow iron, swelled with pride when he spoke of Custer's defeat.

"And now we live on the reservation, penned up like the white man's cattle. Our old men no longer dream dreams. Our young men seek forgetfulness in the white man's firewater. Our women have lost hope. Our children cry because they are hungry." He stared into the distance for a long moment, as if seeing visions of the past. "And so we left the reservation. Here, hidden away, we can live in the old way and pretend we are still free."

Quiet tears tracked Catharine's cheeks as Ohitekah rose and walked into the darkness.

That night, she held Chasing Elk in her arms, her heart aching for what his people had lost.

Chapter 21

They returned to the village nestled in the shadow of the Black Hills the next day. Macawi fussed over Catharine, suggesting she sit outside in the shade and rest.

Catharine assured Chasing Elk's mother that she was fine, but she didn't argue when Macawi insisted she should rest. Though she felt much better, Catharine was content to sit in the shade. After weeks on the trail, breaking Chasing Elk and her brother out of jail, and everything else that had happened, the prospect of having a day with nothing to do was nice for a change.

Chasing Elk had left early that morning to go after Leah, but only after Catharine had promised that she wouldn't leave the camp for any reason.

It was pleasant, sitting there watching the women go about their daily tasks. Most of their work was done outside, and she felt a twinge of envy at the way they talked and laughed together. It occurred to Catharine that she hadn't had a close friend since her family left the East, and she suddenly longed to be a part of the close camaraderie the Lakota women shared.

She smiled as she watched the children at play. The little girls played with their dolls, imitating the work their mothers did. The little boys played at war or chased each other through the camp. The older girls looked after their brothers and sisters or worked alongside their mothers. The older boys practiced with bows and arrows or guarded the horse herd. Only the men appeared idle. Most of them sat in the shade and talked. A few could be seen fashioning new arrows. One man was restringing his bow. All in all, it was a tranquil scene that left her wishing she wasn't an outsider, that she could speak their language, that she might join the three women who were taking their children down to the stream to splash in the cool water.

Gradually, her eyelids grew heavy and she went inside the lodge to take a nap.

It was dark when she woke sometime later.

Going outside, she found Macawi preparing the evening meal. Ohitekah sat cross-legged in front of the lodge. Several children sat around him, listening intently as he told them a story. Catharine listened to the words. Though she could not understand the Lakota language, she loved the sound of it.

She smiled at Macawi as the woman came to stand beside her. When she asked Macawi what the story was about, she learned that it was the same story that Chasing Elk had once told Leah about how the Old Man made men and women.

"The children have heard it many times," Macawi

said, "but they never tire of it and they always ask for more."

But there were to be no more stories that night, as the mothers came one by one to collect their children and take them home.

After her long nap, Catharine wasn't ready to go to bed when Macawi and Ohitekah turned in. She sat out in front of Macawi's lodge, wrapped in a warm buffalo robe, gazing at the stars and thinking how true the story of Old Man was, and how similar men and women were, whether they were white or Lakota, whether they were in the East or the West. Whenever a group of men and women got together, sooner or later they split into two groups, with the women gathering in the kitchen to talk about recipes and children and fashions while the men went into the library or stepped outside to smoke. Perhaps all people were more alike than different, she mused, and she thought it was sad that the red man and the white man didn't spend more time trying to get to know each other instead of trying to massacre each other.

It was late when Chasing Elk returned with Leah. Catharine hadn't expected him to return until the next day. Rising, she dropped the buffalo robe and ran toward him. Leah was asleep in his arms, and she reached up to take the child from him, noting that even in sleep, Leah clung to Gretchen. Smiling, Catharine decided she would have to make Gretchen a doeskin dress and a pair of moccasins.

Dismounting, Chasing Elk kissed Catharine, then took Leah from her arms and carried the child into his mother's lodge. After he settled his daughter in bed, he went back outside to where Catharine waited.

"Are you all right?" he asked.

"Yes, I'm fine. I missed you."

"I missed you, too." He gathered her into his arms and hugged her lightly. "Let me turn the horses loose."

"All right."

She watched as he unsaddled the horses, thinking how glad she was that he had returned safely.

Moments later, he took her in his arms again. "I thought you'd be in bed."

"I couldn't sleep."

"Why not?" he asked, and she heard the concern in his voice.

She shrugged. "I took a long nap today and I wasn't tired. I'm glad now that I stayed up."

"Me, too. Do you feel like taking a walk? I need to stretch my legs."

Hand in hand, they walked away from the camp. It was a beautiful night. A fat yellow moon hung low in the sky. Stars twinkled in the heavens. A faint breeze carried the scent of sage and pine.

"Do you have any idea where you'd like to settle down when we leave here?" Chasing Elk asked after awhile.

Catharine shook her head. "Anyplace you want to go is fine with me."

He grunted softly. "I'd like to settle some place nearby so Leah can visit her grandmother."

"That's a good idea. I never really knew my grandparents. My mother's parents died when I was young, and my father's parents lived in Tennessee. We hardly

ever saw them." She sighed wistfully. "I don't suppose
I'll see very much of Mark now."

Chasing Elk slipped his arm around her shoulders
and gave her a squeeze. "You can write to him when
we get settled. Once we get some money saved up,
we can take a trip to Boston."

She nodded. Of course, she could always get in
touch with Mark through Mrs. Montgomery. And perhaps Mark would come to visit them as well.

Hand in hand, they turned and walked back to Macawi's lodge.

Leah was up bright and early the next morning,
eager to meet her grandmother.

Chasing Elk's throat grew thick as he watched his
mother and his daughter embrace. He smiled as Leah
immediately began asking questions, which his mother
answered patiently and lovingly. Seeing them together,
he noticed that they looked very much alike. They
would stay here for a month or two, he thought, so
that Leah could begin to learn the language and cus-
toms of the People, and then they would find a place
to spend the winter. He had spent his winters here
when he was a young boy, but he doubted whether
either Catharine or Leah, both of whom had been
raised among the whites, would enjoy it. Then, too,
he wanted Leah to go to school. His daughter was
from two worlds. It was important to him that she be
as comfortable among the Lakota as she was among
the whites. In the spring they would find a place to
settle down and build a new life, a place to put
down roots.

A new life. He thought of Ellenora and the few

brief years they had shared, and thanked *Wakan Tanka* for sending him to Catharine, for giving him a second chance at happiness.

And then he thought of Jim Buckner, hoping that the Great Spirit would put the man in his path so that he could avenge Ellenora's death at last.

In the days that followed, Catharine learned much of the Lakota people and their way of life. With each passing day, she learned more of their language. She learned that the little cleared space in every lodge was the family altar. It was known as a square of mellowed earth, and sweet grass, sage, or cedar were burned on it. The Lakota believed the smoke carried their prayers to the Great Spirit.

The Lakota believed that everything was alive with a spirit of its own—earth and grass, trees and rocks, birds and animals, all were part of the Great Mystery. To the Lakota, all life was sacred; thus whenever they killed an animal for its meat or its hide, they offered a prayer thanking the animal for giving up its life.

The Lakota ate animals that Catharine would never have considered to be edible. Skunks, muskrats, squirrels, badgers, and raccoons could be found in the family cook pot, as well as prairie chickens and deer. Buffalo had become a rare treat.

Children were taught to love and respect their parents. Catharine didn't find that particularly strange until she learned that among the Lakota, it meant more than just a child's father and mother. Aunts and uncles were also called mother and father, so that a Lakota child might have several fathers and mothers in the camp, in addition to grandmothers and grandfathers, all of whom gave the child love and instruction.

Children were given their own clothing, bedding, and eating utensils at an early age and were taught to care for those things, thus instilling in them a sense of responsibility. They were taught their place in the village by example, and were expected to imitate their elders.

Old people were revered for their knowledge and their wisdom. It was the old ones who passed the history of the Lakota from one generation to the other by telling stories of days gone by.

The Lakota believed in many gods and goddesses. *Wakan Tanka* was the Supreme Being, but the Lakota believed there were other gods as well. *Inyan*, the Rock; *Maka,* the Earth; *Skan*, the Sky; and *Wi*, the Sun. Each of these were considered to be gods. And there were more: *Hanhepi-wi*, the Moon; *Tate*, the Wind. Evil was personified by *Iya*; *Iktomi* was a deposed god, sort of like Lucifer, who had been cast out of Heaven for rebellion and taken a third of the hosts of Heaven with him.

She learned that the number four was a sacred number. There were four classes of gods and four directions, just as time was composed of four parts—day, night, month, and year. There were four kinds of animals—crawling, flying, two-legged, and four-legged. A man's life was divided into four stages—infancy, childhood, maturity, and old age.

The circle was a sacred symbol. The sun, the moon, the earth, and the sky were round; the four winds circled the earth; life itself was a circle, thus Lakota lodges and the camp circle were round, a constant reminder of the endless circle of life and death and renewal.

The Lakota kept no clocks. Indeed, time meant nothing to them. They ate when they were hungry and slept when they were weary. When they needed meat, the warriors went hunting. The women looked after their homes like women everywhere, eternally busy taking care of their husbands and children, doing the cooking and the sewing and the cleaning.

Leah was learning, too. Macawi made a tunic and moccasins for the little girl. With her naturally dark skin and black hair, it was hard to distinguish Leah from the other Lakota girls except for her hair, which wasn't nearly as long as that of the others. Macawi also helped Leah make a tunic for Gretchen.

To Catharine's chagrin, Leah picked up the Lakota language far more rapidly than she did. Leah blossomed, here in the land of the Lakota, and quickly became a favorite of both children and adults.

Gradually, the women in the camp warmed to Catharine and began to include her in their activities. She grew to love the Lakota people for their warmth and generosity. There was always much to do and the days passed quickly, flowing into each other as one river flowed into another.

But it was the nights she loved best, when she and Chasing Elk walked away from the camp circle to their special place. There, with a warm fur beneath them and the beauty of the heavens above, they shared their love for one another.

And it was there, on a cool night in early fall, when

Catharine told Chasing Elk that she was going to have his child.

He stared at her a moment, and then he placed his hand over her womb. "You're sure?"

She nodded, her gaze searching his in the moonlight. Was he happy?

"Catharine!" He swept her into his arms, his face buried in the wealth of her hair.

"You don't mind, then?"

"Mind?" He drew back so he could see her face. "Of course not. How are you feeling?"

"I feel wonderful. And special." She settled into his arms again, thinking she had never been happier in her whole life. A baby. She was going to have Nathan's baby. She wanted to tell the whole world! She couldn't wait until they reached a town so she could write to Mark and tell him he was going to be an uncle. And who knew? Perhaps in the near future, she would be an aunt! Family. It was what life was all about.

"I suppose you want a boy this time," Catharine said.

He shrugged. "It doesn't matter, as long as it's healthy."

Chasing Elk made love to her ever so gently that night, as if he was afraid she might shatter in his arms. He kissed her tenderly, his every touch telling her how much he loved her. He whispered love words in her ear, sweet words spoken in English and Lakota, as if one language wasn't enough to convey how he felt.

Later, back in Macawi's lodge, she fell asleep in his arms.

Chasing Elk held Catharine close, one hand lightly stroking her hair. She was going to have a baby. Ellenora had been sick every morning during the first few months of her pregnancy and had had to stay in bed toward the end. During delivery, he had feared he might lose them both.

A baby. He smiled into the darkness. He had told Catharine he didn't care whether she had a boy or a girl, so long as it was healthy, and that was true enough, but now, lying in the dark, he found himself hoping for a boy, a son to carry on his name. He shook his head. Another girl would be equally welcome, he thought, a pretty little girl with Catharine's auburn hair and sky blue eyes.

Looking upward, he sent a silent prayer to *Wakan Tanka*, asking the Great Spirit to bless his woman and his child with health and strength.

Macawi and Ohitekah were thrilled with the news when Catharine and Chasing Elk told them the next morning.

Leah was also delighted, and once her excitement died down, the questions began, questions Chasing Elk hadn't expected her to ask at such a young age. Like how did the baby get inside Catharine, and how was it going to get out, and what did it eat, and how did it breathe.

Chasing Elk thought he'd rather spend another year in Yuma than answer his daughter's questions, but he figured if she could ask them, she deserved an answer and an honest one at that. He thought briefly of asking Catharine or his mother to talk to Leah, but Leah was his daughter and she had asked him the questions.

She listened intently as he answered her questions

in the simplest terms he could think of, though he was in no way an expert on the subject of childbirth. Nevertheless, she seemed satisfied with his explanation and ran off to play with her friends and tell them that she was going to have a baby brother or sister.

When she was gone, Chasing Elk blew out a deep breath, and Catharine grinned at him.

"How'd I do?" he asked.

"Very well," she replied, her grin widening. "Now that you have experience, you'll be able to explain it to the next one."

Chasing Elk shook his head. "From now on, wife, that's your job. Once was enough for me."

The next few months passed swiftly and peacefully. Leah and Catharine spent much of their time with Macawi, learning how to cook and sew in the Lakota way. Gradually, without being aware of it, Catharine picked up more and more of the Lakota language.

She remembered how surprised she was the first time one of the Lakota women spoke to her and she actually understood everything that was said. Macawi had helped Catharine make a tunic out of bleached doeskin, and a pair of moccasins. The clothing had felt strange at first, but after a day or two, she wondered how she had ever endured wearing petticoats and stockings and shoes with heels.

Macawi made a shirt and leggings and moccasins for Chasing Elk, as well. Clad in his native dress, wearing a knife in a beaded sheath on his belt, he looked wholly Lakota. And wholly desirable. She never tired of looking at him, touching him.

She had thought that, after a month or two, her

desire for her husband would cool. Instead, it seemed to burn hotter and brighter with each passing day. She couldn't help touching him whenever he was near, whether it was to stroke his arm or run her hand over his back. It pleased her that he couldn't keep his hands off her, either.

It was while they were out walking one evening that he told her they would be leaving his people in a couple of days.

"Winter will be here soon," he said, taking her in his arms. "Ohitekah said most of the people will return to the reservation until spring."

"Is that where your mother is going?"

"They haven't decided yet. But I don't want to stay on the reservation. I told my mother we'd be back next summer, after the baby's born."

"Where are we going to live until then?"

"I was thinking we'd go to Short Rock Creek. It's not much of a town. There are a couple of big ranches, but mostly people just pass through. No one's likely to recognize me there."

"It doesn't matter to me, so long as we're all together."

"It's settled, then. Let's go tell Leah."

It was hard to say good-bye when the time came. Catharine had grown fond of Macawi and Ohitekah and the Lakota people. Leah cried as she gave her grandmother one last hug.

"Do not cry," Macawi said, wiping the tears from Leah's eyes. "I will see you again soon and we will have much to tell each other."

Leah sniffed back her tears. "I'll miss you."

"And I will miss you. Take good care of Catharine. She will need your help now."

"I will," Leah promised.

Chasing Elk embraced his mother. "Look for us in the summer."

"Take care of yourself, *cinks*."

Chasing Elk bid Ohitekah good-bye; then, taking up the reins to the pack mule, Chasing Elk swung up on his horse.

Catharine blinked back tears of her own as she followed Chasing Elk out of the valley. Still, as sorry as she was to be leaving Chasing Elk's family, she was glad to be heading back to civilization. The baby she was carrying was making itself felt more each day. Her breasts were tender, her ankles swollen. She didn't know where they would eventually settle down, but she wanted it to be near a town with a doctor, just in case something went wrong.

Chapter 22

It was raining when they reached Short Rock Creek. Chasing Elk stopped in front of the town's only hotel. Dismounting, he quickly lifted Catharine from the back of her horse and onto the boardwalk. Leah and Gretchen came next.

After tying the horses and the mule to the hitching post, he stepped up onto the boardwalk, shaking the water from his hat.

Entering the hotel, Chasing Elk went to the front desk.

"Welcome to the Lancaster," the clerk said.

Nodding, Chasing Elk asked for two adjoining rooms. Catharine felt a little tickle of excitement when he signed the register as Mr. and Mrs. Nathan Rossiter and daughter. It was the first time she had seen her name linked to his.

"Here." Chasing Elk handed her the keys to the room. "You two go get settled. I'll get our gear and take care of the horses."

"I can have a boy take your mounts to the livery, if you wish," the desk clerk said.

Chasing Elk nodded. "Much obliged."

The clerk rang the bell on his desk. A young boy appeared a few minutes later. "Augie, take this gentleman's horses down to the livery."

"Yes, sir," the boy said.

"I'll go with you," Chasing Elk said. He settled his hat on his head and pulled it down low. "I need to get our baggage."

With a nod, the boy followed Chasing Elk outside, waited on the boardwalk while he removed their belongings from the pack mule. Chasing Elk flipped him a coin, then ducked back into the hotel. He stopped at the desk to inquire about some hot water, then went up the narrow, carpeted stairway to find Catharine and Leah.

Rooms two and four were located at the far end of the corridor. Catharine was drying Leah's hair when he entered room number two.

"Not too bad," he remarked. He tossed his hat on the back of a chair. The room looked clean and well-kept. Starched curtains hung at the windows. There was a double bed and a dresser, a ladder-back chair in one corner. He crossed the floor and looked into the adjoining room.

"What do you say we get cleaned up and then find something to eat?"

"Can I have chocolate cake for dessert?" Leah asked.

"Sure, sweetheart, whatever you want."

They ate in the hotel dining room. It was small and not too fancy, but the food was good. Chasing Elk shook his head as his daughter devoured two slices of cake. Leaning back in his chair, savoring a cup of coffee, he thought about what a lucky man he was. Not long ago, his future had looked bleak indeed. Now he had a beautiful wife and a baby on the way. He had made peace with his daughter and his mother, and the future was looking mighty good.

Leah was ready for bed when they went back upstairs. Chasing Elk tucked her into bed and kissed her good night. With a little sigh, she closed her eyes and she was asleep.

He smiled down at his daughter for a few minutes, then went into the room he and Catharine would share, leaving the door between the two rooms partially open in case Leah woke in the middle of the night.

Catharine was standing at the window, looking out. "It's still raining," she remarked, glancing at him over her shoulder.

He grunted softly. It was really coming down. Lightning slashed across the skies. Thunder rolled overhead, sounding like Lakota war drums.

Chasing Elk moved up behind Catharine and put his arms around her waist. "What would you think about settling down here?"

She shrugged. "It seems like a nice town."

"Tomorrow I'll ask around and see if there's a house for sale anywhere."

"Maybe we could build our own," Catharine suggested.

"Yeah. I'm gonna have to look for a job, too."

"What kind of job?"

"Beats the hell out of me."

"What did you do before . . . before you were arrested?"

"I was training horses for a few of the local folks, and I had a top stallion that I had planned to breed." He grunted softly. He never had found out what happened to that stud horse. "I was just getting established when all this trouble started."

"Can't you do that again?"

"I don't know, maybe. I can always find a job at one of the saloons, dealing for the house."

"Oh."

"What?"

"Nothing, but, well, you'd have to work nights, wouldn't you?"

"Most likely." He turned her in his arms so she was facing him. "Want me home nights, do you?"

She nodded.

"Any particular reason why?"

"So I can do this." She stood on her tiptoes and kissed him. "Or this." She slid her hand inside his shirt, her palms skimming over his chest.

"Good reasons," he allowed, grinning down at her. "I'll try real hard to get a day job."

She laughed softly; then, taking him by the hand, she led him to bed. He sat down, drawing her into his lap. "You happy?" he asked.

"Very happy."

"No regrets?"

"Not one." She cocked her head to one side. "Are you happy, Nathan?"

"Honey, I'm the happiest man this side of heaven."

The next morning after breakfast, Chasing Elk left the hotel to see about finding a job and a place to live. Short Rock Creek might have been a small town with only one hotel and a handful of businesses, but it had five saloons.

He struck pay dirt at the Shamrock. The owner, Paddy Sweeney, was looking for a new blackjack dealer to replace the one who had recently run off to Yankton with one of the dancers.

"I don't allow no fast shuffles," Sweeney said. "No dealing off the bottom or palming aces, nothing like that. I run a straight house here. No tricks."

"Whatever you want," Chasing Elk said.

"You can start tonight," Sweeney said. "Weston worked eight to midnight."

"I'll be here, thanks."

Leaving the saloon, Chasing Elk stopped at a bulletin board beside the barbershop. There, tacked up beside a couple of hand-printed ads for horses and cows for sale, he saw a small notice regarding a house for rent. Plucking the notice from the bulletin board, he went in search of the owner.

"Pack your bags, girls," Chasing Elk said, "we're moving."

Catharine and Leah looked up at him.

"Where are we going, Daddy?"

"I rented a house."

"A house?" Catharine said, rising. "Where?"

"It's located at the end of Third Street. Two bedrooms, parlor, kitchen. It's not much to look at on the outside, but the inside's clean. And it comes with furniture."

"Sounds wonderful," Catharine said.

Half an hour later they were walking into their new house.

"So," Chasing Elk said, "what do you think?"

"It's very nice," Catharine said. And it was. A sofa and two chairs faced the fireplace. Two big windows looked out on the street. The large kitchen was furnished with a square oak table and four chairs. The bedrooms were small but comfortably appointed.

Chasing Elk looked at his daughter. "What do you think, sweetheart?"

She looked thoughtful for a moment, then smiled. "Gretchen likes it."

"What about you?"

"I like it, too. Can I have the blue bedroom?"

"Sure, if you like."

"Can we afford this?" Catharine asked.

"I found a job today, too," Chasing Elk said.

"Oh? Where?"

"Over at the Shamrock Saloon, dealing blackjack. I start tonight."

She smiled at him. "You've been busy."

"Yes, ma'am."

"What time do you go to work?"

"Eight to midnight."

By five o'clock, they had unpacked their belongings and put everything away. Catharine had gone to the general store and bought new sheets, towels, and cleaning supplies, and even though Chasing Elk thought the house looked clean, she had insisted on washing and waxing every surface in sight. She put Leah to work dusting while Chasing Elk had been in charge of washing the windows.

Now she stood in the center of the parlor, her hands on her hips as she looked around the room. "That's better."

Chasing Elk nodded. The house fairly sparkled. The furniture gleamed with a fresh coat of wax. There were clean sheets on the beds. All the dishes had been washed and put away. The carpets had been aired out.

Looking pleased with herself, she went into the kitchen to fix supper. Leah trailed after her.

"I hope Gretchen won't be jealous of the new baby," Leah remarked.

"You'll just have to love her a little more," Catharine said. She glanced at Chasing Elk, who had followed them into the kitchen. For all that Leah seemed happy about the new baby, she wondered if this was her way of seeking reassurance.

"People never run out of love," Chasing Elk said, drawing his daughter into his arms.

"They don't?"

He shook his head. "You love me, don't you?"

"Yes."

"And Catharine?"

Leah nodded.

"And Macawi and Ohitekah?"

Leah nodded again.

"And you still have love enough for Gretchen, don't you?"

Leah smiled her understanding, then went into the parlor to play with Gretchen.

"You're a wonderful father," Catharine said, squeezing his hand.

In their room later, Catherine watched Chasing Elk get ready for work. She was glad he had a job. She just wished it wasn't in a saloon. All that gambling. Men drinking. Saloon girls sashaying around with their arms and legs exposed, flirting and drinking with the customers. Taking them upstairs. Chasing Elk was a handsome man. She didn't like the idea of other women looking at him, especially women who earned a living the way the saloon girls did.

He picked up his hat and settled it on his head. "Guess I'd best be going."

She nodded, lifting her face for his kiss. "I'll miss you."

Putting his arms around her, he drew her close. "I'll miss you, too." He kissed her again, and then picked Leah up in his arms. "Be a good girl. Do what Catharine tells you." He kissed her cheek. "And don't stay up too late."

"Yes, Daddy."

Setting her on her feet, he ruffled her hair, gave Catharine one last kiss, and left the house.

The Shamrock was in full swing when he stepped through the doors. The poker tables were full. He saw maybe a half a dozen men bucking the tiger at the faro table. A man sat at the piano, his head back, his eyes closed as his fingers moved over the keys. Three couples danced in the corner. A thick layer of blue-gray smoke hung in the air.

Chasing Elk made his way to the end of the bar where Sweeney stood, one foot on the rail, one hand curled around a shot glass.

"You're right on time," Sweeney said. "You'll be taking over for Fleming at table two."

"All right."

"I don't allow my dealers to drink anything stronger

than beer while they're working." Sweeney glanced at the gun riding on his hip. "You know how to use that hogleg?"

"I can hit what I aim at."

Sweeney nodded. "Try to keep it leathered."

"Anything else?"

"That's it."

With a nod, Chasing Elk went to relieve Fleming.

He had been working a little over two hours when two new players sat down at the table.

Chasing Elk didn't pay much attention to their conversation until one of the men mentioned the name Buckner. He paused in mid-deal, his eyes narrowing.

"Something wrong?" the man asked.

"I used to know a man named Buckner. Jim Buckner. Would that be him?"

"Could be. I didn't catch his first name."

"Where is he?"

The man shrugged. "I dunno where he is now. He was just some two-bit drunk I met over at the Lucky Deuce the other night."

Chasing Elk stared at the man. Was it possible Buckner was here, in Short Rock Creek?

"You gonna deal those cards?"

"Is he still in town?"

"How the hell should I know?" The man tapped on the table. "I still need a card."

Chasing Elk dealt cards to the two men and one to himself.

The second man looked at his cards and then tossed them in. "Busted," he muttered.

"Nineteen," the first man said, turning his cards face up.

Chasing Elk flipped his cards over. A king and a queen. "Tough luck."

The man dropped a silver dollar on the table. "Let's go."

The second man grimaced, but he put up a dollar, too.

Chasing Elk dealt the cards, his mind only half on the game. Buckner might be in town. He glanced at the clock. Another hour to go. He was tempted to walk away from the table, go to the Lucky Deuce, and ask after Buckner, but he needed this job. He had a wife and a child to look after now and a baby on the way. He couldn't just up and quit on a whim. And it might not be the man he was looking for. Jim Buckner hadn't been a drinking man. Just the opposite, in fact.

But men changed, and Buckner certainly wouldn't be the first man to try and drown a guilty conscience in a bottle of booze.

At two minutes after midnight, Chasing Elk was on the street and headed for the Lucky Deuce Saloon.

Like the Shamrock, the Lucky Deuce stayed open into the wee hours of the morning. Chasing Elk went straight to the bar.

The bartender, a big burly man with slicked-back hair and a trim mustache strolled toward him. "What'll you have?"

"A whiskey and some information," he told the bar dog. "I'm looking for a man name of Jim Buckner."

The bartender filled a shot glass and slid it across the bar. "You a friend of his?"

"I'm from his hometown."

"What town would that be?"

"Tucson." Chasing Elk lifted his glass and took a drink.

The bartender regarded him for a few minutes, then nodded. "He was in here earlier tonight."

"Do you know where he's staying?"

The bartender shook his head. "Couldn't say."

"Do you know if he'll be back?"

The bartender shrugged. "He usually stops by sooner or later. You know how it is with some men. Just can't leave the booze alone."

"Obliged for your help."

"Want me to tell Buckner that you're looking for him?"

"No," Chasing Elk said, slapping a dollar on the bar. "I'd like to surprise him."

Whistling softly, he left the saloon.

It was too late to go looking for Buckner now, but tomorrow. Ah, tomorrow he would at last confront the man who had killed Ellenora. His fingertips caressed the butt of his gun. Tomorrow Jim Buckner would pay for Ellenora's death, and for every hour that Chasing Elk had spent behind the cold walls of Yuma Prison.

He was surprised to find Catharine waiting up for him when he got home.

"Why aren't you in bed?" he asked, tossing his hat on the hall tree.

"I was worried."

He frowned. "Why?"

"It's after one. I expected you home over an hour ago."

"Oh." Unbuckling his gunbelt, he hung it next to his hat.

"Something's wrong," she said, her brow furrowing. "What happened?"

"Buckner's in town."

She stared at him a moment, not comprehending, and then the name rang a bell. Her eyes widened. "He's here?"

Chasing Elk smiled. "Can you believe the luck!" He paced the floor, too keyed up to think of sitting down.

"That's wonderful news," she said slowly. "Tomorrow you can tell the sheriff and they'll arrest him."

"The sheriff! The law didn't believe me before. What makes you think they'll listen to me now?"

"If you're not going to turn him in, then what are you going to do?"

"I'm going to find him and then I'm going to make him pay for what he did."

"You can't take the law into your own hands, Nathan."

"Watch me. I spent four and a half years waiting for a chance like this. He got away before. But not now. Not this time."

"Nathan . . ."

"Don't worry, Catharine, everything will be all right."

Don't worry, Catharine, everything will be all right. Those words played over and over in her mind as she lay in bed that night, unable to sleep, afraid that when her husband found Jim Buckner, he intended to play judge and jury. How could she live with him if he killed a man in cold blood? No matter what Buckner had done, he deserved a trial. She could understand Nathan's anger, even his hatred for the man who had killed his wife and let him go to prison for a crime he hadn't committed, but to take the law into his own hands . . . How could he do such a thing?

She rolled onto her side, blinking back her tears. He couldn't kill Buckner and expect to stay here. They would have to leave town and go back on the run. What kind of life would that be, especially for his children? Maybe he hadn't considered that yet. Maybe, once his excitement cooled, he would think about the consequences and what it would mean to their marriage, to their children. Killing Buckner wouldn't bring Ellenora back or restore the years he had spent in jail. Surely he knew that? Vengeance was never the answer.

She closed her eyes, praying that Nathan would realize that before it was too late.

Catharine woke after a restless night. She hadn't fallen asleep in her husband's arms, and she had missed his closeness, his warmth, the sense of belonging.

Nathan was already up, no doubt anxious to be on his way. She could hear him talking to Leah, though she couldn't distinguish the words.

Rising, she washed her face and dressed, then stood in front of the mirror and brushed out her hair. First she braided it, then she took the braid out and arranged it in a neat coil at her nape. She was stalling, she thought, unwilling to go out and face her husband, knowing what he intended to do.

Finally, she swept her hair away from her face, tied it at her nape with a ribbon, and then went into the kitchen.

Leah was sitting at the table, eating a slice of bread and butter. Gretchen sat in the chair beside her. Nathan sat across from his daughter, a cup of coffee in one hand. They both looked up as Catharine entered the room.

"Daddy says I have to go to school."

"Yes, I think you should," Catharine agreed.

"But I won't know anyone," Leah said petulantly.

"I'm sure you'll make friends in no time at all."

"That's what Daddy said. But what if they don't like me?"

Catharine looked at Chasing Elk.

"Let's worry about that when it happens," he said. "I'll take you tomorrow morning." He drank the last of the coffee in his cup. "Right now, I've got business to take care of." He glanced at Catharine. "You'll look after Leah?"

"Of course."

He kissed Leah on the cheek. "I'll see you later."

"Bye, Daddy. Can I have a new dress for school?"

"Sure." He pulled some money out of his pants pocket and handed it to Catharine. "Take her shopping, will you?"

Catharine nodded, then followed him to the front door. "What should I do if you don't come back?"

"What's that supposed to mean?"

"You know very well what it means. What if Buckner kills you?"

Chasing Elk snorted. "That's not going to happen."

"What if it does?" she insisted.

"I'd like you to raise my daughter. If you don't want to, then see that she gets back to my mother."

Catharine laid her hand on his arm. "Nathan, please don't do this."

A muscle worked in his jaw. He looked at her a moment, then opened the door and left the house.

He checked the saloons first, then the barbershop, but there was no sign of Buckner. Next, he went to the hotel.

"Jim Buckner," the desk clerk said, thumbing through the register. "Yes, he was here."

"Was?" Chasing Elk blew out a breath, unable to believe Buckner had been right under his nose.

"He left in a bit of a hurry early this morning."

"Did he say where he was going?"

"No."

"Did he say if he'd be back?"

The desk clerk shook his head.

Muttering an oath, Chasing Elk left the hotel and headed for the livery.

"Jim Buckner?" the hostler said. "Yeah, he came in a little after sunrise. Bought a horse and saddle and lit out like he had a fire under his tail."

"Did he say where he was going?"

The hostler stroked his jaw thoughtfully for a moment. "He might have said something about Silverton or Durango." He shrugged. "Or maybe it was Virginia City. I don't rightly recollect."

"Do you remember which way he headed when he rode out?" Chasing Elk asked, his impatience growing.

"North, I think it was. Yes, that's it. North."

"Has anybody else ridden out of here since this morning?"

"No."

"Obliged."

Leaving the livery, Chasing Elk studied the ground. The freshest trail did indeed lead north. He followed the horse's hoofprints for awhile, noting the cut of the track, the way the horse tended to drag the toe of one back foot. It was a track that would be easy to follow.

Going back inside the livery, Chasing Elk asked the hostler to saddle his horse. Then he went to the house to tell Catharine he was leaving.

Catharine stared at him. "You're going, just like that? What about your job? What about us?"

"I won't be gone long. And I can get another job."

She blinked back her tears. "I can't believe you intend to go off and leave us here, alone, in a strange town. I can't believe you intend to leave the daughter you just found. I can't believe you intend to leave me!"

"Dammit, Catharine, I don't want to, but this might be my only chance to catch Buckner. Why can't you understand that?"

"I understand your need for revenge is stronger than anything you might feel for me or for Leah."

"That's not true and you know it."

"I don't know it."

"It's something I have to do. Why can't you see that?"

"Then go!" she cried. "You can spend the rest of your life hunting him down for all I care, but don't expect me to be here waiting for you when you get back. If you get back!"

"Catharine . . ."

"Go on! What are you waiting for? He's getting away."

"Dammit, Catharine, don't make this any harder than it is."

"You're the one making it hard," she said coldly, "not me."

He stared at her, torn between his need to grab her and make her understand and his need to extract justice from the man who had murdered Ellenora and stolen four and a half years of his life.

When he reached for Catharine, she turned away. "Don't touch me unless you mean to stay here, with us, where you belong."

Angered by her refusal to understand, he turned on his heel and stomped out of the house. Only then did he realize he hadn't told his daughter good-bye.

Buckner's trail was easy to follow. For the first few miles, Chasing Elk's exasperation at Catharine's refusal to understand how he felt rode beside him. Stubborn woman! Why couldn't she see how important it was for him to go after Buckner? His wife had been killed, and he had been convicted of her murder. He had spent four and a half years in hell for a crime he hadn't committed, missed out on four and a half years of his daughter's life. His hand caressed the butt of his gun. One quick clean shot, that's all he wanted. . . .

He swore softly. Killing Buckner wouldn't clear him of Ellenora's murder. But what else could he do? Dammit, he didn't want to spend the rest of his life looking over his shoulder, wanted for a crime he hadn't committed, wondering if someone would recognize him, waiting for some bounty hunter to find him. But he couldn't just let Buckner ride off scot-free, either.

He blew out a sigh, wishing he knew what the hell he was going to do. One thing he did know: He should have taken the time to go back and tell Leah that he was leaving, to explain to her why he had to go. He should have told her he loved her, in case he never had another chance.

Cussing softly, he urged his horse into a lope. The sooner he caught up with Buckner, the sooner he could return to his wife and daughter.

He only hoped they would both be there, waiting for him.

Chapter 23

Leah looked at Catharine, a frown furrowing her brow, her big brown eyes woeful. "Why didn't he tell me good-bye?"

"He was angry at me," Catharine said.

"Is he angry at me, too?"

"No, of course not. We had an argument and . . . and well, he was just so mad he stormed out of the house. I'm sure if he hadn't been mad, he would have told you he was leaving and kissed you good-bye."

"Where did he go?"

"He went after the man who killed your mother."

"Why was he angry with you?"

"Because I didn't want him to go," Catharine said. "I wanted him to stay here, with us."

Leah hugged Gretchen closer, her expression troubled. "I hope Daddy catches that bad man. I hope he goes to jail."

Catharine blew out a sigh. She couldn't blame Leah for wanting to see Buckner brought to justice. Being a child, Leah probably didn't realize the danger her father was in. Catharine didn't know anything about Jim Buckner, but she doubted he would go down without a fight. She could understand Nathan's desire for vengeance, but why couldn't he see that while killing Buckner might satisfy his need for revenge, it would only make things worse? If Nathan killed Buckner in cold blood, proving he was capable of murder, how could he ever convince anyone that he hadn't killed Ellenora as well? And what if . . . oh, Lord, what if Buckner killed Nathan? Why, oh, why hadn't he stayed home?

"Leah, the day your mother was killed, are you sure you didn't see anything else? Did you hear anything?"

Leah frowned. "I heard Mama and Mr. Buckner arguing. He wanted Mama to run away with him, but she said no. Mama told him to leave. She said she was going out to the barn and that she wanted him to be gone when she got back.

"How did you hear all this?"

"I was in the kitchen. Mama thought I was in my bedroom."

"Go on."

"Mr. Buckner found me in the kitchen. He grabbed me by the arm and pushed me into my bedroom. And then he locked the door. I looked out my window and saw him go into the barn and close the door. He didn't come out for a long time. When he did, he washed his hands in the horse trough. And then he rode away. And then Daddy came home and found me. I was crying."

"Leah, why didn't you tell anyone this before?"

"No one asked me."

Catharine shook her head, amazed that the child remembered so much of what she had seen four and a half years ago. But then maybe it wasn't so unusual.

It had been a traumatic day. She had probably relived it over and over again. It wasn't surprising that no one had asked a four-year-old child if she had seen anything. But it was obvious that Leah Chasing Elk was a bright child, and, over time, she had undoubtedly grown up enough to be able to explain what she had seen in detail. Catharine bit down on her lip, wondering if a court would allow Leah to testify, wondering if a jury would believe the words of an eight-year-old child.

She had a feeling it was Chasing Elk's only hope.

Chapter 24

Jim Buckner rode as if his life depended on it, which it very well did. He pushed his horse hard, certain that Ellenora's husband would come after him, knowing he would probably be dead by now if one of his drinking buddies hadn't warned him that a man had been in the Lucky Deuce asking about him, a man who fit Nathan Chasing Elk's description.

He wiped the sweat from his brow, blinked it from his eyes. He needed a drink. Hell, he needed a whole bottle, but he hadn't dared take the time to buy one.

He glanced over his shoulder again. Was Chasing Elk already after him? Maybe he was worrying for nothing. He had left in the middle of the night without telling anyone where he was going or why he was leaving. But even as he tried to tell himself there was nothing to worry about, he knew it was a lie. Chasing Elk was half Lakota and everybody knew that an Indian could track an ant over a rock in the dark.

Damn!

He drummed his heels against his horse's flanks. Of all the bad luck! What the hell was Chasing Elk doing out of prison? Escaped, most likely. But to turn up in

Short Rock Creek . . . Buckner shook his head. He should have known his luck would run out sooner or later.

He had to run, had to hide, but where to go?

His horse was covered with lather when he reined it to a halt an hour later. He was sweating some himself, he thought ruefully. He had to slow down, had to give the horse some rest if he didn't want to find himself out here in the middle of nowhere on foot.

Dismounting, he walked the animal to cool it out, constantly looking over his shoulder, cursing at the delay.

Guilt ate at him. Why hadn't he taken time to buy a bottle? It was the only thing that kept him sane, the only way to shut out the image of Ellenora—the blood that had spread around his knife in her chest, the way the light had gone out of her eyes . . .

He hadn't meant to kill her. She had been the most wonderful woman he had ever known. He'd taken one look at her and fallen head over heels in love. He'd written her poetry, given her presents, pretended he was fond of her little 'breed daughter, done everything he could to make Ellenora love him in return. She had been so beautiful, her voice soft and sweet, her smile like that of an angel. He had adored her, worshipped her. That last day, he had gone out to her house and begged her to run away with him, but she had refused.

Remembering, he felt all the old anger and resentment rise up within him. She had refused to leave that dirty half-breed! She had told him to go home and not to come back, and then she had gone out to the barn. He had locked the brat in her bedroom, then followed Ellenora out to the barn, determined to be alone with her, to convince her to leave her half-breed husband and brat and make a new life with him.

He hadn't meant to hurt her.

He hadn't meant to kill her. . . .

He stared into the water while the horse drank, seeing it all again in his mind.

He had gone down on his knees, pleading with her one more time to run away with him. He'd had money then. He promised to give her anything she wanted, clothes, jewels, a trip to Europe, anything at all. And still she had refused, saying she was happy to live in that ugly little house with that dirty half-breed. It was then that he had realized that she wasn't good enough for him, that she was nothing more than a harlot, content to sell herself to that Indian and raise his red stick whelp.

His rage at her rejection had choked him. Determined to take her by force if she would not willingly be his, he had thrown her down on the hay. She had struggled against him, biting and clawing like a wildcat. Her nails had raked his cheek. Somehow she had gotten hold of a knife. He hadn't meant to hurt her. He loved her, even then. He had wrenched the knife from her hand so that she couldn't use it on him and then . . . He sobbed at the memory. He hadn't meant to hurt her. He didn't remember plunging the knife into her breast, still could not believe he had done such a thing.

Guilt and remorse overwhelmed him anew as he pictured it again in his mind. He remembered being at her side, staring down at her in disbelief, seeing the pain and the accusation in her eyes.

He had begged for her forgiveness, declared that he loved her, but it had been Chasing Elk's name she had murmured with her dying breath. And then, with a sigh, the life had gone out of her eyes.

Horrified by what he had done, he had run out of the barn, her blood still on his hands. He had quickly washed in the horse trough, then vaulted into the saddle, knowing he had to get away before her husband returned. He had almost made it. Even now, he could hear Nathan Chasing Elk's voice calling his name, hear the whine of a bullet close to his ear.

With a jerk, Buckner glanced over his shoulder. There was no one there.

Swinging into the saddle, he took up the reins and urged his horse into a lope.

Chapter 25

He was closing the distance between them. The thought filled Chasing Elk with a cold sense of satisfaction as he squatted on his haunches near a shallow stream. Buckner had been here, and not too long ago. Judging from his horse's droppings, the man was less than two hours ahead.

"You won't get away," Chasing Elk muttered grimly. "Not this time."

Stretching out on his belly, he drank from the stream. Soon, he thought, soon he would have the man who had killed Ellenora.

Rising, he waited for his horse to cool off before he let the animal drink, and then he was back in the saddle, riding steadily onward.

By tomorrow, Buckner would be his.

He rode until dark, then made camp alongside a shallow stream. He ate jerky and hardtack for dinner, and washed it down with water from his canteen.

Later, he cleaned and oiled his gun and holster, then sat with his back propped against his saddle, staring into the distance, remembering Ellenora. . . .

He had been uncomfortable meeting her parents

that first night. They were polite but distant. In spite of their efforts to disguise it, he was aware of their disapproval. He was equally uncomfortable in their presence. Ellenora's parents were well-to-do and dinner was a formal occasion. He took one look at their table and had a strong urge to bolt from the room. He watched Ellenora carefully and copied her choices in her use of silverware.

After dinner, he followed the family into the parlor, his discomfort rising as her father questioned him about his parents, his prospects. When the evening was over, he was certain Ellenora's parents would never allow her to see him again, and he had been right. They had forbidden her to see him and so she did what lovestruck girls had done since time began. She met him on the sly.

Two weeks later, he asked her to marry him and she accepted. Needless to say, her parents were appalled. They argued. They threatened. They wheedled. In the end, they had begged, but to no avail. Ellenora was old enough to do as she wished, and she wished to marry him. When she did, her parents disowned her. A year later, they moved to Colorado.

Chasing Elk blew out a deep sigh of regret. If she had listened to her parents, she would be alive today, no doubt living in a fine house with an equally fine, upstanding young man. And yet he couldn't be sorry for the years they had spent together, or for the child born of their love. Ellenora had hoped that Leah would breach the gulf between herself and her parents, but they remained stubbornly remote. Their only concession had been to send Leah a gift every year for her birthday.

Muttering an oath, he thrust the unpleasant thoughts

away and summoned Catharine's image to his mind. Pulling his hat down low over his eyes, he fell asleep thinking of ways to win her forgiveness.

He was up with the dawn. A quick cup of coffee, and he was in the saddle again, riding hard.

The sun was setting when Chasing Elk caught sight of a rider ahead. He felt a rush of adrenaline. Buckner! He clucked to his horse, and the big bay lined out in a dead run.

The rider ahead glanced over his shoulder, then slammed his heels into his mount's sides.

But Buckner's horse was almost played out. Chasing Elk's long-legged bay easily closed the distance between them.

Buckner glanced over his shoulder again. Chasing Elk saw the panic in the other man's eyes, the certain knowledge that the chase was over and he had lost.

And still Buckner refused to give up. He kicked his horse again, and the game little animal surged forward.

But it was no use. Chasing Elk urged his horse up alongside Buckner's. Reaching out, he grabbed the horse's bridle by the cheek strap, gradually slowing both horses from a gallop to a trot.

Panicked, Buckner tried to hit Chasing Elk across the face with the end of the reins.

Muttering an oath, Chasing Elk gave a sharp tug on the bridle. Buckner's horse came to an abrupt halt. With a startled cry, Buckner flew over the horse's neck. He landed in the dirt, face down, and lay still.

Dismounting, Chasing Elk drew his Colt, then rolled the man over onto his back.

Jim Buckner stared up at him, his expression one of sullen defeat. "You gonna kill me now?"

Chasing Elk eared back the hammer of his gun. "It's no more than you deserve," he retorted. Here, after four and a half years, was the moment he had been waiting for.

Buckner's eyes grew wide as he stared death in the face.

Chasing Elk's finger curled around the trigger. One shot and it would all be over. Jim Buckner would be dead. Ellenora's death would be avenged.

Just one shot. And he couldn't do it. Ellenora wouldn't want him to. He knew it in the deepest part of his being. He could almost hear her voice telling him it was not the answer. And Catharine . . . If he killed Buckner now, he would lose her.

"I can kill you now," he said, his voice hard, "or you can ride back to town with me and turn yourself in."

Rising cautiously, Buckner said, "I didn't mean to kill her."

"Save it for the judge," Chasing Elk said. "Turn around."

Holstering his gun, Chasing Elk quickly searched Buckner for weapons, surprised when he didn't find one. "Get on your horse."

Buckner groaned as he put his foot in the stirrup. Once he was in the saddle, Chasing Elk removed the man's kerchief and used it to tie his hands together.

"Is that necessary?" Buckner asked sourly.

Chasing Elk shrugged, then swung up on the bay. Taking the reins to Buckner's horse, he headed back to town with his prisoner in tow.

They rode for about an hour in silence before Buckner remarked, "It's your word against mine, you know. You've got no proof that I killed her."

"That's why you're going to confess."

"And if I don't?"

"Then I'll gun you down. I've got nothing to lose," he said. Except his wife and his daughter and his freedom. He was taking a hell of a chance in trusting that Buckner would confess, but what other choice did he have? "I'll be watching your every move. You won't see me, but I'll be there."

Proof, Chasing Elk thought. He needed proof that Buckner had killed Ellenora and he had none. No proof and no witnesses. No one but Leah had seen Buckner at the house that day, and he doubted a jury would give much credence to the testimony of an eight-year-old child, especially when that child had been four years old at the time of her mother's death, and was his daughter, besides. Even if a jury believed that Leah had seen Buckner at the house, it was her father she had seen holding the knife that had killed her mother.

For a moment, he considered turning Buckner loose, but he couldn't do it. Until he cleared his name, he and Catharine would never be able to settle down. As long as he was wanted by the law, he would always be looking over his shoulder.

Chasing Elk swore softly. He was putting his life in Buckner's hands. He just hoped he didn't regret it.

Chasing Elk's feeling that he was doing the right thing in bringing Buckner in alive quickly faded as he rode toward the sheriff's office. He had a sudden premonition that his worst fears were about to be realized. Reining his horse to a halt, he was about to turn and hightail it out of town, but it was already too late. Even before he reached the sheriff's office, he found himself surrounded by armed deputies. Looking past the men, he saw that there were wanted posters tacked to just about every post in town, all bearing his likeness and description.

"Keep your hand away from that gun," one of the deputies warned.

With a nod, Chasing Elk raised his arms. One of the deputies relieved him of his gun and rifle.

"Get down," the deputy said.

Chasing Elk lifted one leg over the saddle and slid to the ground. He jerked his chin in Buckner's direction. "This is the man who killed my wife."

"Cletus, bring him along," the first deputy said. "We'll let the sheriff sort this out when he gets back from Yankton."

Moments later, Chasing Elk found himself behind bars once again. Buckner was locked in the adjoining cell.

"I want someone to notify my wife," Chasing Elk told the deputy known as Cletus.

"Sure. Who she is?"

"Catharine Rossiter. She lives on Third Street. The last house."

With a nod, the deputy left the cell block.

Chasing Elk blew out a sigh. If this wasn't the stupidest thing he had ever done, it was mighty damn close.

"I'll be out of here in no time," Buckner said

smugly. "You should have killed me when you had the chance."

Chasing Elk didn't bother to reply, but he had a feeling Buckner was right.

Catharine and Leah arrived twenty minutes later.

"Nathan, are you all right?" Catharine asked anxiously.

He grunted. "Do I look all right?"

She glanced at the man in the next cell. "Is that him?"

"Yeah."

She reached through the bars and took her husband's hand in hers. "I'm glad you didn't kill him."

"Yeah, well . . ." He shrugged. "There isn't a hope in hell that they'll convict him. I doubt if he'll even go to trial."

"It'll work out. I know it will." Catharine drew him to the far end of the cell, away from Buckner, and lowered her voice. "I've been talking to Leah. She remembers quite a bit of that day. She remembers seeing Buckner go into the barn. She heard him asking Ellenora to run away with him. She heard them arguing about it."

She was grasping at straws, but he didn't say so.

"Maybe we could get you a new trial?"

"Maybe." Even if it was possible, he doubted it would do any good. He thought bleakly of the last one. It had been over in thirty minutes. No one had believed a word he said. The jury had listened to the prosecutor, they had listened to the Watkins woman's testimony, they had examined the knife, heard his side of the story, and found him guilty as charged.

He ruffled Leah's hair. "How are you, sweetheart?"

"How long are you going to be in here?"

"I don't know."

Tears welled in her eyes. "They won't send you away again, will they?"

He took a deep breath. "I hope not. But if they do, Catharine will take care of you." He wiped the tears from her eyes. "Don't cry."

She reached for his hand. "I love you, Daddy."

"I love you, too." Her hand felt small and warm in his. "Listen, Catharine. If the worst happens, I think you should take Leah and go back to Boston. Mark is there. He'll look after you."

"No! I'm not leaving you. If . . . if they send you back to prison, we'll come visit you every week."

He shook his head. He didn't want Leah anywhere close to Yuma, didn't want her to see the ugliness of it, or Catharine, either. It was bad enough that his daughter had already seen him behind bars twice.

Catharine glanced at Leah. "We'll talk about it later. Can I get you anything?"

"A good lawyer."

Catharine took him at his word, and the next morning Robert Glass showed up at the jail. He requested he be allowed to speak to Chasing Elk in private, and the deputy agreed to let them use the sheriff's office.

Robert Glass was a small, wiry man with wispy gray hair and sharp blue eyes. He listened carefully to everything Chasing Elk had to say, making copious notes all the while.

"So," Chasing Elk said when the lawyer stopped writing, "how's it look?"

"Not good," Glass said frankly. "You're certain no one besides your daughter was aware that Mr. Buckner was at your home that day?"

"Yeah."

Glass tapped one finger against his chin. "Assuming we could get a new trial, I don't think it would be wise to put your daughter on the stand. I'm afraid her testimony would be more incriminating than helpful."

"So there's no hope?"

"I'm afraid not. I can always move for a new trial but, frankly, I think it would be a waste of time."

Chasing Elk told Catharine as much when she came to visit him that night.

"We'll think of something," she said, forcing a smile. "Wait and see."

"Sure," he said.

But they were both lying.

That night, Catharine sat up long after Leah had fallen asleep. Getting a lawyer had been a last-ditch effort at best. Even knowing nothing would come of it, she'd had to try. Chasing Elk had already been tried and found guilty of killing his wife. He couldn't be tried again, but she had hoped a lawyer might find a loophole somewhere or find grounds for a new trial. But that wasn't going to happen. Their only hope now was that Buckner would confess. And she was sorely afraid that wasn't going to happen. But she couldn't give up hope. It was all she had.

Her heart ached for Nathan. It grieved her to see the look of despair in his eyes. She could hear it in his voice, the hopelessness that he felt, his dread of going back to Yuma.

She tried to recall everything he had told her about

the day Ellenora had died, trying to find some clue, something they had overlooked, no matter how seemingly insignificant, that might prove he was innocent, or at least prove reasonable doubt, but there was nothing.

The sheriff returned to Short Rock Springs five days later. He talked with his deputies and then he took Buckner into his office to talk to him.

Twenty minutes later, the sheriff stood outside Chasing Elk's cell. "My deputies say you brought Buckner in claiming he's the man who killed your wife."

"That's right."

The sheriff held up a flyer. "Says here that you escaped from prison."

Chasing Elk nodded. There was no point in lying.

"Also says you were convicted of murdering your wife."

"I know what it says. I didn't do it. Dammit, I didn't do it!"

"Well, now, that's what they all say."

Chasing Elk clenched his hands.

"I'm afraid I don't see any need for a new trial." The sheriff rolled the poster up and tapped it against his thigh. "I'll be notifying Yuma to come and pick you up."

"What about Buckner?" Chasing Elk asked, his voice tight.

"Unless you've got a good lawyer and some new evidence against Mr. Buckner that will stand up in a court of law, I've got no reason to hold him."

No reason to hold him.

Those five words killed whatever hope he'd had.

"I can't believe it," Catharine said later. "I can't believe they just let him go. It isn't fair." She blinked rapidly, and he knew she was trying not to cry. "It just isn't fair!"

Chasing Elk shrugged. He'd been a damn fool to think this would end any other way. "Finding me guilty was the same as finding him innocent. Dammit, I should have killed him when I had the chance!"

For once, she didn't argue.

Chapter 26

The days that followed passed too slowly and, at the same time, too fast. His first thought each morning was that he was one day closer to returning to Yuma. His last thought at night was that he was one day closer to never seeing Catharine or Leah again. He couldn't eat, couldn't sleep, couldn't do anything but pace the floor or lay on his cot staring up at the ceiling, thinking what a fool he'd been to think this would turn out any other way.

It got harder and harder to tell Catharine and Leah good night. Each hour, each moment he spent with them became more and more precious.

Leah clung to him each night, her hand squeezing his.

And then it was the last night. The sheriff had told him that the prison wagon from Yuma would arrive the following afternoon.

That night, just before they left, Leah thrust Gretchen through the bars. "Here, Daddy," she said, her voice thick. "Take Gretchen with you. She'll keep you company."

Chasing Elk looked at his daughter and knew he had never loved her more than he did in that instant. "Thank you, sweetheart, but I can't take her with me," he said.

"Why not?"

For the first time in days, he felt like laughing. He could just imagine the looks and remarks he'd get if he showed up back at Yuma carrying a rag doll.

"It isn't allowed." He handed the doll to his daughter. "You take good care of her for me, all right?"

"All right."

Chasing Elk glanced at Catharine. "Have you written to Mark yet?"

"No."

"Dammit, Catharine, you can't stay out here on your own."

"I'll write him when you're . . . in a day or so, I promise. Don't worry about us, we'll be fine."

"You're thinking about going back home, aren't you? Back to that rundown farm."

She shook her head, but he saw the truth in her eyes. Before he could argue, before he could tell her it wasn't safe, the cellblock door opened and the sheriff stepped in.

"Time's up."

"We're coming," Catharine said.

"Good night, Daddy."

"Good night, sweetheart." Bending down, he kissed his daughter's cheek.

"I love you," Catharine whispered.

"I love you, too."

She leaned forward for his kiss. "Good night, Nathan."

He watched his wife and daughter walk away, feeling as though they were taking his heart and soul with them.

In the morning, Catharine made Leah ham and eggs and toast for breakfast, but neither of them ate.

"How soon until we can go see Daddy?" Leah asked.

"Soon," Catharine said. "You're not going to cry, are you? It will make him unhappy if he sees you crying."

"I won't cry." Even as she spoke the words, tears dripped down her cheeks.

Catharine blinked back tears of her own. She had to be strong, for Nathan. She could cry later. She had a feeling that for a few days, that's all she would be doing.

"Come on," Catharine said, "we might as well go."

Outside, she stood on the boardwalk, holding Leah's hand.

"Look," Leah said, pointing across the street. "There's that bad man."

Catharine glanced across the street. Jim Buckner was standing in front of the bank. Feeling her gaze, he turned to look at her. For a moment, she thought she saw shame and sadness in his eyes before he blinked and turned away.

Jerking her hand from Catharine's, Leah ran across

the street. Holding Gretchen tight in one hand, she stopped in front of Buckner.

"I hate you!" she said. "You killed my mama!"

"Go away, kid." Buckner glanced up and down the boardwalk.

"You killed her!" Leah said, her voice rising. "I heard you fighting with her and then you followed her into the barn and shut the door. You killed her, I know you did. And now my daddy's going to jail for something you did and I'll never see him. . . ." Tears welled in her eyes and coursed down her cheeks. She sniffed them back. "I'll never see him again, and it's your fault!"

"Get out of here," Buckner growled.

"Please don't let them send my daddy back to jail," Leah said, her tears coming harder and faster now. "Please make them let him go."

Buckner looked at the gathering crowd and shrugged his shoulders. "I don't know what she's talking about."

"You're a bad man," Leah said, sniffling. "A very bad man."

"Come, Leah," Catharine said, taking her by the hand. "You'll get no help here."

Chasing Elk was standing at the bars waiting for them when they arrived. He hugged Leah and then Catharine, wishing he had the words to tell them how much he loved them, how much they meant to him, but the words wouldn't come.

For once, Catharine had no words of hope, no words of comfort. She could only cling to him, cherishing each moment.

And then, as if realizing she might never get to tell him again, she whispered, "I love you, Nathan. I'll love you until the day I die."

"I know," he said, his voice thick.

"Don't worry about Leah. I'll take good care of her, I promise. And I'll write you every day. We both will. And I'll take Leah to see your mother every summer. . . ."

He nodded, unable to speak past the lump in his throat.

He swore softly when he heard the cell block door open and then the sheriff's voice.

"The wagon's here."

Chasing Elk hugged his daughter one last time, then drew Catharine into his arms. He kissed her, one long, lingering kiss that said everything he couldn't put into words.

And then the sheriff was there, cuffing his hands behind his back, leading him out of the jail to the prison wagon.

Chasing Elk climbed inside and sat down.

Catharine stood on the boardwalk, her arm around Leah's shoulders. She forced a smile, not wanting the sight of her tears to be the last thing he saw.

She held the tears back until the wagon was out of sight. And then, not caring if the whole world saw her, she wept.

Jim Buckner watched the prison wagon rumble down the street. He saw the woman's tears, saw the child bury her face in the woman's skirts.

Muttering an oath, he stumbled down the street to the nearest saloon, afraid that all the whiskey in the world wouldn't wash away his guilt or drown out the words that echoed relentlessly in his mind.

He bought a bottle, carried it to a back table, and sat down in the shadows. He didn't bother with a glass, just tilted the bottle up and let the whiskey pour down his throat.

You're a bad man, accused the voice in his head. *A very bad man.*

Yuma Prison was just as Chasing Elk remembered it. Gray walls. Iron bars. A hard, lice-infested cot. And Fat Tom was there, waiting for him. So, Chasing Elk thought, he hadn't killed the bastard, after all. More's the pity, because Chasing Elk knew he would have to pay in blood sooner or later for the beating he had given the guard.

"I knew you'd be back," the guard said. "Just like I know that sooner or later you'll bend one of the rules or make a break for it, and then your ass will be mine."

Chasing Elk ignored him, just like he ignored everything else. A week went by. A month. Two. Three. He did what he was told, ate the slop they fed him, and kept his mouth shut. The only things he had to look forward to were the letters from Catharine and Leah. He wasn't going to do anything that would deny him that privilege, and that included running afoul of Fat Tom.

The days passed in a sea of sameness. He focused all his energy, all his thoughts on whatever task he was doing, refusing to think about Catharine or Leah or what might have been. It was only at night that he allowed his memories to surface. There, in his cot, shrouded in the darkness, he let himself remember the softness of his wife's skin, the beauty of her smile, the sound of her laughter. He relived every moment they had spent together. It was agony, knowing he would never see her again, never hold her again, never taste her sweetness again. He thought of his daughter, his heart aching for all that he would miss. She would grow to be a young woman, marry, have children of her own, children he would never see.

He lived only for letters from home, letters that brought him joy and pain. Letters that he read every chance he had until he had them memorized. They were his only reason for living, and as the days went by, he wondered if they were reason enough.

Catharine wrote him long, chatty letters filled with love and hope. In contrast, his tended to be brief. There was little that went on in the prison that he wanted to share with her. After telling her that he was doing all right, that he was trying to hang on to his temper, there was little to say except that he loved her.

Sitting down on his cot with his back to the wall, he wrote a reply to Catharine's last letter.

Catharine sat back in her chair, reading what she had written.

Dearest Nathan: Another week has gone by, and I miss you more than ever. I think of you always and pray for you every night, pray that you will find the strength to endure what must surely be unendurable. I know you have lost all hope, but I continue to hope and pray for a miracle. Please do not be discouraged. I cannot believe that life would be so cruel as to keep us apart. Please take care of yourself and know that I love you more and more with every passing day.

I know you have been worried about us being back here on the farm, but please put your fears to rest. Dooli, the warrior who has taken Marteen's place as chief, has adopted Leah as his daughter. We are well protected now. Dooli brings us fresh meat every night.

I have been schooling Leah and she is doing very well. She is such a bright child. She loves to read and to make up stories.

I wrote to Mark to let him know what has happened and that we are at the farm. He wrote back to tell me that he and Bonnie Lee are doing well. Mark is working at a bank in Boston and they have bought a small house not far from Mrs. Montgomery. Bonnie Lee is expecting their first child. . . .

Catharine sat back, one hand pressed to her stomach. Should she mention that she had felt the baby move? Would it cheer him, or remind him of how much he was missing? She loved it when his letters came, and yet each one left her feeling more depressed than the last. His unhappiness, his bitterness were evident in every line.

She tapped her foot. Perhaps she would just say she was feeling well and let it go at that for now.

With a sigh, she leaned back in her chair and closed her eyes. She seemed to be tired all the time. Her breasts were tender, her ankles swollen, and she was nauseous every morning. Leah was excited at the thought of a new baby, buy Catharine had warned her not to mention the baby in any of her letters.

"Why not?" Leah had asked. "Don't you think Daddy is happy about it?"

"Of course he is," Catharine had replied. "But I'm sure it makes him sad that he can't be here right now. If we talk about it, it might make him feel worse, do you see?"

Leah had frowned. "I guess so."

Catharine sighed. She hoped she was making the right decision. Nathan hadn't mentioned the baby in any of his letters. She would take her cue from him, for now.

If he hadn't said anything about her pregnancy when her time was near, she would mention it.

But it would not be today.

Chapter 27

"Hey, Injun, you've got a visitor."

Chasing Elk looked up from the letter he was reading. A visitor? Who would be coming to see him here?

The guard unlocked the cell door and motioned him outside.

His curiosity growing with every step, Chasing Elk followed the guard to the main building and into a small room where prisoners were allowed to receive visitors. In all the time he'd been locked up, no one had ever come to visit him before.

Chasing Elk stepped into the room and the guard closed and locked the door behind him.

A man stood at the room's single window. He turned at the sound of the door closing.

Chasing Elk stared at the man. "Do I know you?" he asked, thinking the man looked vaguely familiar.

"No. I'm Andrew Buckner. Jim was my brother."

"Was?"

"I buried him two weeks ago."

And buried my last hope of getting out of this hell hole with him, Chasing Elk thought bleakly.

Andrew Buckner sat down and motioned to a vacant chair. "Why don't you sit?"

Chasing Elk dropped into the chair he indicated. "So, why are you here?"

"Jim hanged himself two weeks ago. He left this note." Andrew pulled a piece of paper out of his coat pocket and handed it to Chasing Elk.

Andy, I can't live with the guilt any longer. Please contact the proper authorities and tell them that Nathan Rossiter is innocent of any crime. I'm the one who killed Ellenora Rossiter. It was an accident. We had an argument and, well, it doesn't matter what we were arguing about. I never meant to kill her but it happened. Please tell the family I'm sorry for the shame I've brought to them. And tell Rossiter that I'm sorry as hell for everything that happened. Hell, I guess that's where I'll be going. Oh, one more thing. Ask Rossiter to tell his little girl that I'm not really a bad man. Your brother, James.

Chasing Elk read the letter a second time, then looked at Andrew Buckner.

"The warden is processing your release. I wanted to meet you and give you this." Reaching into his coat pocket again, he withdrew a large envelope and passed it across the table. "Go ahead, open it."

Frowning, Chasing Elk opened the envelope and withdrew the contents. "I don't understand."

"There's forty thousand dollars there," Andrew

said. "Ten thousand dollars for every year you spent in jail."

"I can't take this."

"I wish you would. I know it's not enough to make up for all the time you spent here, but we'd all feel better if you'd keep it and use it to make a fresh start."

Chasing Elk stared at the money. He remembered Ellenora telling him that Jim Buckner's family was wealthy. He had dismissed it as idle talk, certain that Buckner had just been bragging to impress Ellenora.

"I really wish you'd take it."

He hesitated a moment, then said, "If you're sure."

"Believe me, Mother can afford it. She feels terrible about all this." Andrew stood. "Our family is extremely sorry for what James did, and for the misery that he caused you and your daughter."

Chasing Elk nodded.

"If you ever need anything, please don't hesitate to get in touch with us."

Chasing Elk rose, his mind reeling with all that had happened in the last ten minutes.

Andrew Buckner extended his hand. "Good luck to you, Mr. Rossiter."

"Thank you."

With a nod, Buckner left the room.

Chasing Elk was still trying to absorb all that had happened when the warden entered the room.

"You're a free man, Rossiter." He dumped Chasing Elk's clothing on the table. "As soon as you get changed, come up to the office. I've got some papers for you to sign before you leave."

Chasing Elk nodded.

He glanced at the money spread on the table. It was more money than he'd ever seen in his life, more than he'd ever expected to have. And it was his.

He glanced at his clothes, and then he looked at the open door.

It hit him then. He was a free man.

Catharine sat on the porch putting the finishing touches on a quilt she was making for the baby. She smiled, her hand dropping to her stomach as she felt the baby move.

She was contemplating possible names when she saw a plume of dust off in the distance. Frowning, she watched as a rider came into view. She stared as he came closer. Heart pounding, she rose and moved to the edge of the porch.

It couldn't be. Oh, Lord, had he escaped again?

"Nathan?" She descended the stairs as the rider reined his horse to a halt. "Nathan!"

He swung out of the saddle, his arms wrapping around her, holding her so tight she thought her ribs might crack.

And then he was letting her go, stepping back, his gaze settling on the swell of her belly. "Are you all right?"

"Yes, I'm fine."

"Have you seen a doctor?"

"Yes. He said there's nothing to worry about."

"You never mentioned the baby in any of your letters."

"Neither did you."

"I know." He shrugged. "I just couldn't talk about it."

"It's all right." She hugged him tight. "You escaped again, didn't you? We'll have to leave here right away."

Before he could answer, Leah came flying down the stairs. "Daddy! Daddy!"

He scooped her into his arms and swung her around. "Hello, sweetheart."

"I missed you, Daddy."

"I missed you, too. Come on," he said, taking Catharine by the hand. "I've got a lot to tell you."

As quickly and succinctly as possible, Chasing Elk told them how Andrew Buckner had come to visit him in prison and all that had happened.

"Buckner left his brother a letter. In it, he asked me to tell you that he wasn't a bad man," Chasing Elk told Leah. "Do you know what he meant?"

She nodded. "I told him he was a very bad man for killing my mama."

"I guess he believed you."

"I'm sorry he's dead," Leah said solemnly, and then she smiled. "They'll never take you away from us again, will they?"

"No." He drew his wife and his daughter into his arms, a prayer of thanksgiving rising in his heart. "Nothing will ever take me away from my girls again."

Epilogue

Five years later

Catharine sat in a rocking chair on the front porch, watching Chasing Elk lead a pretty little paint pony around the corral while their three-year-old daughter asserted that she was old enough to ride by herself. Janie was a natural rider, but Chasing Elk wasn't ready to let her ride alone just yet. Catharine didn't blame him. Their son, Nathan, Jr., sat on the rail, encouraging his little sister. Nate, now almost five years old, was the spitting image of his father and very protective of his sister.

Life had been wonderful since Chasing Elk had been cleared of Ellenora's murder. They had moved to Yankton and built a spacious home. Chasing Elk was training horses again, and in a short time had built quite a reputation for himself. Leah, now thirteen, had blossomed into a beautiful young lady.

As promised, they went to visit the reservation every summer so that their children could get to know their father's side of the family.

Mark and Bonnie Lee had come to visit them twice.

Next year, Chasing Elk had promised Catharine that they could go to Boston.

She smiled as Chasing Elk left the corral, a child on either side of him.

"Nate, take your sister inside and tell Leah to fix the two of you some lunch," Chasing Elk said, climbing the stairs.

"All right," Nate said, taking his sister by the hand. "Come on, Janie."

Chasing Elk knelt beside Catharine. "How are you feeling, beautiful?"

"Beautiful! I just feel fat. I wish this baby would hurry and get here."

"You're beautiful to me, fat or thin."

She smiled, knowing it was true. Here, beneath the bold Dakota skies, she had found everything she had ever dreamed of in his arms.

Dear Readers:

I hope you enjoyed *Dakota Dreams*. I've always loved cowboys, Indians, horses, and the Old West, and it's always fun to let my imagination wander into the past and see where it will lead. One of the sources I used for information was the Phoenix Valley History page on the Natural American Web site (http://www.thenaturalamerican.com/phoenix_history.htm).

I'm sorry to say that *Dakota Dreams* will most likely be my last historical for a while, but I hope to revisit the Old West somewhere down the road. In the meantime, Amanda Ashley has a book coming out in February 2006.

Time certainly flies by. When I sold my first book back in 1985, I never thought that twenty years later I'd have published thirty-one historical romances, ten paranormal romances, nine anthologies, four Silhouette romances, and three fantasy romances.

My thanks to those who have sent me letters and emails. I love hearing from you!

May God bless you and yours.

Madeline
http://www.madelinebaker.net

New York Times
bestselling author

Madeline Baker
Under Apache Skies

When a rugged stranger darkens the door of her
family porch, Martha Jean Flynn can tell right away
that Ridge Longtree is nothing like the other cowboys who usually show up in search of work. But
when tragedy strikes, Marty must flee with the half-
Indian loner—and she discovers a love that threat-
ens to set her heart aflame.

0-451-21282-7

**Available wherever books are sold or at
penguin.com**

S903

All your favorite romance writers are
coming together.

SIGNET ECLIPSE